I0636681

Published by BookPop Media LLC

Edition 2

ISBN 978-1-956918-08-3

24.6.4.1R

1st Edition date of publication: April 15th, 2022

1st Edition eBook ISBN: 978-1-956918-03-8

1st Edition Print ISBN: 978-1-956918-04-5

Cover design by Fay Lane (https://faylane.com/)

Symphony of Crowns and Gods Official Website:

https://www.theauthorbrian.com

A NOTE ON SERIES THEMES:

Symphony of Crowns and Gods is an intricately woven fantasy series filled with unexpected twists and turns. This narrative explores a rich and complex world, including sudden transitions to themes and motifs that may provoke strong emotions or discomfort for some readers. These elements include, but are not limited to, dark magic, violence, moral complexities, psychological manipulation, trauma, and crises of identity. Characters in this series must overcome the darkness within themselves and confront the harsh realities of their world to ultimately discover their inner strength and resilience. Their journeys will not be without their scars.

JOIN BRIAN A. MENDONÇA'S EMAIL NEWSLETTER

WHY SIGN UP?

It's simple: fans on this email list get my official updates before anyone else, including any other blogs and social media websites. Here's the news you can expect:

- Upcoming releases and previews of upcoming books
- An open dialog about my author journey
- Deals and sales
- Opportunities for ARCs (Advance Reader Copies)
- Info about fantasy books from other indie authors

Sign up link:

https://theauthorbrian.com/join-brians-newsletter

Or use this QR code:

Greater Events of the World

as verified by Iris Thorne, Councilwoman
of Internal Affairs of the Second Darian Kingdom

The Human
Uprising
(Years 1 - 171)

Scourge of the
Dragon Slayers
(Years 171-401)

The First
Great War
(Years 441-449)

Downfall of
the First
Darian Kingdom
(Years 441-446)

Lucidian
Civil War
(Years 445-449)

Founding of
the Second
Darian Kingdom
(Year 450)

The Blooming of
All Nations
(Years 450 -   )

Scheduled:
Marriage
of Darian Princess
Lydia von Stonewall
and Throatian Prince
Thane Asche
(Year 474)

THROATLAN ISLAND

WHITE BOAR'S LANDING

HOMES OF THE SON SEER VRAI

MOUNT SEPHORR

LOYALTY CIRCLES & BREEDING FARMS

TEMPLE OF WHITE

SOUTHEAST YAENIA

WARGONNE

GALE VILLAGE

SKY TOWER COAST

HILLSIDE REACH

THE LOWLAND GRAVES

NEW GINSTOWN

HAVENTOWN

LAST HOPE

EMIL

LUCIDIAN ENCLAVE

THE LEILA KINGDOM

STARLIGHT BEACH

GRAVITY

OF

OBEDIENCE

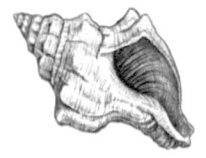

SYMPHONY OF
CROWNS AND GODS
BOOK TWO

BRIAN A. MENDONÇA

THE ASCENSION

T he sun crept over the horizon. With it came warmth and light, peeking between the clouds and through the Temple of White's glassless windows. Sitting cross-legged on the black marble floor with his head bowed, Prince Thane wrinkled the corners of his eyes slightly as he took a few deep breaths. Then he jerked upright and inhaled deeply, as if making up for lost air, before suddenly exhaling with all his might.

In front of him, smoke from various incense sticks meandered between a trio of obelisks. Words in a foreign language he couldn't identify covered each of the pillars from top to bottom. Despite their resemblance to the Throatian language, the scripts were meaningless to him. Even Cereene, who was highly knowledgeable about the old texts, couldn't decipher the hieroglyphic writing. Thane's father seemed to know the history and secret significance of the obelisks and the writings, but he refused to share the details whenever Thane asked.

Outside, the bells tolled from a nearby Loyalty Circle, declaring the completion of another sacrifice. A Son See'er had grown closer in their faith.

"Sheiaa Kaaduul," whispered Thane.

He continued his meditation for another hour, finding inner peace in the rising heat of the stone floor until Elder Hrodspire's arrival interrupted him.

"Prince Thane, I'm sorry to trouble you again about this," said Hrodspire, bowing to the obelisks and then to Thane. "Your mother, she's—"

"I know she's worried," Thane said, "but Father told us not to disturb him on his pilgrimage. We know this. He might be late, but he's not in danger."

Often loose-lipped, Hrodspire relished being the first to share the latest gossip and tales. Perhaps spreading hearsay had become his preferred entertainment in his old age. "But it's been two weeks longer than ever before. Compared to the rest of our island, the icy winds of Mount Sephorr grant no accommodation. He must have run out of food days ago."

"Then he'll fast as needed until he completes his quest," Thane replied. "When he's finished praying, my father will return. Why do you and my mother persist in over-analyzing his actions and making a fuss about nothing?"

"It's not about questioning," Hrodspire said. "Like the other Elders, we're concerned for his safety."

"Which Elders, specifically, Hrodspire?" Thane snapped.

"Several of them, I'm afraid."

Thane scowled. "Send them all to a Loyalty Circle. It will remind them of Zann-Xia-Czul's protection and the consequences for those who lose their faith."

Hrodspire gulped, perhaps finally realizing that he was bothering him. "I intended no lack of faith, my prince. This might be a test for our king, or maybe even for you."

"A test, old Elder? I doubt it. You're reading far too much into this."

"I apologize, Prince Thane. Please forgive my intrusion. But I urge you to talk to your mother soon. It will reassure her."

Both of Thane's parents, as the highest-level Son See'er Vrai, had already proven themselves during their trials in the Loyalty Circles. The Throatian queen was stronger than Hrodspire acknowledged. It was nearly insulting that he would suggest she was someone who would needlessly worry about her husband. There no point in wasting further breath on the Elder. Thane had come to the Temple of White for meditation, not to indulge in pointless conversation.

"You're forgiven," Thane said. "Now go."

Undisturbed, he closed his eyes again and continued his meditation until midday, when he finally rose from the floor. Blood rushed through his numb legs, painfully easing the cramps he'd developed while praying. Near the exit where he'd left his brown leather sandals, he lit a stick of incense, letting it burn over a small metal bowl on the ground. Satisfied, he gave a final bow to the obelisks and left.

Outside, the winding path down the grassy hill led to where the highest castes of families lived. Being royal, rich, or powerful correlated with one's devotion to Zann-Xia-Czul compared to others who lived on their island. Through growing loyalty or faltering faith, individuals moved throughout the rings of society as instructed by their god. Zann-Xia-Czul could read their minds, ensuring no secret stayed hidden.

The Asche house, standing nearest to the temple, served as a constant reminder of the expectations laid upon them. Homes without doors signaled to other Son See'ers that a family had nothing to hide. After all, their island's small stone huts embodied their religious principles: mindfulness, transparency, and sacrifice.

Thane stepped into his single-room home through a tall archway. No one was inside, and the kettle was absent from the stove, prompting him to turn around and resume his walk down the gravel path away from the Temple of White. A quarter mile north of his home, amidst the huts scattered about the hill, he found his mother kneeling beside a small river.

"Shivanna Adul, Mother," Thane called to her.

Urith Asche, standing taller than any other female Son See'er Vrai, shifted toward him, clutching her kettle. Sunlight reflected off the lengthy scar on her face as she nodded. "Shivanna Adul. I'm at peace, though I don't know for how much longer. Your father has never been gone for this long."

Thane took the kettle, carrying it for her as they ascended the hill. "I'm certain he's spending his time in isolation productively. Elder Hrodspire mentioned last week that we were lagging in our annual harvest. Father is likely praying about that."

"I hope you're right," Urith said, "but I sense something else is amiss."

"I've never believed those rumors about Mount Sephorr. If our god can read our thoughts and intentions from anywhere, why would he only communicate with Father while he's on top of the mountain?"

Urith jabbed his shoulder, causing some of the

kettle's water to splash onto the grass. "It's not your place to question it," she growled. "Your grandfather, and his father before him, said the same. Tradition outweighs your imagination."

"Sorry," Thane said, rubbing his arm.

They returned home and brewed tea from some nearby yellow wildflowers. As it steeped, Urith unstrapped her sword from the wall and grabbed a whetstone from the cupboard. She grunted as she sat down and began sharpening her blade. Tiny sparks flew as she angrily ground stone against metal.

"Are you planning to carry that up Mount Sephorr and look for Father?" Thane asked. "You know it's forbidden."

"I'm going to contribute to a Loyalty Circle."

"As if you haven't been going there every day lately."

"It keeps my mind off things. Don't you get any ideas about climbing Mount Sephorr either."

"I'm not the one who's worried about Harkbin," said Thane. "And believe me, I'd rather climb any mountain other than Mount Sephorr. Give me heat and humidity over a blizzard any day."

"Watch your tongue," Urith said. "You're not too old to be punished by your mother. I won't hesitate to make you kneel on broken seashells again until you learn respect."

In silence, Thane took the kettle from the fire

and poured their drinks. He sat down beside her and stared at the bear pelt strung across the wall. A month ago, his mother had downed the beast with an arrow, finishing her hunt with her blade. Their family savored the meat for weeks until his father announced his need to begin his journey up the mountain earlier than usual.

The impulsive decision to ascend so early was likely the root of Urith's concerns; Harkbin rarely deviated from his routines and rituals. She had packed him some bear meat, and that same night, he'd ventured off without even informing the Elders.

"I'm going to the Loyalty Circle now. Do you want to come?" Urith asked through a mouthful of smoked rabbit jerky.

Loyalty Circles were perhaps the most poorly thought-out demand of worshipping Zann-Xia-Czul. While it was clear their god required blood sacrifices, Thane couldn't understand why animals weren't suitable for their rituals. It made no sense for a god to want his followers murdering each other. Indeed, the Breeding Farms kept the Throatian population steady, but it never appeared to grow beyond that. Neither the Elders nor his father could answer why only human blood was acceptable either.

Thane watched the steam rise slowly from his cup. "I'm going to White Boar's Landing to check on my new armor. The craftsman is behind schedule and I'm curious why he hasn't contacted me about it."

"Why not just send a Son See'er? You needn't do such trivial fetch quests on your own."

"As if I would allow a mere servant to touch it," Thane scoffed. "They'd cover every piece of the suit with their greasy fingerprints. The artisan imported most of the materials from Wargonne in the Darian Kingdom. It's going to be the most spectacular suit in the—"

"Fine. I'll see you tonight then."

His mother downed the rest of her tea in a single shot and wiped her face with her arm. She set her cup down on the table next to a pewter handbell, which she then picked up and rang so loudly that any Son See'er within a quarter mile would hear her summons. A moment later, a young servant girl appeared and carried Urith's armor and weapon for her as they left down the hill.

Thane took a while longer to finish his tea, then headed down a separate road toward White Boar's Landing. Off in the distance, ships came and left from the beach. Various crates of food and other supplies were stacked neatly along its piers, and the crews hastily sorted them to prepare for trade. The squawking of gulls clashed against the sound of ocean waves as Thane entered the bustling market.

Son See'ers made their way past him, nodding in greeting as they carried wares to their carts. Foreigners from the Silent Deserts paid him no mind, unaware of Thane's royal status.

The laws and their enforcers prevented strangers from delving into the Throatian culture or venturing further into the island beyond the port's gates. Similarly, merchants who conversed with outsiders were only taught enough Common Tongue to do their trading, nothing more. Therefore, there was no exchange of culture. Thane suspected the restrictions were for hiding Throatian religion from other nations. Human sacrifice likely wasn't acceptable in other ways of life. Some of the sailors that came through White Boar's Landing lacked the physical aptitude required to survive a Loyalty Circle. Chances were the sacrificial arenas were exclusive to their island.

Zann-Xia-Czul used his magic to enforce the secrecy of religious matters. When Thane was a child, Hrodspire told him stories of how their god summoned thunderstorms for over a hundred days straight. The nonstop wind and rain engulfed the island, forming a barrier of cliffs around it, leaving White Boar's Landing open as the sole means of entering the country. Despite the restrictions, the port flourished with carts, shops, and trade.

As he entered a small armor and weapons shop,

the elderly smith Thane had commissioned several weeks ago appeared through the rear door. The man quickly set the box of scrap metal he was carrying onto a nearby workbench.

"Shivanna Adul, my prince." The armorer grinned, wiping his spot-covered hands on his apron. "Thank you for coming."

"Shivanna Adul, Son See'er," Thane replied. "How is my armor? Is it ready?"

The man scratched his head and glanced at the door. "Alas, it is yet incomplete. I'm still waiting for the material I need to glaze the surfaces. Without it, the armor will easily scratch."

Thane lifted his shoulder in half a shrug. "So, it is out of your control until you have the missing component. How much longer will you need once it arrives?"

"I'm expecting it here in a few more days. Making the protective coating will be easy, and then I'll paint the surface with it. Once it all dries and hardens, you'll have the greatest armor I've ever crafted. Would you like to see what I've done so far?"

Although he hadn't answered Thane's question or given a timeframe, seeing the progress was at least worth checking on. "Yes, I would."

The armorer rubbed some sweat off his forehead, and his hand left a streak of greasy polish behind. "It would be best if you tried the main parts on now while it's still possible to make adjustments. I tailored everything as we planned, but it wouldn't hurt to make sure everything's comfortable."

He led Thane to the back room, where various tables and shelves displayed partially completed projects. A pearl-white breastplate and matching helmet sat on a mannequin, glistening and beautiful. Thane knew they belonged to him and couldn't contain his grin.

"Yours is easy to spot among the rest of them, isn't it?" the craftsman commented. "Since you gave me creative freedom on the design, I've taken inspiration from the Temple of White and our island for the color and style."

Thane lifted the armor off the display. It was the lightest cuirass he'd ever held. His eyes closely traced over its intricacies. Someone had meticulously painted pale blue fish across the snow-white suit. Lines of the same color curved between the fish, mimicking the ocean waves. Fish held no significance to him, but with this new armor, perhaps they could become part of his reputation and identity. As the craftsman had promised, the suit was unique and beautiful. The texture, however, felt no different from glass or seashells.

As he held the armor in front of him, he kept his eyes unblinking. "Will this truly protect me? It feels too light to block arrows or heavy blows."

The man nodded and pointed his wrinkled finger at the breastplate. "Your curiosity honors me, my prince. You asked for powerful protection, but with feather-like weight. I've made it exactly as you requested. Even without the scratch-resistant seal, it can defend you just as well. Still, it is best we do not compromise its beauty by testing it yet."

Thane slid the armor on and tightened the straps. After he finished adjusting the parts for his upper body, he moved on to his new leggings. Although every piece was solid, the complete kit was as light as cloth. He would be able to dash quickly in a fight, almost unfairly fast. Best of all, everything fit perfectly.

"Your work is astounding. How did you make this?"

"I'm sorry, I can't reveal my trade secret," the man said, idly twirling a small hammer in his hands. "You have my word; this is the finest armor you'll ever own."

There was something unsettling about the man. Perhaps he was nervous because his prince had shown up to his shop unannounced, and the project wasn't yet complete? Nonetheless, it wasn't worth pressing the man further—at least not until the armor was finished and it was time to ensure that everything was crafted as it should have been.

"Thank you," Thane said. "What about the other pieces?"

"Everything else is in my storage drawers, but they are of the same quality and beauty. You'll have all the parts when it's done, of course."

"Then I'll come back next week to collect the armor. Thank you for your diligence. I'll ensure you're paid as we agreed and that your See'er rank rises."

The armorer dropped his hammer. "My See'er rank? Prince Thane, you are too kind! Such is worth more than all the gold you could give me! Thank you, my lord. You are so much more flexible than your father. So much—"

"Best not to compare me to him," Thane warned. "Until next time, Shivanna Adul."

"S-Shivanna Adul," he stammered. "Thank you again for your business!"

Thane returned to the calmest area of the pier, avoiding the hustle and bustle of the day traders. Wandering alongside the docks, his eyes drifted out to the sea. As the ocean's waves caught his gaze, Thane yearned to leave the island and explore the world.

Although his father and ancestors had decreed that Son See'ers never leave their homeland, they had never justified why. Despite Thane's devotion to his god, he sometimes worried that some of the required practices and instructions might have been misinterpreted. Whenever he asked his father about why everything had to be done a certain way, he was told to trust and obey the Throatian traditions. Those who were less skeptical than Thane attributed anything out of the ordinary to "the will of Zann-Xia-Czul."

"Only through me does our god give his orders," Harkbin had told him. "Beware of your private thoughts, for Zann-Xia-Czul sees everything within our minds. He always knows when the Son See'ers doubt his ways and calls them to be tested."

Naturally, being tested, according to Harkbin, meant being killed by lightning; there was neither a trial nor a chance to object when someone's faith was in question. Zann-Xia-Czul simply gave Harkbin the names of the Son See'ers who were unworthy of sacrifice, and they would be lined up in a field together. Harkbin would read them their faults and sins, then magical lightning rained from the sky to perform the executions. It was a dreadful fate, but perhaps less painful than bleeding out in a Loyalty Circle. Thane sometimes worried that excessive questioning might cost him the favor of Zann-Xia-Czul. However, Hrodspire had once counseled that small doubts were often forgivable so long as they didn't lead to action.

A nearby shout interrupted Thane's contemplation of his god's nature. He glanced over at several guards who were running toward the gateway leading to the island's center. Had someone breached the perimeter? He jogged to where the men and women were gathering. Whatever incident was transpiring seemed out of the ordinary.

"What's happened?"

"There's a fire on Mount Sephorr," a middle-aged guard said. "We suspect it might be your father calling for help."

Dark smoke lingered near the mountain's summit. The cause of the blaze, which seemed larger than a mere campfire, appeared to have consumed at least a handful of trees.

"It couldn't be a message!" one of the younger guards added. "The king knows it's forbidden for anyone to ascend, even for a rescue. We can't violate the sacred orders."

"Shut up," the first guard said. "It's not your job to whine and complain."

"I'll seek the Elders' counsel," Thane said. "If my father is truly in danger, they might bend the rules. Assemble your troops and prepare to ascend—I might instruct you to search for him."

The men shared nervous glances. None dared to challenge his direct order, even if it contradicted the commandments of their god. Finally, their leader stepped forward.

"Yes, sir," he said, pounding his fist on his chest. "Shivanna Adul."

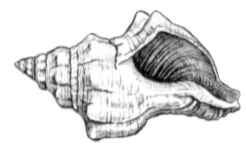

THANE RETURNED HOME IN SEARCH OF HIS MOTHER OR any of the Elders. However, upon arrival, all the nearby huts were vacant. Chances were they were all still at one of the Loyalty Circles. The next most likely spot to find anyone relevant was at the Temple of White, so Thane hastened up the road to where he'd spent the morning praying.

As he approached the massive stone building, Hrodspire trudged out to meet him halfway, huffing and puffing.

"I saw you ascending the hill, my prince," he wheezed. "Are you aware of the fire? It's raging on—"

"But is it from my father?" Thane scowled. "What are the details?"

He slowed his pace, allowing Hrodspire to keep up with him as they walked toward the Temple of White. Frowning at their reduced speed, Thane moved as quickly as Hrodspire could follow.

"Elder Kaelgeth saw several lightning bolts strike the top of the mountain," Hrodspire said. He took another moment to breathe. "Therefore, it's most likely that King Harkbin is in danger."

As they crossed beneath a large archway, Thane's heart faltered. "Would Zann-Xia-Czul have a reason to harm Father?"

The Elder scratched at the last remaining gray hairs on his head. "Come. Your mother and Kaelgeth await us. They're praying by the obelisks."

After removing their sandals, they entered the main worship room where Urith and a middle-aged man in a purple hooded robe were kneeling before the three obelisks. The man next to her was Elder Kaelgeth, the Temple of White's keeper. Like Hrodspire, the island's sun had withered his skin over the years, leaving behind various brown spots and wrinkles. Such were the marks of the highly ranked Son See'er Vrai—it was extremely rare for anyone to live long enough to approach the age where one would die of natural causes. Elders, hand-selected by their peers, served Zann-Xia-Czul and the island for life.

As Urith arose from the ground, Elder Kaelgeth greeted them with a silent nod. She turned a quick bow to the pillars and blood dripped down her armor onto the white marble floor. The mess didn't worry Thane at all, as he knew none of the blood was hers.

"Thane," she said, "this time, we cannot let tradition limit us. Someone should ascend Mount Sephorr and find your father."

Kaelgeth, spotting the blood on the ground, removed a polishing cloth from his robe and started wiping up the mess at her feet. Though the Elders were ranked higher than most other people socially, the royal family was still the highest, and it was his job to look after the religious structures and monuments.

"Respectfully, my queen," he said, "you cannot climb. We permit only the Throatian king to approach Zann-Xia-Czul on Mount Sephorr. The laws clearly forbid it."

The scar covering most of her face bulged as she growled back at him. "We must make an exception! My husband, your king, is likely in danger."

"It's not our decision," the keeper of the Temple of White countered. He rose from the floor and pocketed the bloody polishing cloth. "You dare question the command of Zann-Xia-Czul?"

Hrodspire rested his hand on Kaelgeth's shoulder. Whenever he laid his wrinkled hand on someone in that manner, it signaled that whatever he said next was not to be disputed. "Queen Asche may have a point, though for the wrong reason. An exception is necessary, and in this case, I propose allowing Prince Thane to ascend."

It couldn't be right. Mount Sephorr, the massive,

snowy summit that dominated nearly a third of their otherwise tropical island, was sacred. Kaelgeth was correct that the rules were simple: only the king could climb the mountain. Everyone else, the Elders included, couldn't.

"Me?"

"You think so, too, Hrodspire?" Kaelgeth asked. "And why should we allow Prince Thane to break the law?"

Hrodspire chose his next words carefully. "Because Thane might now be the king. There's a strong possibility King Harkbin is already dead. If that's the case, Thane can rightfully ascend Mount Sephorr."

"Explain yourself," Urith barked. "There's no way my husband is dead!"

"Kaelgeth, you saw the lightning with your own eyes, correct? You didn't learn of this from another Son See'er?" Hrodspire asked.

"Correct. There were several strikes, but no sound."

"Then you can understand the implications here," Hrodspire said, staring firmly at the queen. "Pardon me for considering the worst possibilities, but acknowledging this is the only way to allow Thane to search for his father."

Thane glared at the Elder. Suggesting his father

was dead meant only one thing: Zann-Xia-Czul, their god, had killed him with lightning.

Before he could utter a word, Urith closed the distance to Hrodspire, her face scowling inches from his, and gave him a slight shove. The old man wavered in surprise, then shrank back from her.

"Harkbin would never turn against Zann-Xia-Czul!" Urith yelled. "I should kill you where you stand for even suggesting such a thing!"

"Calm down," Kaelgeth warned. "The Temple of White is no place for violence."

"I don't like the idea of Father being dead either," Thane said. "Still, we must acknowledge the possibility. Lightning without thunder means our god created it. We can't deny it happened, but we have to figure out why."

"I agree with Prince Thane," Hrodspire said, still cowering. "I propose we grant him provisional kingship until we learn the fate of King Harkbin."

"Seconded," the queen grunted after a moment that was thick with silence and scowls. She turned to Kaelgeth, who was straightening his purple robe. "Will the Elders let Thane ascend?"

"I don't believe there's enough evidence," Kaelgeth said. "Nonetheless, despite my personal disagreement, I'll permit it in my capacity as an Elder."

Thane nodded. "We need to understand what

happened. If ascending Mount Sephorr is the only way, I'll do it."

So long as there was a chance his father was alive, he would take it, no matter how steep the climb.

"Very well," Hrodspire proclaimed. "With two Elders and the queen present, we hereby grant you the temporary privileges and powers of the king. This proclamation will either expire or extend upon your father's return. Shivanna Adul, Thane Asche."

"Be safe, my son," Urith said. "Return to us unharmed."

"Shivanna Adul," Thane said. "With any luck, I will be back with Father soon."

THANE JOGGED TO THE FOOT OF MOUNT SEPHORR where the trail began. He looked back toward the Throatian huts that dotted the neighboring mountains, wondering if it would be his last time seeing them. If Zann-Xia-Czul truly did not want him to reach the mountain's peak, death by lightning was inevitable.

Ascending Mount Sephorr presented its own challenges. Wild bears and other predators thrived there, unchallenged by hunters. Armor was a necessity, yet Thane opted for his old, rusting suit instead of the new set. The craftsman had warned that risking scratches before he'd applied the final coat of protective paint was not worth it. Thane agreed with him. After all, what was the point in having such an elegant white suit if there were a chance it would become battle-scarred in its first use?

"I look more like a commoner than a prince," Thane muttered, glaring down at his chest. "This isn't proper attire to meet my god." His old armor set had suffered from years without polish, slowly deteriorating under the sea breeze. Despite the metal surface's cloudy appearance and patches resembling brown sand—results of his neglect—it would still offer him protection.

As he ascended Mount Sephorr, the dirt path gradually transitioned into snow. Shivering, he pushed forward through the freezing wind, higher and higher, toward the summit. As his shoes filled with the iciest moisture he'd ever encountered, he quickly developed a strong disdain for snow. His armor offered no warmth, and since he had encountered no wild beasts, he discarded it in the sleet. It would provide little protection against a lightning strike anyway, and Thane ultimately didn't want anyone to find his body dishonored by such attire, should he die there.

After trudging up the hill for three hours, he took

a break, sitting down on a cold log. Though he'd seen plenty of squirrels, rabbits, and other game so far, Thane opted to eat the jerky he'd brought instead. Despite their religious mandate to consume raw meats, he preferred the taste and dry texture of the jerky over any cold, squishy, and lifeless alternative. Supposedly, centuries ago, the earliest Throatian people struggled to digest uncooked meats, but Zann-Xia-Czul had continued requiring it anyway. Enduring the hardship of their meals served as a test, leading to adaptations in their bloodlines that enabled future generations to follow these practices without falling ill. However, in the snowy ranges of Mount Sephorr, raw meat would resemble the taste of an animal's corpse even more than usual. The relentless cold surrounding Thane was unyielding, and he had no desire to partake in consuming uncooked meat.

"I should have brought more clothes," he growled. It was too late to make up for his lack of proper planning. He would need to endure the weather until reaching the summit. The fires at the top would help him warm up. He stood and resumed his journey.

As the intensity of the wind gusts increased, they pierced his lungs and caused his nose to run. Amidst the cold, he picked up a subtle hint of smoke. At least he was nearing its source now. Another series of zephyrs blew past him, and the sound of chanting echoed off in the gales somewhere far up the road. His father was nearby.

Thane's heartbeat surged as he broke into a run. No longer weighed down by the armor, his energy had been renewed. The onset of sunset and ensuing darkness soon caused the path to become unclear. Thane could see nothing, so he let the chanting sounds guide him through the mountain's forest.

"Shivanna, Shivanna, Shivanna…" the voice echoed against the howls of the wind. As Thane neared the summit, he confirmed that the chanting voice belonged to his father. The repetition meant only one thing: the king was in danger and begging for peace.

The path ended, and Thane found himself in a clearing dominated by a large, white, stone plateau. Surrounding it were eight vast trees, ablaze and smoking, as if they were sticks of incense. His father knelt in the plateau's center, both hands extended in the air as he chanted to a cave's dark opening. Whatever was inside likely held greater significance than the burning timbers surrounding the plateau.

"Harkbin!" Thane called out, still balking at the strange surroundings.

The Throatian king, either ignoring him or unable to hear him, continued his chanting unbothered.

"We have to go now!" Thane said. He coughed heavily as smoke filled his lungs.

With his father remaining undisturbed, it prompted Thane to climb onto the plateau and run towards him. Thane grabbed his shoulder, but Harkbin fearfully shoved him away. What was going on?

"No, you cannot trick me with these illusions!" Harkbin yelled. "Zann-Xia-Czul, I'll pray here until this is right!"

"Father, it's me!" Thane yelled. "I climbed Mount Sephorr. I'm really here!"

Harkbin lowered his arms and turned to his son. His face was gray with ash. "How did you...? It's forbidden. Our god... h-he would have—No, wait... You coming here could have been his intention. But that would mean—"

"What's happening?" Thane asked. "Why are the trees on fire?"

"They're omens of what's yet to pass," Harkbin said. "We're all in great danger. You shouldn't have come, Thane. You really shouldn't have come..."

"Why not? We need to go home. When did you last eat or drink anything?"

"Since our god didn't strike you down during your ascension, you've confirmed your role in this," his father replied tearfully. "I'm so sorry, my son."

Before Thane could respond, Harkbin turned

back towards the cave, raising his arms again to resume his chanting. It was the first time Thane had ever seen his father truly afraid of something. His delirium was likely from a lack of food and water. Yet could Zann-Xia-Czul be living inside that cave? What had they discussed to cause Harkbin to lose his normally unshakable composure?

Thane placed himself on the ground beside his father and gazed at the cave's entrance. Perhaps now he could finally have a conversation with his god and understand the reason for Harkbin's mysterious behavior.

"Shivanna Adul, Zann-Xia-Czul," Thane said, raising his arms in worship. "Please tell me what's happening. What's this—"

"Quiet, you twit," Harkbin said, shoving his elbow into Thane's ribs and knocking him over. "Zann-Xia-Czul only speaks to me. You haven't the right to question or command him!"

"Please!" Thane begged, ignoring Harkbin's reprimand. "I need to know what's happening."

"Thane, know your place!"

The prince's eyes narrowed as he studied his broken father, his king.

"What did he say to you?" Thane asked, pushing himself from the ground. He looked over at the trembling shell of a man upon whom his people relied on the most. "Everyone's been worried about you. We need to return home and talk about it."

"I can't go yet." Harkbin shook his head, his voice cracking. "The plan needs to change. Otherwise, our island will become—"

His king's despair and refusal to return home were unsettling. He wished he could do something—anything—to make his father understand the danger of their situation. Somehow, there had to be a way of getting through to him. But first, he had to figure out what was happening, even if not why.

"What plan?" Thane asked. "What did Zann-Xia-Czul ask of you?"

Turning away, Harkbin said, "The Loyalty Circles... we need more. Far more than we have now."

"That's nothing worth fretting about," Thane said. "We'll have the Son See'ers build more of them and increase our Breeding Farms, too, if needed. It'll take time and effort, but—"

"You don't understand," Harkbin interrupted. "Yes, we need more sacrifices, but they won't be enough. If we can't increase our yield, Zann-Xia-Czul can't protect us."

"What?"

"The blood supply—it'll be too low. There's not enough of it!"

His father wasn't making sense. The traditions of

Loyalty Circles and Breeding Farms were nearly as old as the island itself. So long as they made expansions and gained enough resources, the infrastructure supporting their population would accordingly scale.

"Why does he need blood at all?"

"We have no place questioning his needs," Harkbin retorted.

"Did you see him?"

"Who?"

"Our god."

"We humans aren't fit to see him. We are just—"

"Did you ever actually lay eyes upon Zann-Xia-Czul, yes or no?" Thane snapped.

Despite never setting foot on Mount Sephorr before, he sensed something was terribly wrong and out of the ordinary. The crackling of the burning trees echoed in the background, and he swore he could hear the snowflakes hiss as they landed among the flames.

"No."

Throughout Thane's life, his father, the Elders, and everyone else in power had insisted that Zann-Xia-Czul existed in physical form at Mount Sephorr's summit and forbade entry to anyone but a Throatian king. Why hadn't Harkbin ever witnessed their god if the ordinances were indeed accurate? Was there something their people were missing?

Regardless of the possibilities, everything would be unclear until Thane could meet their deity directly.

"We have to verify the truth," he said. "We need to confirm whether Zann-Xia-Czul is legitimately a god. Why else would he need the blood?"

"How dare you!" Harkbin exclaimed. "Have you no faith?"

"It doesn't add up!" Thane said. "He needs us to bring him more blood but won't explain why or show himself. Even at Mount Sephorr's summit, why must he hide? Something is wrong here. He might just be a Lucidian. His powers bear resemblance to the rumors about those people."

"No, Thane! You're wrong!"

"He's obviously been living alone up here the whole time," Thane said. "I'm going into that cave."

"Don't!" Harkbin reached out to stop him, but Thane was already running across the platform toward the entrance.

"Stay where you are, Father," Thane called over his shoulder. "I'll be back in a moment."

Though the cave had an enormous opening, he guessed the cavern inside was shallow, given the nearby cliff. He peered through the entrance and saw only darkness and faint shadows. Going inside was the only way to discover Zann-Xia-Czul's identity.

Thane grabbed a burning branch from the

nearest tree and held it in front of him. As he approached the cave's entrance with his new light, a bolt of lightning shot from the sky and sizzled through the snow where he was about to step. The strike narrowly missed him, clearly a supernatural warning.

He froze, and his eyes darted upward. The lighting was magical, but was it truly a god's power? He'd heard rumors of a group of humans far across the sea who'd learned how to use magic, but that their powers were weak. Being so close to his god's presence, yet denied a meeting with him, made Thane hesitant. The prince considered whether the entity he worshipped was only a fraudulent sorcerer after all.

"Zann-Xia-Czul!" Thane bellowed into the cave. "My faith in you wavers! Show me you aren't merely a Lucidian! Prove to me you are truly a god!"

"Shut up, you fool!" Harkbin yelled. "You're not thinking clearly!"

More lightning bolts rained down, this time forming a circle around Thane. Despite his upper body's uncontrollable shaking, his legs found the strength to sprint toward the cave again. The attacks were magic, but they were only warnings.

"Thane! No! Our god isn't a Lucidian!" Harkbin's warnings were useless; Thane was already in the cavern's mouth.

"I need proof!" the prince yelled, his determination preventing any desire to retreat. "Lucidians use their own blood to make their magic. We can't know who Zann-Xia-Czul is unless we see!"

He carefully extended his torch as he stepped into the cave. The flame's light reflected off the back wall, proving the interior was shallow—only fifty feet from end to end. Zann-Xia-Czul was in there somewhere, but where? There was no evidence of anyone hiding inside.

As Thane neared the rear wall, the floor disappeared from under him. He jerked backward and fell onto his backside, accidentally dropping the burning tree branch into the dark pit. The dwindling light, reduced to a distant pinpoint, momentarily cast a glow on the pit's edges. Several seconds went by before the light winked out completely and he heard the torch thud on the ground below. Thane gasped, for if he'd taken another step, he would have died.

Embarrassed, he crawled over to the edge and peered down below. Even though the torch had extinguished just a moment ago, the pit's bottom now glowed orange as growing flames climbed higher and higher at an alarming speed. He rolled back again and the fires rapidly subsided, narrowly missing his head.

"You've proven you have magic," Thane called

into the darkness. "That much is clear. But who are you really?"

He tried to look down the hole again, but fire erupted from the bottom once more, blocking his efforts. Suddenly, a scream shook inside his ears.

"WHITE ARMOR CANNOT PROTECT YOU FROM A BLACK STORM. OBEY ME OR YOU'LL PERISH WITH THE REST."

Thane quickly turned around, but nobody stood behind him. He swore that someone had yelled directly into his ear. Few people were aware of his new armor—only the armorer and perhaps the Son See'er Vrai that served him. Thane's suspicions of Zann-Xia-Czul being a Lucidian were put to rest. Though none of his questions were truly answered, Thane concluded for now that whatever hid within the cavern was, at the very least, a reclusive yet powerful magical being. A real god or not, it was too strong to challenge.

"I understand," Thane called out, trying to hold his composure and conceal his faltering voice. He'd been tested but spared. "I remain your loyal Son See'er. Thank you for showing me the way."

He held this position for a long while, waiting for acknowledgement, but Zann-Xia-Czul did not say another word.

2
THE DEMAND

Blood poured from his legs onto a small mountain of shattered seashells as Thane reached his fourth hour of meditation. Despite the thousands of cuts along his knees and shins, it was hardly a painful punishment. Kneeling on broken shells was nothing new.

His parents' method of discipline, applied whenever he disobeyed, had been far more uncomfortable during his childhood. Back then, his nerves were unaccustomed to the stern reminders of obedience and compliance. Now that Thane was in his early twenties, the suffering barely felt different from kneeling on bare ground. Resting on broken manilla seashells was less physically painful, but more embarrassing because all the Elders would know of his disrespect and corresponding punishment.

"Rise, my son," Urith commanded as she entered the Temple of White's cathedral and glared down at him. "Do not wipe your knees."

"As you wish, Mother," he replied. His hands instinctively reached to dust the shards off his legs, but he caught himself and stopped. "How is Father?"

Taking her time, Urith retrieved a new bundle of incense from the obelisks' bases and carefully set it next to the half-burned sticks. She lit the new sticks, placed them among the ashes, and then bowed. The lavender fragrance filled the spaces between the obelisks as she coughed from the smoke.

"He's still shaken by everything he saw, including what you did at the cave," Urith said. "However, a bath, some bone broth, and a tankard of mead are speeding his recovery."

Those things would ease his father's body from the hike, but the source of Harkbin's strange behavior came from whatever he and Zann-Xia-Czul had been discussing before Thane arrived. Never had he seen his father so upset. In a best-case scenario, rest and some reassurance from their god would relieve his unusual state of panic and frenzy.

"Did he say what Zann-Xia-Czul wants us to do?" Thane asked. "I'm still unaware."

"Your father has spoken of nothing other than his disappointment in your blasphemy."

"I'm sorry about that," Thane sighed. "When I

approached the plateau and didn't see our god, it gave me doubts. But in the end, Zann-Xia-Czul spoke to me! His words sounded within my mind!"

Urith nodded her approval. "Perhaps he forgave your moment of weakness. Maybe he recognized your role as the future Throatian king."

"We have no way of knowing," Thane said, waving some of the incense smoke from his eye. "I now respect Father's pilgrimages more than ever. Mount Sephorr is very, very cold."

A cough echoed behind them as Hrodspire entered the cathedral. At his side was Valenti, another Elder.

"Shivanna Adul, Prince Thane and Queen Urith," the woman said, holding a large, dirt-covered book. "I apologize for our tardiness. There was an incident at one of the Breeding Farms I needed to resolve."

Disruptions and altercations were commonplace in the daily activities of the Breeding Farms. Regardless of sex or gender, compelled procreation led to a mixture of emotions and strife among the people involved. Above all else, their duty sustained the island's population and refined the bloodlines to only Zann-Xia-Czul's most loyal. The Elder's direct control over the birth rates was necessary, as the Loyalty Circles demanded so many deaths. Aside from the Son See'er Vrai, the Elders, and a few other exempted families, most of the population followed a simple pattern: birth inside a Breeding Farm, proving themselves in a Loyalty Circle, and then contributing to the cycle's repetition.

Elder Valenti managed every aspect of the Breeding Farms, including selectively pairing Son See'ers to reduce the spread of any inherited diseases. She also ensured smooth execution of everything, from planning to childbirth, regardless of the participants' pleasures or displeasures. In situations where neither of the paired Son See'ers desired to fulfill their duties, complications arose and Valenti needed to intervene.

"Was it another Son See'er Fohh?" Urith asked her.

"Indeed. We moved him to Loyalty Circle Fourteen. While there's no room for false worshippers within our bloodlines, he'll serve Zann-Xia-Czul in life or in death."

Urith grinned and gave her a light tap on the shoulder. "Your delay was justified, Isola. Well done."

Meanwhile, Valenti narrowed her eyes at Thane. "I hope you've learned your lesson, my young prince. Your temporary appointment as king had limits."

"I wasn't even considering my title," Thane said. "I sought the true face of our god, but now I recognize my skepticism as a problem."

"Proof isn't the foundation of religion—faith is," Valenti continued. "It's best that—"

"I'm certain Thane understands the concept now," Hrodspire said as the prince held his tongue. The Elder gestured to a doorway at the other end of the cathedral. "Come, let's all sit together and wait for King Harkbin's arrival."

In the next room, empty plates, drinking glasses, and a pewter handbell were set out for them. A moment later, Kaelgeth joined and rang for the servants. On cue, the Son See'ers brought out a fresh pitcher of wine for their meeting in the dining chamber.

"What's tonight's meal?" Hrodspire asked the person filling his glass.

"Rabbits, sir."

Hrodspire nodded. "Okay, bring them in when King Harkbin arrives."

"King Asche is already here, sir," the servant replied. "He hasn't entered the cathedral yet because he walks among the gardens. Pardon me for saying, but he was deep in thought, muttering to himself."

"He was likely praying or preparing for this meeting," Urith said. "Pay no mind to his talking."

"Of course, my queen."

The four of them drank their wine in silence. Finally, just as Thane believed his father wouldn't be joining them after all, Harkbin burst into the room.

"Shivanna Adul," the king greeted. He screeched his chair against the ground and sat down. A dark purple bruise surrounded his left eye. Thane hadn't noticed the wound when they'd been atop Mount Sephorr, so he suspected his father had recently taken part in a Loyalty Circle.

Everyone else replied in unison, "Shivanna Adul."

Harkbin sniffed his wine before taking a sip. "Much is amiss on our island, and so I'll be straightforward about what I've learned: Zann-Xia-Czul needs our help as much as we need his."

Urith wiped some wine off her upper lip with her arm. "Something's wrong, isn't it?"

"Blood is the fuel that allows Zann-Xia-Czul's miracles to manifest in our world, and so blood has always been our offering. We've never known why it was this way, but our lives and culture revolved around it."

Valenti nodded. "I think we all suspected this, even though it was never explicitly stated."

"His confirmation was no surprise to me either," Harkbin said. "The problem is that Zann-Xia-Czul now needs a higher volume of it than we can produce."

"Do you mean he requires it, or asks it of us?" Hrodspire said. "It was my understanding that the sacrifices were optional, but we did them anyway to please him."

"We've met the quotas all along without realizing it—that's the way it's always been," Harkbin said. "Our tradition of giving blood to Zann-Xia-Czul, as a means for him to protect and provide for us, goes back generations. Over time, following the normalization of the Loyalty Circles, we lost these details."

"Why does he need more?" Thane asked, idly fiddling with the white tablecloth. "If it's always been this way, then he'll only need the same number of sacrifices every year, right?"

"A calamity is approaching," Harkbin answered. "A sorceress from another world intends to destroy our people. She'll be here within a year. We won't be able to defeat her on our own, and Zann-Xia-Czul needs the extra blood to protect us from her magic."

Hrodspire scratched at his beard. "I know nothing of sorceresses, but what you say about blood is correct. Lucidians need it for their talents. Even if Zann-Xia-Czul needs more to protect us, being able to use such high quantities goes beyond what any Lucidian can do. We have the advantages of the Loyalty Circles for this."

"The Breeding Farms give the Loyalty Circles vast amounts of blood for the rituals, yes," Valenti said. "Tangents aside, how much blood do we need, exactly?"

"The blood equivalent of a hundred thousand people," Harkbin said, "besides what we're already producing."

"What?!" Kaelgeth said, dropping his drink. "That many? There's no way... we could never—"

"It's impossible to expand that fast," Valenti interrupted, passing him a napkin. "Even if I opened more Breeding Farms and forced every able-bodied woman to pledge, it wouldn't bring the population to a hundred thousand more per year. There wouldn't be enough time. Even in perfect conditions, we'd need at least five years, if not longer. And even if we could enlarge our population that quickly, how would we feed and house them all?"

"I am aware of all this," Harkbin said. "That's why I need your cooperation to figure something out."

The servants re-entered the room, this time carrying platters of raw rabbit for dinner. After dishing out the cold meat, another Son See'er brought in a large bucket, filled three-quarters of the way with blood from earlier in the morning. Setting it on the table next to Harkbin's plate, the servant provided his king with a golden-bladed knife. Harkbin grasped the red-jeweled hilt and held his free hand over the bucket, then sliced his palm and let a few droplets of blood fall in with the hare's.

"Sheiaa Kaaduul," he intoned, handing the dagger to Urith.

Like her husband, Urith mixed her blood with the animal's.

"Sheiaa Kaaduul," she echoed.

The others followed suit. Last in line for the ritual, Thane solemnly nodded to the nearby servant. The young girl quickly retrieved the offering to place in front of the obelisks, where it would stay overnight.

"Such traditions are as refined as the Throatian civilization itself," Harkbin said, wiping his palm and sealing it shut with a tourniquet. "We must never forget what it means. Thane, please remind us."

The prince took a quick breath before reciting the answer he'd repeated since he was a child. "The blending of our blood with that of the animals we consume symbolizes our shared suffering, life, and spirit. Suffering and death are unavoidable parts of life."

Though he'd answered perfectly, Harkbin gave him no acknowledgment. He simply took a long drink. The table remained silent for what seemed like a full minute before Elder Valenti spoke up.

"So, what is our plan to increase the blood offerings? Ignoring this problem isn't an option."

The table sat quietly for a few more moments, except for the brief clangs of their silverware and glasses. Now Thane understood why his father had been so mentally shaken at Mount Sephorr's summit. Their island's design and infrastructure revolved entirely around Breeding Farms and Loyalty Circles—all for their devotion to Zann-Xia-

Czul. To suddenly learn that their offerings were actually requirements all along—and not only that, but learning they'd have to increase offerings to a hundred thousand more people within a year—was incomprehensible.

"Could we possibly bring in people from overseas?" Kaelgeth suggested. "The blood doesn't need to be from Throatians alone, does it?"

"It just needs to be human blood," Harkbin said, stabbing his fork into the raw rabbit meat.

"But how would we gather and transport a hundred thousand people to our island?" Hrodspire said. "Even if we had more ships, we couldn't conquer that many people."

"Perhaps we could just transport the blood instead of the people themselves? Shelves and shelves of bottles might work," Kaelgeth suggested. "I'm not sure it's even possible to collect so many people and deliver them to our island. Still, we'd lack the controlled environment of the Loyalty Circles."

"I agree with Kaelgeth," Thane said. "The Breeding Farms and Loyalty Circles are the most efficient methods to produce and gather whatever we require. Regardless of the location, we need to confine it to those systems. It's a waste of resources otherwise."

"Our existing facilities are already full," Hrodspire warned. "We couldn't hold twenty more people, not to mention a hundred thousand more."

"Even with sufficient infrastructure," Valenti said, "achieving this goal is biologically impossible. There's no way of making it happen faster than it can already be accomplished."

They were right. Expanding the population by so many people within a year wasn't possible. However, if only the blood mattered, perhaps killing people in the Loyalty Circles didn't matter. Collecting the blood a little at a time would leave the Son See'er alive at the end of the ritual.

"What if we just take ten percent of each person's blood at once?" Thane asked. "This would allow them to donate more in the long term."

His father shook his head slowly and set down his fork. "When I was on Mount Sephorr, I also considered that option. Leaving the Son See'ers alive still wouldn't produce enough before the deadline. The problem is that everything needs to be delivered together in about a year. A hundred thousand people, ready to give their lives, is what's asked of us. Stockpiling it won't work."

Thane stared at the dead rabbit on his plate. Chances were high that Zann-Xia-Czul already knew his demands were impossible, but was their god purposely being cruel by making them run in circles? Was all this somehow a greater test, with an overlooked conclusion? Why couldn't their god defeat a sorceress on his own? There had to be more to it than what Zann-Xia-Czul had revealed to Harkbin. True, human blood gave magic. But why would a god depend on it for his powers?

Hrodspire nodded. "We agree that it's impossible to sacrifice people we don't have. Perhaps if we knew more about the sorceress's threat to our island, we could—"

"Zann-Xia-Czul gave us all the information we need," Harkbin interrupted. He cleared his throat, but his voice was still raspy from chanting so much. "This plan transcends us all, and we each have a specific role to play. We must trust our god to manage the remaining details."

"Did he provide any hints on how to accomplish our task?" Hrodspire asked. "We're talking about a hundred thousand new people, my king. That's over double the current population of our entire island."

Everyone resumed their silence for a moment, until a servant returned with a large ceramic jug. The liquid sloshed inside the bottle as, with shaking arms, the boy nervously tilted it over Urith's shoulder and refilled her glass. Satisfied that he'd topped off the queen's drink, the boy quietly lugged his wine over to Harkbin, but the king shooed him away.

"What if we stopped doing the Loyalty Circles?"

Valenti said, holding up her empty glass for the servant to fill. Both Harkbin and Urith shuddered at the idea. The Elder scratched the top of her dark hair. "Closing them would be temporary, of course. Achieving our goal depends on the number of Son See'ers. So, if we stopped the sacrifices and put everyone into Breeding Farms instead, it might help. Once there's enough blood, we could resume the normal operations of Loyalty Circles."

"That would disrupt the balance," Urith said.

"We can't let that happen," Hrodspire said. "Breeding Farms and Loyalty Circles rely on each other to keep Son See'ers obedient. Getting rid of one will break their symbiosis."

"At least I'm contributing new ideas instead of declaring everything impossible," Valenti countered.

"Just a moment ago, you yourself declared it impossible!" Hrodspire said.

Harkbin slammed his fist on the table. "Calm yourselves, both of you! Let us recess for now. If nobody comes up with a viable plan by morning, I'll return to Mount Sephorr and beg for more help. We'll get Zann-Xia-Czul the blood he needs. Somehow…"

He rose from his chair and left his meal behind, unfinished. Urith followed him back toward the cathedral, leaving Thane alone with the three Elders. Hrodspire, Kaelgeth, and Valenti had all served their positions since long before he was born. They had become his de facto family—almost like aunts and uncles. The Throatian prince had no siblings and, as a child, had remained isolated from all but a few Son See'er Vrai to allow him to focus on his studies. Tightly bound by religion and necessity to rule, it was destiny that the Elders and his parents would work together so closely. Still, their expectations of the prince were high, often leaving little room to deviate from the island's doctrines.

"You're awfully quiet, Thane," Hrodspire commented.

Thane had been shuffling his food around his plate without eating it. It seemed as if Zann-Xia-Czul was intentionally causing them to panic. The goal was a pointless demand only meant to agitate them all.

"I dare not speak my mind," Thane said. "Yesterday's events shook my faith, and I'm taking care to reconcile everything I witnessed. I don't want to worry any of you while my spirit falls back in line."

Kaelgeth rested his elbows on the table and leaned forward. "Your desire for mindfulness is admirable, but if you have any helpful ideas, put them forward. Just because they pass through your lips does not mean we'll have to implement them."

"Are you sure it won't cause trouble?" Thane asked.

"We are all failures in the worship of our god," Hrodspire said, "in some way or another. Humans are imperfect. So much is true in every religion. Whether we are unaware of it, admit it, or conceal it, consistent attempts at obedience are more realistic to achieve than constant success."

Thane gave him a slight grin. Despite Hrodspire's incessant need to share gossip, his lips occasionally let out a helpful truth. Somehow, he suspected he'd just heard something worth remembering. He looked toward the doorway into the cathedral. Satisfied that only the Elders could listen in on their conversation, Thane rested his forearm on the table and leaned in.

"When I discovered my father on Mount Sephorr, he was trembling with fear, chanting for peace," Thane whispered. "Our god's demand is a puzzle without an actual solution. Harkbin also knows this, but he won't admit to it. Eventually, he's going to have to concede that we can't accomplish this task. Seeing him so distraught makes me wonder why Zann-Xia-Czul bothered asking us for this at all. There's got to be some ulterior motive behind it."

Hrodspire took a sip from his drink. "A god may test his people, but I'm certain he wouldn't ask for anything unattainable," he said. "We can overcome his trials if—"

"If it's Zann-Xia-Czul's will, then so be it. However, we already know we can't meet the blood quota without his help, so what's the actual point? Was the purpose of his demand just to trap us into needing to compromise with him? Is the sorceress even real?"

"My prince, you're overthinking it," Valenti replied. "Our god would never manipulate his people in such a way."

"He knows our thoughts and every detail of our island," Kaelgeth added. "Even asking the impossible of us, it wouldn't be for a nefarious purpose. It would be for our growth."

"Again, righteousness is all about effort toward obedience," Hrodspire affirmed, "not the ultimate success or failure."

"Everything you've stated is fair," Thane said. "But if the threat of a sorceress is true, how will we sacrifice over a hundred thousand people's worth of blood?"

"None of us have an answer for that yet, Thane," Hrodspire said. "Trust me—somehow, we'll find a way."

Thane couldn't blame the Elders for lacking a solution. The problem was unprecedented; to his knowledge, their island had never faced an outside threat before, let alone a magical one. Only one other person might have a deep enough understanding of their island's history to potentially contribute something valuable: Cereene Cirixaa.

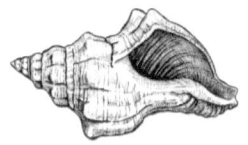

HAVING REACHED NO SOLUTION WITH THE ELDERS, Thane left the Temple of White. The cold ocean breeze blew across his pale cheeks as moonlight covered the sandy pathways leading from the temple over the hill. Rather than returning to his own hut, Thane walked toward where Cereene Cirixaa lived. Despite her home being roughly the same size as the one he, Harkbin, and Urith all shared, she lodged alone. The rest of her family members had waned away long ago during their participation within the Loyalty Circles.

As he entered her home, Cereene was busy at her small wooden desk, scribbling the writings of an old, sacred book into a new volume. She was a Son See'er Vrai, a noted loyal follower of Zann-Xia-Czul. Her status gave her the privilege of learning to read and write in the Throatian native script. The upper class expected their Son See'er Vrai to copy, memorize, and preserve several books every week. Thane and Cereene often hiked along the island's mountains to archive the volumes deep within remote caches hidden in the wilderness. Without such measures, religious texts and lore risked being lost to time.

"Thane!" Cereene dropped her quill and quickly embraced him with the warmth of her petite figure. "I'm glad you're okay!"

From the moment they'd met a year ago, their blades pointed at one another, Thane knew he wanted her. They both knew, because of the circumstances, that she owed her existence to him. Cereene appeared to return his feelings, but Thane often prayed that sparing her life wasn't the only reason for it.

"I've been better," he said, abandoning his thoughts. Right now, he needed her level-headedness more than anything.

Cereene released him, then studied him over. "What happened to your legs? They're all bloody!" She rushed over to the modest fire pit in the corner of her room and fetched a steaming kettle. She poured the water over a thick cloth and promptly returned to him. "This will clean you up," she said as she knelt and began dabbing at his legs.

He couldn't help but blurt out what he'd done. "I disobeyed my father while I was at the top of Mount Sephorr."

"The rumors are true, then. You ascended. But what did you do there?" Cereene finished cleaning the blood and broken shards of seashell from his limbs, then led him over to her bed. He sat down as she brought him some bread and water. Despite its simplicity, there was less pressure around this food than his previous meal. Here seemed more like home.

"So, what happened?" she repeated.

He explained all that had occurred since before hiking Mount Sephorr, sparing no details regarding his newfound questions about their religion.

"Harkbin isn't saying everything he saw," Thane said. "I don't know what he's hiding, but there's something else at play that I cannot define."

"Of course, your father is just worried about you and everyone else," Cereene said. "I don't think he has anything to conceal. The king wants to do what's best for everybody, the same as he's always done. Such struggles help us grow."

"To be honest, I've often felt the blood sacrifices were wrong somehow," Thane said.

"Huh?"

He set down the bread and gulped the cup of water in a single chug. "The Loyalty Circles only end in death, and I can't help but feel they are immoral, even if they're to benefit our god."

"Part of believing in Zann-Xia-Czul is letting go of your personal beliefs and trusting in the plan he has laid out for us," Cereene said.

He gazed into her fiery, emerald eyes. "If I'd

followed his intention, we wouldn't be resting here together now."

After all, it was with his influence as a royal family member that he'd saved her from the Loyalty Circle's fate. Cereene would never set foot in a Loyalty Circle again, but her newfound privilege came with a consequence. Son See'er Vrai were bound to lifelong servitude to the upper-class Throatians, no matter the nature of their requests. Thankfully, the Elders and his parents had turned a blind eye to what he'd done.

"None of us can stop what's meant to be or what's coming," Cereene reminded him. "Life and death are natural states. We have only what we can control."

"But why do we have to keep killing one another?"

"It's a sacrifice by definition," she said, placing her hands on her hips.

"What?"

"It's about giving up something that you'd rather keep. We mustn't forget that suffering is as inevitable in life as it is in death. Sheiaa Kaaduul."

"Sheiaa Kaaduul," Thane replied automatically. "I once heard that, across the sea, they worship a different god named Asura. His followers put out food and wine for their god in offering instead of killing each other in his name. Why do we require so much violence, forcing people to breed, and only to support more bloodshed?"

"Our conviction is stronger than those who pray to other gods," Cereene said, raising her chin up. "Asura is a false god, created by those who aren't able to discipline themselves for the greater good. His followers don't understand the meaning of suffering, death, or what it means to sacrifice for a higher purpose. Throatian hearts can handle what's needed for that—we're so much stronger, and our souls burn with a passion to do the right thing. That's why we're the only humans capable of serving Zann-Xia-Czul. Therefore, we do as we're told. We are the only ones who are able."

Even if he hadn't made her a Son See'er Vrai, she deserved to be one. Still, regardless of her status and rank, it wasn't good to serve anyone so blindly, even Zann-Xia-Czul.

"So, you'll obey whatever your god commands, even if it goes against your personal opinions?" Thane said.

"That's correct," Cereene nodded. "While climbing Mount Sephorr, you became lost among the trees, if you understand what I mean. You're overthinking."

"It came more from general curiosity than doubt," Thane admitted. "It was only after I saw my father's desperation and couldn't meet Zann-Xia-

Czul that I recognized the gaps in what I thought I knew."

"That's all it took to cause your faith to crumble?" She sat up in bed. "Everyone knows that our god will only communicate with the Throatian king. You're still a prince, and it's the only reason he kept you alive. He's not obliged to change the rest of his rules just because he made an exception once. You're lucky he spoke to you at all."

"It makes sense now. My curiosity got me carried away. Still, there's one last thing I don't follow."

The two of them changed into their clothing for the night and slid into Cereene's bed together. Though the sheets were small and could barely hold the two of them, close contact assuaged the worst of the chills on the coldest nights.

"It's normal for one's faith to waver," Cereene said, wrapping her arms around him. "I trust you, even though some of what you're saying goes against what our beliefs should be. So, what else is there you don't understand?"

"About what he said to me—how white armor won't protect me from a black storm. What does it mean?"

"That's easy," Cereene said. "Before Mount Sephorr, you were checking on the new armor that's being crafted for you. It's white. The black storm is an allusion to the sorceress's magic. Zann-Xia-Czul cautioned that your faith in him is more important than anything material. By speaking into your mind, he proved he was real."

Despite their differing backgrounds, Thane hoped he could marry Cereene someday. Perhaps after this crisis was resolved, he would have the chance to settle down with her. She had a knack for understanding exactly what he needed. Her gentle warmth was something nobody else on the island possessed.

"Why is it you always find such obvious answers to my questions?" Thane teased.

Cereene beamed at him. "I spend days on end with my head inside those books so that you don't have to. You're welcome."

"Oh, I see how it is," Thane grinned. "Let me thank you for it, then…"

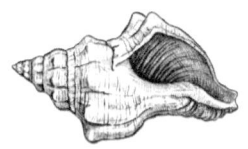

LATER, DEEP INTO THE NIGHT, THANE AWOKE. THE fireplace had burned out hours ago, and the ocean winds pushed a heavier breeze than usual through the open doorway. As Cereene continued sleeping next to him, Thane quietly crept out of bed and placed more logs onto the ashes of her dying fireplace. As he fanned the cinders, the fire gradually reignited.

He stayed squatted, holding his hands close to the warmth. Crickets chirped outside, as the ocean waves crashed against the cliffs in the distance. Despite the evening's lingering quietness, something still didn't seem right.

Tension plagued his neck, leading him to gently press his fingers against his jawline. Tilting his head to the left, he inhaled deeply for a few seconds before releasing the air. Although the exercises relieved some of the pressure, they were insufficient to completely alleviate his tension. Nevertheless, Thane repeated his controlled breathing and stretching a few times, then tried meditating.

As he inhaled and exhaled slowly beside the gentle crackling of the flames, ten minutes passed. Just as he started feeling centered again, Zann-Xia-Czul's voice yelled directly into his mind:

"REMEMBER, THANE: GOOD SON SEE'ERS ALWAYS OBEY MY DECREE. ARE YOU A GOOD SON SEE'ER?"

Thane's heart skipped a beat, and he quickly jolted his head away from the fireplace, scouring the room. He and Cereene were still alone in the small hut.

"What do you want?!" he yelled toward the ceiling.

"Thane!" Cereene cried out, awoken in a frenzy. "What's wrong?"

He let out a long breath, and the hairs on his neck rescinded. "Sorry, Cereene. I fell asleep while meditating and had a bad dream."

"It's a tad late to be contemplating, isn't it?" She looked through the doorway, out toward the sky. "Or perhaps a bit early."

"I couldn't sleep. Sorry for waking you."

"Come back to bed. Tomorrow is going to be busy for you, I think."

"Yeah." He unfolded his legs and returned to the bed.

"Goodnight, Thane," she said, pulling the blankets over his body.

"Goodnight."

Thane continued gazing into the flames until sunrise. Zann-Xia-Czul's magic was undeniably real, as was his god's disappointment in him. The night steadily transformed into morning, refusing to yield another moment where Thane could peacefully sleep beside Cereene. As he surrendered to the daylight, he took a piece of bread and chewed quietly. Cereene woke up shortly after him, proceeding to put a kettle of water on the boil. As the flames fluttered around the steel, she resumed copying the religious book sitting on her desk.

"Did you sleep okay the rest of the night?" Cereene asked.

"Yes."

She put down the quill and turned to face him. "I can tell when you're lying to me. What's on your mind?"

Thane glanced toward the ceiling, sighed, and then returned his attention to her. "Zann-Xia-Czul is going to test me soon. He spoke to me again last night."

She frowned at him. "Test as in... as in lightning?"

"If I fail whatever he's about to ask of me, then yes, he might kill me." He grabbed his sandals and strapped them on.

"Wait, Thane! Where will you go?"

"To a Loyalty Circle," Thane said. "I need to calm myself down."

3

THE LOYALTY CIRCLE

Half an hour later, Thane approached a tall stone building, Loyalty Circle Nineteen. Though the original Loyalty Circle from generations ago remained a primitive fighting pit, the designs of the subsequent iterations had advanced over the years. The fourth version optimized the collection of the sacrificial blood. Battles took place on rooftops with grate-like floors, and whenever blood spilled, funnels below them captured and deposited it into buckets below. Blood was the motivating force of the island, and their country had established twenty of these buildings throughout the centuries.

Above all else, Loyalty Circles functioned as a test of devotion to Zann-Xia-Czul. This didn't change the fact that some of the long-term winners

—or survivors, depending on who you asked—chased the thrill of the fight, and had established careers and fame from their victories. Some Loyalty Circles, such as number nineteen, had received modifications to their rooftop structure to provide more excitement for the spectators. The Loyalty Circles had an entertainment factor the Elders could not deny, so they controlled the idea rather than outright banish it.

There were two ways a Son See'er could take part in the ritual: a Reminder of Suffering or a Reminder of Death. The first option simply meant to fight another Son See'er in the Loyalty Circle until only one remained. The second required the participant to collect the filled buckets at the bottom floor and place them on an altar as an offering to Zann-Xia-Czul. Either way, the mantra "Sheiaa Kaaduul" encapsulated the significance of the events that occurred there several times a day.

Thane approached the line of Son See'ers waiting to enter the building and went straight to the front. Being a member of the royal family, he enjoyed the advantage of not needing to wait to spectate or perform the rites. The people behind him fell into two groups: those addicted to the suspense of the events, and those terrified of engaging. No matter which group they fell into, the will of Zann-Xia-Czul compelled them all to be there.

"Shivanna Adul, Prince Thane," the young coordinator said. He held a large scroll to record the names of the Son See'ers passing through the great wooden doorway. Should someone have failed to check into one of the Loyalty Circles at least weekly, it would be Elder Hrodspire's responsibility to follow up with them. Armed guards, ready with their chains, typically handled those with frequent absences. For the common citizen, there was no avoiding the religious call to participate.

Thane glanced at the growing line of people behind him. "Shivanna Adul, Son See'er. It's a busy morning for you, isn't it?"

The young man lowered the scroll to his side. "Contributions are always welcome here. Have you come for a Reminder of Death or Suffering?"

"To spectate," Thane replied. "Watching the other Son See'ers helps me clear my head and feel closer to Zann-Xia-Czul."

The coordinator frowned, moving his oily face next to Thane's. "Is it true you ascended Mount Sephorr?"

"I had to find my father. He'd taken longer on his monthly pilgrimage than normal. The Elders gave me their blessings to ascend."

"What was it like up there? We always see the whiteness of it from a distance, but what about the weather? Is it truly cold, or is it only white sand?"

"Both," Thane answered. "There's no other place like it. Unless Zann-Xia-Czul calls me back, I have no plans to return there until I am king and my duties require it."

The young man's mouth hung open in disbelief. A moment of awkward silence passed before Thane bid him farewell and made his way through two giant wooden doors. Inside, his footsteps echoed down a cobblestone hallway until he reached a spiral staircase. Guided by the orange torches mounted along the wall, he moved up them and arrived on a landing bathed in sunlight from the roof exit. A Son See'er standing at attention opened the door for him and ushered him towards the stone benches perched above the arena.

"Water or wine today, my prince?"

"Wine."

Thane sat down and waited for the next round of the ritual to begin. Aside from various swords, shields, and spears left behind by previous participants, the grated floor was clear for now. What made Loyalty Circle Nineteen special, however, were three stone moats that formed a circle around the arena's center. Almost a foot tall, each rested above the metal flooring, their insides stained black and filled with ash. An attendant, bearing a bundle of straw and twigs, walked along each canal, stuffing her tinder and oils inside. As she finished preparing the stone rings, another coordinator approached the stands, carrying a scroll filled with the names of the people waiting in line.

"Shivanna Adul, honorable Son See'ers," he announced. "This next round of the ritual will be a unique event. Almost fifteen years ago, a foreigner from the Yaenian continent visited White Boar's Landing and attempted to steal from one of our market stalls. We captured him, and have held him prisoner since then, attempting to convert him to the ways of Zann-Xia-Czul. The outsider doesn't speak much of our language but recently grasped the value of cooperation. His reward is an opportunity to show whether he's willing to step into the light and begin his life anew as a true follower."

The people in the crowd bowed their heads in silence as Thane sipped his wine. A thief wouldn't last long in the Loyalty Circles. His time in prison had come to an end and he had neither atoned for his crimes, nor learned the Throatian tongue, nor contributed anything worthwhile to society. Nobody would dare admit it, but to bring a foreigner into a Loyalty Circle only served as an officially sanctioned way to kill them. Whoever this criminal was, he would only fight for his life, not to honor and sacrifice for Zann-Xia-Czul. To give the prisoner any more credit or benefit of the doubt was a lie.

Armed with spears, guards moved forward, each

gripping the arm of a thin, middle-aged man in a gray tunic and black trousers. His long, dirty, red beard hung down, and his eyes burned with anger. The escorts shoved him forward into the Loyalty Circle's center and provided a rusty, old blade.

"Don't even think about turning it against us," the guard warned. The prisoner stared at the weapon without acknowledging him. Chances were he hadn't understood a word of what they'd said.

The coordinator gave the red-bearded man a disapproving scowl before refocusing his attention back to the scroll. "Facing the convict will be the Son See'er born of Breeding Farm Ten, Mornne Tharkk."

Moments later, a Son See'er entered from the opposite end of the arena. He had a medium build and several burns all over his face. It likely wasn't his first time in Loyalty Circle Nineteen. Armed with a sword, he was ready to fight. Armor was forbidden in the ceremonies unless the Elders arranged it in advance. Normal clothing, usually vulnerable cloth tunics, were the norm. Son See'ers who could afford them wore leather, but most could not.

"Now is the time to say your last words, if you have any," the coordinator said. "If you survive three rounds, or Zann-Xia-Czul strikes down your enemy with lightning, I will deem you innocent."

Mornne Tharkk cast a menacing glare at his opponent. "Anyone who steals from a Throatian steals from our god himself. We should have executed the prisoner the moment we captured him, not rewarded him with fifteen years of food, water, and shelter."

The crowd erupted in applause. As they calmed down, the announcer asked the foreigner to speak if he wished, but the language barrier prevented any understanding. Fortuitously, Thane knew Common Tongue and was in the mood to talk. He stood from the bench, still holding his wine.

"Prisoner," Thane said in the speech the man would understand. "You're about to engage in a battle to the death. Only one of you will walk out of here. Do you have any last remarks?"

The orange-haired man gaped in astonishment. "So, you blood-mongers can speak the common language after all. Fine, I'll give you some last words, then... I'm Ibiram Lionheart and I've committed no crime. I stole nothing from you, but you've stolen my life away. My family at home waits for me." He pointed his sword at Thane, then shifted it toward his opponent. "I'll duel for my freedom, no matter how many battles it requires."

Thane frowned and then spoke in Common Tongue once more. "That's not how it works. The Loyalty Circle is a never-ending cycle to remind us of suffering and death. As in life, both are inevitable."

Ibiram returned a fearless grin. "Then I suppose

I'll have to fight you all, one at a time, until I'm the last man standing on your bloody little island. Did you know that before all this, I was a mercenary? I've killed pirates all along the coasts of the Silent Deserts, slavers, and their guards too. I'll cut down anyone who stands—"

"Enough of your long-windedness," the prince interrupted. He waved his hand at the coordinator and switched back to his native tongue. "Ring the bell."

The Son See'er complied, and another servant carried a torch to the stone canals, igniting the tinder. Fire quickly enveloped the circle, starting the round. The oils that had been poured into the fixtures were special, allowing the flames to rise as walls taller than any Son See'er.

Mornne Tharkk wasted no time in initiating the engagement. "Death to infidels!" He swung his blade horizontally at Ibiram, but the foreigner parried it.

"Burn in the black sands of Tornaa!" Ibiram Lionheart yelled in Common Tongue, bouncing to the left before taking his first swing back at Mornne Tharkk.

The Son See'er charged forward, blade pointed directly ahead, but Lionheart performed a strange spin to evade the attack. As quickly as Mornne had come from the front, Ibiram slid to his side and successfully poked his ribcage. The Son See'er growled in pain before taking another wild, but futile, swing.

"It's over now," the foreigner taunted. "You're going to bleed out."

The coordinator approached two of the servants who were conducting the arena and murmured some instructions to them. A moment later, an archer lit an arrow on fire and shot it into the second-most ring. The battlefield grew smaller as a second wall of flames edged the two fighters closer to each other.

Thane continued observing Mornne and Ibiram until something thudded down next to him. The head of a silver war hammer had landed on the ground to his left.

"Shivanna Adul, cousin," the young man holding the weapon said. "Waiting to see if you'll have the chance to punish the foreigner?"

Thane failed to hide his grimace. It was Desaii Egon, the nephew of Urith Asche, and the most annoying person Thane had ever known. Though Desaii had a strong build, plenty suitable for lifting the war hammer he carried with him everywhere, his lack of focus and attention to detail made his weapon mostly useless. Above all else, Desaii had a reputation for provoking the weakest Son See'ers into joining him in the Loyalty Circles, then being unable to handle himself in battle. He'd had so many near-failures that Hrodspire ordered anyone who faced him to be drugged with a sleeping weed, stabbed in the leg beforehand, or disadvantaged in whatever way would guarantee Desaii a win. His blood connection to Urith was all that protected him, for he couldn't properly defend himself. Nobody dared tell him the truth, for Desaii's inflated ego would flare up if they did, and it wasn't worth the hassle of getting pestered to join him in a Loyalty Circle. Though Desaii was Thane's cousin, he avoided him whenever possible. Supposedly, Desaii's blood brother, Grimm Kathaar, was more level-headed, less provocative, and a formidable warrior, but Thane had avoided interacting with him over the years just for the sake of avoiding Desaii.

"I doubt there'll be an opportunity for me to fight the thief," Thane said. "Surely Zann-Xia-Czul won't allow him to advance further."

Desaii took a seat next to him, placing the war hammer between his legs. He stank of fish grease and alcohol. "I heard you've recently advanced further than you should have."

"What?"

"Mount Sephorr. You climbed up even though you're not the king. That's illegal, you know."

"The Elders told me it was in our best interest," Thane said. "Besides, Zann-Xia-Czul didn't strike me down. He could have, but he chose not to."

68

Desaii moved closer and whispered into Thane's face with his smelly fish breath. "You should stop grasping for so much power before it's due. Your family possesses a history of bending the rules for their personal benefit. Ordinary Son See'ers are noticing, and they aren't taking too kindly to it."

"They're welcome to their opinions. It's up to Zann-Xia-Czul whether their thoughts betray their faith," Thane shot back. "My family has nothing to hide. We've always been transparent and acted in the interest of all Son See'ers."

His cousin grunted and gripped the handle tightly. "Everyone noticed that you're only taking part in Reminders of Death recently. You've been avoiding killing anyone in the Loyalty Circles. And when was the last time you had a Reminder of Suffering? If you go on without risking your own life, other Son See'ers won't want to do it either. That's going to be a problem. Plus, you made that Cirixaa girl a Son See'er Vrai, and I know you're sleeping with her. Did she turn your heart soft, my prince?"

"Watch yourself, cousin," Thane warned. "My decisions don't concern you."

"Your rule-bending is getting out of hand," Desaii continued. "You begged the Elders to let you search for your missing father, but regular Son See'ers saw it was self-serving. Your choices have nothing to do with what Zann-Xia-Czul asks of us."

"Shut up."

A collective gasp rippled through the crowd, drawing Thane and Desaii's attention back to the arena. Mornne Tharkk had collapsed onto the ground, a sword now through his chest. Ibiram Lionheart stood over him, a triumphant grin on his face as he pointed the other blade at his defeated foe. The foreigner had somehow taken hold of both weapons and ended the ritual. To conclude the round, the Loyalty Circle coordinator rang the bell once again.

"Sheiaa Kaaduul," the chant echoed from every Son See'er as the fiery rings gradually subsided.

Blood dripped from Mornne Tharkk's body, funneling into the system within the building below. The orange-bearded prisoner pulled the blade out of him and confidently held both weapons. In Common Tongue, he bellowed to the crowd, "Who's next?"

Desaii picked up his war hammer. "I'll challenge the prisoner."

Thane grabbed his cousin's shoulder. "No, I will."

He knew his courage was only half-hearted. Truthfully, he wasn't sure whether Desaii was lying about the rumors. But if it was true, it was time for Thane to prove himself to his people. Plus, there was always the chance that this was the test Zann-Xia-Czul had in store for him. It was the first opportunity in his life to battle a foreigner too.

With a smile, Desaii sat down again. "As you wish, my prince. May the better man be victorious."

The coordinator rushed over to them. "Prince Thane, I thought you were only here to spectate? We already have Son See'ers lined up to partake in the Reminder of Suffering. There's no need for you to join unless you feel called to do so."

Thane hoped Zann-Xia-Czul was watching. Calmly, he stated, "As a prince, I cannot pardon a foreigner who spills a Son See'er's blood."

The coordinator replied, "We'll procure some weapons for you. Follow me."

As he stepped away from the bench, Thane swore he heard Desaii murmur 'fraud' under his breath, but he ignored him, continuing his stride. The supervisor led him over to a large bin filled with various swords, shields, axes, and spears.

"Are you certain you want to enter this round?" the young man asked.

"I am." He selected a spear and crossed over the now-extinguished rings into the arena.

"The Common-Tongue-speaker came to have a chat with me!" Ibiram yelled with a wild grin.

"That's Prince Thane to you."

"You're the Throatian prince? I doubt it. But

either way, you're a fool for risking your life with me."

"We'll see about that," Thane said. "I've visited these places since I could walk."

Lionheart stepped forward, scraping his two swords against one another. "Asura's ass. Everyone knows if they kill you in these games, they'll get executed afterward anyway. Nobody walks freely after murdering royalty, even if it was a fair fight."

Despite the intriguing conversation and his opponent's surprising intellect, Thane decided it was best to conclude their conflict swiftly. Thankfully, the spectators didn't understand the words he and the prisoner were exchanging. It surely would have given Desaii more fodder to taunt him with later.

Thane twirled his spear as he circled the arena. "I doubt you're going to want to go down easily for me. Just one of us can walk out of here, you know."

"I intend to kill you and anyone else who crosses my path," Lionheart declared. "Then I'll steal a boat and return to Starlight Beach—to my wife and daughter, Rosalyn."

The abrupt ring of the Loyalty Circle's bell and the rekindling of the first perimeter of fire made Thane flinch, and their figures bathed in an unsettling warmth. In three minutes, the servants would light the second ring.

"Your wishes are honorable, but they won't free

you from here," he said. "The only way off this island is through the cycle of life and death. That's how it's always been."

"Prove it, boy."

They slowly circled the arena, eyes locked, keeping their distance. Despite his spear having the advantage of reach, the prince couldn't determine whether the foreigner truly knew how to use two swords simultaneously. Dual wielding was a technique of high risk and low reward. Son See'ers who'd tried it typically failed miserably and paid for their naivety with their lives. The problem was, this man was a foreigner and there wasn't a way to know how he'd been trained, if at all. Was the claim of being a mercenary a lie?

Thane advanced two paces toward Lionheart, the tip of his spear aimed at his chest. Holding a blade alongside the spear, Lionheart charged toward him. Thane reacted fast enough to pivot the shaft away and resume the advantage, but it was a trap. Lionheart suddenly threw his other sword forward, forcing Thane to duck. Never had a Son See'er fought so recklessly!

As Thane straightened back up, the prisoner reached into his pocket and flung a handful of dirt at him. Eyes watering from the dust, Thane swung his spear in a wide horizontal arc. How and why the man was carrying sand around in his pockets was a mystery, but there was no time to think about it; Thane was losing the fight and suspected the wine he'd been drinking had something to do with it.

The second ring of fire sprang up, grazing Thane's rear and consequently shrinking the playing field. He jumped out of the way and repositioned his weapon, locking the sharp point back onto Lionheart's chest. His enemy was fighting with strange tactics, so Thane would try the same.

Instead of charging forward with the spear, Thane leaped backward through the wall of fire, then quickly picked up the discarded blade on the other side. Trying the same trick as his foe, Thane threw the sword back through the flames toward where his enemy had been, then sprinted ahead with his spear. The foreigner skillfully deflected the airborne weapon but inadvertently left an opening.

Thane impaled him through the chest. The spear's tip slid cleanly out through Lionheart's back, sealing his fate. Thane leaned into it, and half the weapon had come out the other side before he let go and watched his foe drop to the ground.

"Asura, please watch over... Rose," Lionheart gasped, his blade clattering to the ground.

"I'm sorry," Thane said in Common Tongue, picking up the sword. "Zann-Xia-Czul is the one true god, and these are his ways. Sheiaa Kaaduul."

Concealing his regret with a false smile, Thane

plunged his second weapon through Ibiram's "lion heart." It would give the man a swift death.

"Sheiaa Kaaduul!" the crowd echoed as the prince let go of the handle. He looked back toward Desaii, who was frowning from the observation benches. Servants quickly extinguished the fiery rings, and the Loyalty Circle's coordinator approached.

"Excellent work, Prince Thane," he proclaimed, inscribing the battle's outcome onto his extensive scroll. "You've done the island a great service—justice and sacrifice in the name of our god."

"Such is customary, my faithful Son See'er," Thane managed through gritted teeth. "This is a Reminder of Suffering, nothing more." He hurried toward the stairway, nodding to Desaii on his way over.

"You got lucky today," his cousin muttered, with a scowl that made him even uglier than normal. He didn't stand. "Maybe not so much next time."

The prince considered ignoring Desaii's taunt, but as he reached the downstairs door, he spoke up anyway. "Loyalty is proven through actions, not luck. The sole consequence of this battle is the affirmation that I am meant to survive."

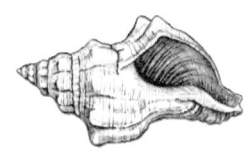

ONCE AGAIN, THANE FOUND HIMSELF ENTERING THE Temple of White. Harkbin, Hrodspire, and Valenti were all kneeling in the presence of the obelisks, praying diligently. Silently, Thane approached from the side and knelt next to his father. His forehead grazed the frigid stone floor as he joined the others in addressing the stone pillars. Though he'd won his battle within the Loyalty Circle, something about the fight had awakened an abrupt recognition of his own mortality. Lionheart would have taken his life if he'd had the opportunity. That exchange, along with Desaii's accusations, tied knots in Thane's chest.

"Son." Harkbin's voice echoed in the marble cathedral.

Finishing his bow, the prince said, "Shivanna Adul, Father."

"We need to talk. Come with us." Everyone arose from the floor and offered the obelisks one last nod.

The four of them proceeded outside into a garden, where a worn stone pathway guided them to the beach. In silence, they sauntered across the cliffs, looking over the ocean and White Boar's Landing. Far off in the distance, along the coast, ships were arriving and departing the trade port. As Harkbin, Hrodspire, and Valenti remained silent, the rustling of lizards scrambling among wild bush branches competed with the distant echoes of the sea. The wind howled against Thane's face, reminding him how high they were above the Loyalty Circles and Breeding Farms—the nest of death in the valley below.

"It's time I reveal the full truth to you, my son," Harkbin said as they neared a small area where travelers could rest. Surrounded by hedges, three identical stone benches sat arranged in a triangle. Thane's father gestured for them all to choose a seat.

"And what's that?" Thane asked, suspicion edging his voice. "You've been hiding something from me, haven't you? What's the truth about Mount Sephorr?"

His father sighed and leaned his elbows onto his knees. "I didn't do it because… I didn't think… Well, I mean… What happened up there is complicated."

"Just say it. Why is Zann-Xia-Czul angry with me?"

"He's not angry with you, I promise you that," Harkbin replied. "So, here's the truth: our god's original demand was far more difficult for us to fulfill. Sacrificing a hundred thousand people's worth of blood was the compromise."

"A compromise? But how? How much blood does Zann-Xia-Czul actually need to protect the island? Why is the amount somehow negotiable?"

His father sat up again and exchanged a wistful glance with Hrodspire and Valenti before turning back to Thane.

"Please calm down and listen to me," he said. "We were mistaken about everything. How much blood we dedicate to Zann-Xia-Czul has less effect than we originally thought. Who it comes from matters more. Some people's blood converts to magic more strongly than others."

"For over thirty years, I've managed the Loyalty Circles," Hrodspire continued. "Not all human lives are equal. Your father didn't know this detail until recently, either."

If the quality mattered, surely it meant Lucidian blood had the best potential. How many of them would they need to match a hundred thousand Throatians' worth of blood, though? Even if it was possible to calculate, it still didn't seem appropriate to consider.

"Assuming the Lucidian people have the most magical blood," Thane said, "the problem is that they've confined themselves to their Enclave since their civil war. To sacrifice their populations, we'd have to sail across the ocean, break down their walls, and overcome their powers to capture them. Then there'd be the obstacle of transporting them all back home. Even if we could accomplish it, is it moral? Until earlier today, we'd never sacrificed prisoners either, to my knowledge."

Valenti shook her head, then turned to her king. "Watching this conversation play out is burning my heart. Please excuse me." She straightened her dress and retreated toward the cathedral.

"What's wrong with her?" Thane asked. Valenti oversaw the Breeding Farms; it was unlike her to be bothered at the idea of forcing people to do anything against their will.

Hrodspire cleared his throat. "While it's true that the Lucidians are suitable candidates for sacrifice, you're right—they aren't the solution to our dilemma." He turned to Thane's father. "My king, shall we?"

Harkbin wiped the sweat from his brow. "Our god requested we bring three things before him to protect us from the sorceress. Across the sea in Yaenia, the Darian king secretly holds a collection of powerful magical stones known as the Tears of Asura. We also need the blood of his eldest daughter. With those in hand, we can return home and present them to Zann-Xia-Czul."

"Stealing magical stones is straightforward," Thane said. "Abducting a princess will be more complicated. Still, it's easier than a hundred thousand people's blood. What's the third item we need?"

"The third piece is—" Harkbin choked on his own words. "It's you, Thane. Your blood. I wasn't aware of it until Mount Sephorr."

He blinked a few times to make sure he wasn't dreaming. "My blood? But why?"

"Your blood and the Darian princess's are magical enough to support what he needs, according to Zann-Xia-Czul," Harkbin said. "On the mountaintop, I refused our god's demand when he told me about you. I couldn't live with myself if I sacrificed my son... so I begged him to find another way, and he told me that a hundred thousand people's worth of blood was the only alternative means of protecting us."

"This...it can't be this simple," Thane argued. "Are you saying two royals and some magical stones equate to countless sacrifices? I can't believe these are the only options."

"Unfortunately, they are," he affirmed with a regretful sigh.

"Father, surely this can't be true," he protested. "Zann-Xia-Czul must be testing your loyalty. I don't possess any magic." Thane turned towards Hrodspire and pointed at himself. "You know I'm nothing more than a title. Tell me that's the truth."

Hrodspire nodded solemnly. "You aren't magical, at least as far as we can tell. The same applies to Princess Lydia in the Darian Kingdom. Still, Zann-Xia-Czul called for the two of you. He knows all, so whatever his reasons are, we must trust him. You two are the key to our defenses."

"But if I die, you'll be left without an heir to the throne," Thane blurted out.

Harkbin's lips curled inward as though he wished he could never have started their conversation. Hrodspire was about to speak again, but the king quickly placed his hand on the Elder's shoulder and shook his head. His wrinkled face frowned, giving another somber nod of acknowledgment. Whatever the Elder had wanted to say, Thane guessed Harkbin didn't want him to say it.

"There are already laws written to handle such a situation," Hrodspire said, choosing his words carefully. "But stating this doesn't mean we want you to die, either. We'd rather have you alive, despite your occasional snappiness."

Thane's eyes darted back to his father's. "So, do I even have a choice? There's no way we can come up with a hundred thousand more sacrifices."

"The freedom of deciding is a burden itself, but I'll grant you the choice if that is what you wish," Harkbin said. "A resolution in either direction has the potential for regrets. If you don't want the burden of choosing our island's outcome, I can relieve you of the decision. It's the least I can do. Regardless, allowing the sorceress to attack us without a challenge is unacceptable."

Was putting Thane's name down with the Darian princess's just a means of tormenting his father? Perhaps it was some kind of sick joke? There was no way his blood could help thwart a sorceress. The idea of Thane being called upon was too preposterous; there had to be something else behind it all.

"I need to take a walk," Thane said, storming off toward the temple's entrance.

"Wait, Thane!" Harkbin yelled. "What we've discussed remains between us. Don't let your mother know that you're… that you're—"

"I won't."

Death was inevitable. Thane knew he couldn't resist sacrificing himself for the greater good. He'd willingly set himself on fire, stab his own heart, look up at the sky and wait to be electrocuted, or any other action his god asked of him if it were needed— all those years of facing trials within the Loyalty Circle had permanently ingrained that devotion in him. The only question was whether he was throwing his life away for nothing.

4

THE NEXT COMMAND

Nearby, gulls squawked and battled amongst themselves over a slice of bread. On the pier ahead of them, foreign traders went about their daily negotiations with the locals. Such ordinary people wouldn't notice that a prince was among them, and Thane was thankful for it. Watching them go about their routines as an unnoticed observer was calming. It was better that few recognized him for the time being. He might soon be gone anyway, so perhaps none of it mattered.

"Why do you think I'm so special, Zann-Xia-Czul?" Thane whispered to the sea. Cold water washed against his legs, stinging the cuts from the day before. He leaned his upper body against one of the mossy posts, absorbing the glow of the beating sun.

"Why does the sorceress want to attack our island?" He sighed, the calm ocean waves ebbing and flowing beneath him. "My faith in you remains strong, but I need to know... I need assurance that if I do this, my life won't be in vain."

Despite the uncertainty of the answer, Thane already knew his fate. Pushing against the wooden deck, he grunted as he lifted himself up again. Water dripped down his knees, and he stared in the opposite direction of the ocean, back to where the Temple of White sat on its hill. It was still too soon to return there and face his father and the Elders.

He strolled through the crowded market streets. If Thane's destiny was to die so soon, he at least wanted to be buried in his beautiful, white armor. The bell above the door rang as he entered the artisan's boutique. In a dark corner, the owner sat at his workbench, fiercely pounding a sword with his hammer.

"Shivanna Adul, Prince Thane," the craftsman said, looking up from his work. "My apologies, but the shipment hasn't arrived yet. Can I assist you with anything else?"

"Do you have any idea when it will arrive?" Thane asked.

The armorer set aside his tool and removed his

faded brown work gloves, then approached Thane at the front of the store. His face was sweaty and covered in dirt and soot.

"I'm sorry, my prince. The situation hasn't changed," he said, absently scratching his nose with his oily hands. "If you'd like, I can send one of my apprentices to you the moment I get what I need. Once I have it, the rest is easy."

"That will suffice," Thane said. "Thanks again."

"I apologize for the delays. I just need more time."

Thane let out a half-hearted chuckle. "It's beyond your control."

Behind him, the shop's bell rang again. "Thane! What are you doing here?" It was Cereene, grinning cheerily at him.

"I came to check on my armor," the prince replied. "But what about you? As a Son See'er Vrai, you need nothing from this shop."

"You're right. It's actually something for you." She met eyes with the shop's owner. "Sir, is my order ready yet?"

The elderly man nodded as he let his shoulders relax in relief. "It is."

"Why are you getting me a gift?" Thane asked. "I don't need anything."

"The secret's out, I guess," Cereene replied. "Almost a year has gone by since you saved me from the Loyalty Circle. This is a thank-you."

The shop's owner approached one of the many shelves spanning his walls and retrieved a modest package. He handed the paper-wrapped parcel to Cereene, who quickly inspected its contents with her dainty hands.

Thane looked curiously at the item. "It's so small. Is it some sort of weapon? Or perhaps armor?"

"The best kind one can possess," Cereene replied, extending the package towards him. "Here, open it."

Thane took it from her warm, soft fingers. He pulled the red string, tying the package tight and unwrapped it to reveal a small cerulean gem embedded within a silver amulet. Engraved into the jewel piece was the Throatian symbol Thane knew very well.

"Zann-Xia-Czul," Thane said, reading the character he would see every day when praying to the obelisks.

"For your protection and blessing as you carry out the will of our god," Cereene said.

"Um... thank you." Thane forced a smile. A necklace seemed insignificant compared to the more important matters. "It's quite beautiful."

"And unique," the armorer said. "Your partner designed it special for you. I don't normally forge jewelry, but you'll notice a level of perfection with the quality."

"Happy one year of being together, Thane!" Cereene beamed.

"Thank you." He unraveled the chain and placed the amulet around his neck. Despite its elegant style, its weight seemed heavier than standard silver, perhaps because of the cerulean gem inside. It was a wonderful gift, though he couldn't treasure it as much as he wanted. Everything else in his mind had consumed any potential joy.

"Cereene, shall we go have some tea?"

They thanked the armorer and set off down the pier together. As they moved along the busy streets, Cereene jumped up and down as she told him about the rare textbook she'd been copying for the Temple of White's library, about an ancient stone archway called a World Vein gateway that rested, hidden, in one of the Temple of White's lower levels. Nobody knew how to control it. Cereene theorized it was likely built before any of the original Throatian people had even set foot on the island.

Despite it being an interesting topic, now wasn't the moment for it. Thane's impending fate gnawed at him, leaving no room to postpone the inevitable conversation he needed to have with her.

"Cereene, we need to talk," Thane finally interrupted.

"What's on your mind?"

"There's something you should know."

Cereene halted abruptly. "Is it the necklace? You don't like it?"

Thane turned back and put a hand on her shoulder. "The amulet's great, Cereene. Really, it's perfect. There's nothing wrong with it. But the thing is, I've got some bad news—"

"About... us?"

"Yes." He let go of her and stared at his feet. "I... don't think we should see each other anymore."

Cereene's face went white as his words sank in. "W-what? Why not?"

"It's for the best," Thane muttered. His eyes darted around, looking anywhere but at her. Harkbin had told him to keep the truth about Zann-Xia-Czul's actual demand secret, even to Thane's own mother. Cereene couldn't be an exception to that promise. Splitting up with her before she learned his fate would make it easier for them both in the long term.

"It's not for the best. You don't believe it," she said. Her voice faded somewhat, and she took a deep, deep breath. "What's wrong with you? You were okay this morning."

He gritted his teeth, focused on the center of her forehead. "I-I don't know. I can't say. But we have to stop this."

"But why? Stop what? We're doing fine."

"Yes, but—"

"What did you do?" Cereene interrupted. "If it's about Mount Sephorr, don't worry about that. I don't care that you got in trouble. Everything will be fine. We're going to be okay."

She didn't understand—nor could she, unless he told her the truth. But he couldn't disobey his father either.

"What's bothering me isn't something I can say to you. But I know we won't be fine."

"Thane," she said, grasping his wrist, "please tell me what's wrong and why you're acting so depressed. We can fix this."

Tension slowly crept up his shoulders. "Unfortunately, this is unrepairable. It's not your fault, but we can't keep going."

"Thane!"

His mind was bereft of all thoughts, save for the tormenting truth that he couldn't wipe away. "I'm just trying to protect you. There's—"

"I don't need your protection," Cereene said. "What we have is real. There's no shame in it. I'm a Son See'er Vrai and you're my prince. It doesn't matter that I'm obligated to do what you want. I want this!"

"Reputation doesn't matter to me."

"So, what's stopping us from being together?"

"It's..." His mouth hung open, but he couldn't finish his sentence.

"Thane! Are you out of excuses? What do you really want?"

"Here's the full truth," Thane confessed. "Both the Darian princess and I possess magical blood. If we die, there won't be a need for a hundred thousand people to replace us. Please, don't share this with anyone."

Cereene covered her mouth in shock as her eyes filled with fear. Every trace of her scowl crumbled into a frown.

"That's everything," Thane continued. "The two of us will sacrifice ourselves so that you'll be safe from the sorceress."

She stared blankly back at him, and he couldn't tell whether she was upset or relieved about what he was willing to do.

"You really were just trying to protect me," she replied. "Thane, I'm... I'm so sorry. I shouldn't have been angry with you. I-I completely misunderstood the situation."

"No need for an apology. You couldn't have known. I just learned the news too."

"Oh..."

"It's the only way I can protect everyone. I have to do it. I'd be selfish not to."

"I don't want to lose you," she whispered. "There has to be an alternative."

"There isn't," Thane said. "The Elders and I

considered every possible means to gather a hundred thousand new sacrifices. It can't be done within a year."

"And since you and the princess are the only ones with the magical blood, you mustn't ignore the call." She swallowed. "I-I understand. But you... I love you."

"You deserve better than me," Thane sighed.

It was the truth—he hadn't even considered Cereene or the future of their relationship until he'd bumped into her at the armorer. So, how could she be as important to him as he was to her?

"Who deserves whom doesn't matter—only the choice. It's always been that way."

"I'm sorry everything turned out like this. I didn't mean to lie to you, either. There's too much to think about."

Cereene glanced down, lost in thought for a moment. "I'll read as many books as I can to figure this out. What makes the blood you and the Darian princess possess so unique? There must be a reason."

"Thank you for trying to help," the prince replied. "Nobody but Zann-Xia-Czul seems to know what makes our blood special, but this is what the Darian princess and I are being called to do. We're the only ones who can."

"It isn't fair that you should have to die," she

muttered, "but if it's the only way to help our god save the island, what else can we do?"

"It was you who reminded me what a sacrifice is, after all," Thane said. "Giving something to Zann-Xia-Czul that you'd rather keep is how we offer loyalty and obedience."

Opting against tea, Thane returned to the Temple of White to formally announce his intention to sacrifice himself in the effort against the sorceress. From there, Harkbin, Urith, and the Elders spent the next three months locked away in meetings, devising a way to apprehend the Darian princess and obtain the magical stones her father held. The Elders excused Thane from their deliberations and gave him summary updates of their meetings instead. Harkbin had insisted that Thane make the most of his last remaining days.

With his temporary freedom, he opted to spend most of his time with Cereene. As she completed her weekly book duplications, Thane helped her search within other volumes for any shred of information that might help preserve his life. Unfortunately, mentions of magical blood were nonexistent in all

Throatian records and literature. Similarly, their lore lacked any historic special requests from Zann-Xia-Czul. Thane was, perhaps, the first individual destined for sacrifice outside a Loyalty Circle.

Over those three months, Thane established a routine of praying within the sunbathed chambers of the Temple of White before venturing into the nearby hills to visit Cereene. On one particular day, however, his father interrupted this routine to once again partake in a new, unexpected turn of events.

"Yes, my lord," said Harkbin, rising from the marble floor. As Zann-Xia-Czul continued speaking into his mind, another moment of silence crawled by. "As you wish. We'll close ourselves off from the world. We'll spread such rumors. If this will lead to us completing our mission, we'll do it."

"Father, what did he say?" Thane asked. Although the temple cathedral's silence was calming, Thane found it bothersome that everyone relied solely on Harkbin yet again to relay Zann-Xia-Czul's information. "What rumors?"

"Effective tomorrow, we are closing White Boar's Landing indefinitely," the Throatian king declared. "We need to stop all trade with other countries. Isolating ourselves from the rest of the world is our new command."

"Why would you do that? It's borderline insanity," Thane said. "Most of our food and supplies come from foreign countries. We can't live on spices and tea alone!"

"There's more to it than that. However, adopting this sensitive position opens more opportunities than it shuts."

"It seems counterproductive and irrelevant to capturing the princess."

"Trust and obey Zann-Xia-Czul," his father warned. He uncrossed his legs and stood. "These actions are the keys to defeating the evil sorceress."

"I trust him, but I just want to comprehend everything," Thane said. "We could avoid a lot of trouble if we only knew the whole plan."

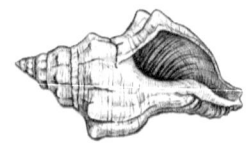

THANE AND HARKBIN QUICKLY REPORTED TO THE Elders and issued the decree about shutting down the island's single trade port. Upon discovering that they'd be severing their country's only supply line, Urith, Hrodspire, Kaelgeth, and Valenti concurred with the prince.

"If we close off White Boar's Landing, it's going to be exceedingly troublesome to restore everything later," Hrodspire warned. "Once we send our customers away, they'll find other markets."

"Not only will our patrons suffer, but our own communities as well," Valenti said. "You're damaging our domestic markets if they can't trade. Their livelihoods are at stake too. How can we obey Zann-Xia-Czul while also protecting our people?"

"Isolating our homeland comes with repercussions, I'm aware of that," Harkbin said.

"Why confine ourselves, then?" Thane asked.

Harkbin carefully surveyed all the Elders, who stared back at him in disbelief. "We're going to spread some misinformation about our island. Closing our borders supports the rumors."

"What rumors?" Urith growled.

The king gave them all a restrained grin. "Whenever people approach our island and get turned away, we will let slip that we've discovered how to use magic."

"My king…" Valenti said with a resonating voice. Her body quivered, but it had nothing to do with the cold sea breeze passing through the glassless windows of the temple. "Respectfully, perhaps Zann-Xia-Czul is out of touch with the skepticism we'll face from foreigners. Our communities are less… How should I put this…?"

"They're trained to accept whatever we say," Thane finished. "Foreigners won't believe the lies as easily."

"Yes, perhaps that's what I meant," Valenti said,

examining Harkbin's face for any sort of reaction. "People won't think we have magic unless we're able to prove it. Only our god himself can conjure such evidence. Will he provide it, though?"

"There won't be such proof from Zann-Xia-Czul, but our actions shall speak loudly enough in its place," Harkbin said. "We must trust that closing our ports and declaring independence from foreign countries is ample evidence. You all agree that doing so is absurd otherwise."

Hrodspire broke out into a coughing fit. He looked as if he'd just lost several years of his life. "We must tread carefully as we move forward," he wheezed. "A thoroughly laid-out plan to accompany these directions can spare us the burden of repairing our economy later. We'll also call for everyone's support at the docks."

"Closing the port means it'll be necessary to scale down the overall population too," Valenti said. "Without trade, our food and other supplies will dwindle. I'll need to limit the Breeding Farms to conserve resources."

"Lack of details aside, we'll move forward with the closure this evening," Harkbin said.

"This evening? My king!" Hrodspire gasped. "That's so sudden. Shouldn't we wait just a little longer until we can—"

"Go to White Boar's Landing this instant,"

Harkbin commanded. "Spread the message to the patrols and merchants. Tell them Zann-Xia-Czul himself delivered this order, not just me."

Hrodspire gulped. "Yes, my king. I'll have it done as you said, with no hesitation on my part. I'll instruct them to spread the stories of magic too."

"If any of the traders protest or dispute, send them to the Loyalty Circles as a reminder that their god, not their money, rules over them. A Son See'er Vrai messenger will contact you later as we come further along with the logistics."

Without saying another word, Hrodspire exited the cathedral and trudged down the steps toward the beach. Thane suspected angry traders and merchants would confront the Elder once he gave them the news. Regardless of the command's source, it still seemed reckless to close everything immediately and indefinitely.

"King Asche, shall we continue this conversation at our appointment?" Kaelgeth said. "We're running late." They were supposed to be at Loyalty Circle Seven.

"The king is never late," Urith snapped.

"My apologies."

The five of them left the temple and moved down the hills toward a broad two-level building made from gray stone bricks. Painted in red on the longest wall, large enough to read from a quarter mile away, was the number seven.

Several archers stood on the rooftop, ready to shoot any Son See'ers who might lose their way or try fleeing from the entrance. A pair of spear-armed guards carefully patrolled the ground level, monitoring the lines of shivering men, women, and children waiting their turn to enter. A scream resounded from the Loyalty Circle's roof, then was silenced just as abruptly. Such was the universal—if unofficial—sign of a ceremony's completion. A moment later, the bell rang, confirming the result.

"Sheiaa Kaaduul," the mantra echoed hundreds of times as those within earshot commemorated the sacrifice.

Thane, Harkbin, Urith, Kaelgeth, and Valenti continued their course to the building entrance, and a staff member approached and greeted them.

"Shivanna Adul, my king, queen, prince, and Elders," the organizer said. "Are you here for the Reminder of Suffering, or Death?"

"Death for all of us," Harkbin answered.

"Please proceed. The next round will start in a few minutes. We've already arranged your accommodations."

The group made its way through a separate archway from where the other Son See'ers were lined up. Their footsteps echoed along the wet stone floor. The building was holy, yet the passages were narrow and dark. Candles were mounted on the walls every few feet, and despite the difficulty to see too far ahead, Thane had the layout memorized. One of his sandals crunched a wandering beetle as he led everyone into the central chamber where they would serve.

Sunlight pierced through the grate-like roof where the most violent parts of the Loyalty Circle took place. Suspended from the ceiling was a complex network of red-stained wooden funnels that led down to several buckets filled with blood. The system filled some canisters closer to the brim than others—it all depended on where someone above had died. Their group split up and began merging the liquid into fewer containers. A fresh set rested along the room's walls, ready for replacement. Meanwhile, a shrine awaited the group just outside another doorway where they'd make their distributions.

"Now, about the Darian princess," Harkbin said. His arms trembled as he carefully poured a bucket of blood into another.

"Speak louder, please," Valenti called out.

Harkbin cleared his throat. "As we spread our claims of discovering magic, we need to consider how this can aid in our effort to abduct Princess Lydia."

"Threatening or intimidating their king might work," Urith said. "He'll give us his daughter, or we'll plague their land with the storms of Zann-Xia-Czul."

Harkbin returned the empty bucket to its place under one of the wooden funnels. Swords clashed above as two Son See'ers fought to the death in the roof's arena. Ten seconds later, there was a grunt, then a moan. Calls of Sheiaa Kaaduul echoed as a body thudded against the metal grate. Blood dripped through the ceiling and into the funnels, slowly filling the buckets.

"It's true that fear is a powerful motivator," Harkbin said, stroking his beard and watching the crimson liquid flow through the tracks. "The Darians only need to believe the magic is legitimate. It doesn't matter whether it actually comes from us or Zann-Xia-Czul."

Thane sifted through the buckets, extracting a chunk of an ear. Finding random fragments of Son See'ers wasn't an unusual incident, given how the grates allowed even something the size of a chicken's egg through. It was essential that the blood be as pure as possible for the offerings, so he dropped the lump of cartilage onto the floor. Another Son See'er would tidy it up later.

"Forcing the Darian king's hand will not work," Thane said. "We don't know what the princess looks like. What guarantee do we have that King von Stonewall won't just send us some peasant girl?"

"He's correct," Valenti said. "We need to ensure that the young woman we gather is undoubtedly the king's eldest daughter."

"Let's first spy on them," Urith suggested. "Then, if they don't give us the right person, we'll wage war."

"Fighting won't work," Thane said. "We don't have the resources to force their entire continent into submission. Mounting a surprise attack against a coastal city is our limit."

"Conflict isn't a wise move, at least not until we have secured the princess," his father added. "White Boar's Landing is our only entrance and exit. The Darian fleet would just need to park at our doorstep and starve us out."

For the next step of their tasks, Thane, Harkbin, and Urith carried six full buckets outside to a small stone plateau. At the center of the platform lay a large, hollowed-out pool filled with the previous day's blood offering. Yesterday's sacrifice was complete and ready to be replaced by the current day's deposit. Taking the lead, Harkbin grabbed a shovel and cleared away the pool.

"Would Zann-Xia-Czul protect our island from Darian soldiers, though?" Thane asked, as he emptied his bucket. "He should be able to destroy armies easily, if he's willing."

Harkbin returned to the shrine and squatted down to meditate. He crossed his legs, closed his eyes, and raised his hands in prayer. A moment passed before he resumed their conversation. His ability to converse with Zann-Xia-Czul outside of Mount Sephorr was a recent phenomenon. Perhaps this was due to the urgency of the mission, but their god no longer seemed to expect his father to ascend for the purposes of communication.

"He'll protect us from all armies," Harkbin said. "The blood required for that is negligible compared to fighting the sorceress."

"Surely there's an alternative to war," Thane said. "Do we have existing relations with the Darian Kingdom?"

Urith came forward with another bucket. "We've always been neutral," she replied, setting the empty container behind her. "They know we live here, and we know they exist there, but that's the extent of it."

"Perhaps we can forge an alliance, then?" Thane said. "If they knew our predicament, we could persuade them to turn over their princess. We could trade them anything else they'd want."

Harkbin laughed. "My son, you are too optimistic. The king would never give up his eldest daughter, even in the unlikely event she willingly committed to our cause. No, we need to take her regardless of her father's—"

The king's eyes suddenly closed again, as if he'd fallen into a deep trance. Another long moment of silence passed before Thane's father relaxed his shoulders and gave a sigh of relief. "Our god says that if we convince King von Stonewall to marry his daughter to Thane, it will lessen our risk."

"A marriage?" Thane asked. "Under false pretenses?" Cereene wouldn't like the idea of him marrying someone else, even if it were a lie.

"If von Stonewall accepts the proposal, that could work," Urith said. "Once Thane and the Darian princess return, we can sacrifice the princess and claim she succumbed to a disease. Nobody would suspect that we were responsible for her death."

Thane bit his tongue. He had almost suggested that they claim their ship sank, and that both he and the Darian princess had perished together. He'd mention the idea to his father later, privately, when it didn't mean revealing his fate to his mother.

"So, how do we persuade the princess to marry me?" Thane asked as he emptied the fifth bucket of blood.

Valenti approached them, carrying two overfilled containers. Red liquid sloshed onto the dirt path and her sunflower-yellow dress. She gave a quick bow to the obelisk and set her offerings down beside Thane's.

"Let the rumors of our magic spread first," Harkbin said. "Ether von Stonewall will trade his daughter for an alliance to protect his kingdom. From his point of view, we're better suited to protect her than he is, thanks to our supposed magic."

"Are you referring to the Lucidian civil war?" Kaelgeth said.

"Both wars." Harkbin replied. He retrieved his red-jeweled knife from his pocket. As he sat with his legs still crossed, his exhausted eyes admired the intricate design of the handle.

"Whoever wields magic rules the future," Urith nodded. "Ether von Stonewall knows this. Now we can take advantage of his kingdom's history."

"But are the political tensions alone enough to compel him to marry his daughter to me?" Thane said.

"He can't ignore the possibility that we'll rival the Lucidians," Harkbin said. "If he refuses, he'll have two magical kingdoms who are neutral to him at best and enemies at worst."

"And what if the sorceress hears these false rumors?" Kaelgeth asked.

"Let me ask Zann-Xia-Czul," Harkbin replied. For the third time, he closed his eyes and awaited a telepathic response. After a moment, he opened them and shook his head. "Our bluff won't fool her. She'll likely ignore the rumors of our magic and remain hidden until she's ready to strike. Like Zann-Xia-Czul, she's using this time to gather her power."

"So, a wedding allows us to bring the princess here without bloodshed," Urith said. "It's an ideal plan, if we can survive with a closed border for that long."

"We'll make do," Harkbin said as he moved closer to the red pool. "Our ancestors survived on this island with no outside help. Besides, all we need is Zann-Xia-Czul. He'll provide everything else we need."

His faith was impenetrable, and Thane wished his own resolve could be so firm.

"Valenti, you'll need to work on reducing the overall population," the king added. "Can you handle this on the Breeding Farm's end?"

"I'll lower the growth rate by eighty percent, starting with next week's output."

"Next week's output?" Thane echoed, his mouth agape.

She seemed to have no remorse for what she'd volunteered to do. Then again, perhaps she'd been doing it for so long that the unborn lives were nothing more than numbers to her. "Yes. Once the port reopens and we've resumed our usual supply of imports again, I'll recover everything back to normal."

"You can send any surplus people to Loyalty Circles Thirteen and Nineteen," Urith said. "They had capacity, last I checked. Confirm with Hrodspire."

"Consider it done," Valenti said. "Unless there are any objections, I'll take my leave now."

"Thank you, Isola," Harkbin said, "for staying true to the cause of Zann-Xia-Czul."

"Let's finish up here," Urith said. "I too want to join in the Reminder of Suffering."

"We're already here, so we might as well," Thane said. He grabbed two of the empty buckets and carried them back toward Loyalty Circle Seven.

His father cleared his throat. "Thane, I thought you had something else to do today?"

Thane turned back to him, brow furrowed. "I do?"

"You do. Perhaps you can partake in the Loyalty Circle another day. There's no point in risking being late for what you've already planned for this afternoon."

"Oh, right!" Thane said. He quickly thought up an excuse. "I-I forgot I have to meet Cereene."

Harkbin offered his red-jeweled knife to Thane. "Indeed. Come, let's complete our duties and then you can meet her."

Thane took the knife from his father and held his palm over the pool. Quickly, he gave it a slice and let the blood spill into the mixture. "Sheiaa Kaaduul."

"Sheiaa Kaaduul," Harkbin repeated as he took the knife back and sliced his own palm as well. Urith approached and followed suit, then Kaelgeth.

"Harkbin, what are you trying to sneak past me?" Urith said as she wiped her hand on her brown leather shirt.

"Past you?"

"We both know Thane isn't a good liar," she said. "You're obviously in on it too, so what are you hiding that's so important? Why can't Thane enter the Reminder of Suffering?"

Kaelgeth, who had been quietly observing, swiftly made his excuses and withdrew from the scene. The truth was inevitably on its way out, and the Elder clearly wanted no part in the upcoming reaction.

"I need to avoid getting hurt before executing the plan with Princess Lydia," Thane said, hoping that sliver of truth alone would be sufficient.

His mother's eyes narrowed. "Might be true, but why hide what I already know from me? What else is there?"

Thane glanced at his father, who shrugged. "There's no point in concealing it from her if she's already suspicious, I guess," he said. "Thane, are you okay to say?"

Thane nodded and turned back to his mother. "To effectively counter the sorceress, I must also sacrifice my life to Zann-Xia-Czul. He needs my blood. Mine and the princess's. It's... special, somehow. Magical."

"Impossible," Urith grunted, her right hand forming a fist. "Your blood can't be special. If it was, then why can't we sacrifice your father or me instead? If you have magical blood, then so must one of us."

"Zann-Xia-Czul says it isn't the case," Harkbin said. "Only Thane's and Princess Lydia's blood will work for what he needs."

"It can't be," Urith said, turning to her husband. "We've done everything right over the years. We've paid the price, over and over again. Surely Thane isn't meant to be taken away from us after—" Her voice broke.

"After what?" Thane asked.

"It doesn't concern you what happened. It's all in the past now," Harkbin replied. "Before you were born, your mother and I sacrificed more than anyone and paid our dues to Zann-Xia-Czul. Let's leave it at that."

For the first time in his life, Thane saw tears streaming down his mother's face. What had his family given up that could actually make his mother cry?

"I've already accepted my fate," Thane offered. "If my life can safeguard everyone else's, it's a sacrifice I'm prepared to make. For the greater good."

Harkbin smiled proudly at the queen, though Thane could tell he, too, was holding back tears. "We've raised Thane to trust and obey the will of Zann-Xia-Czul. This is his calling. This is his test."

"So be it then," Urith muttered. "But what of our heir? I can bear no more children. Who will be our successor if not Thane?"

His father stared up at the cloudless blue sky. "Zann-Xia-Czul and I have yet to make a decision. If we keep the leadership within our bloodline, Thane's cousin Desaii is next in line, but I have my doubts about him."

"Desaii Egon, my brother's son?" Urith said after wiping her face. "He's got his war hammer, but that's about it. He lacks anything related to leadership or serious devotion to our religion. A block of wood would serve as a better king. Would fight better too."

"Zann-Xia-Czul knows this as well," Harkbin said.

"Who's next after Desaii then?" Thane asked.

"Grimm Kathaar, his brother by law," Harkbin said. "He's competitive within the Loyalty Circles and follows our traditions. But the problem is his... tastes. You know how he is."

"You're wrong," Urith said. "If given the authority, he'd raise an army and try conquering the Silent Deserts, the Yaenian continent, or both. There's no way he'd uphold our island's isolation. Grimm is the furthest from a traditionalist as it gets. But he'd do well by it until it catches up with him."

"Still, he's better than Desaii," Thane said, recalling his cousin's fish breath and arrogance.

"There'll be plenty of time for pondering later," Harkbin said. The three of them returned the emptied buckets to the inner chamber of the Loyalty Circle and made their way back home. "Until we bring Princess Lydia to Zann-Xia-Czul, nothing else matters."

5

THE MIRACLE OF THE AGES

Once White Boar's Landing closed itself off from foreign traders, the next months flew by. As the port turned approaching ships away, rumors of Throatian magic spread rapidly throughout the world. With the seeds of their lie flourishing, Harkbin sent King Ether von Stonewall a letter of introduction and asked to form an alliance by marriage. A messenger ship bearing the von Stonewall sigil—a golden sun spread across a maroon backdrop—brought the acceptance ten weeks later.

The wedding between the two nations would happen in six to eight weeks, depending on how long it would take the royal family to sail to Starlight Beach on the Yaenian continent. Harkbin and Urith collaborated with the Elders on the logistics of transporting three ships of Son See'ers to accompany them on the journey. The days passed quickly, and the time felt more like a week instead of months, which gave Thane little chance to come to terms with his fate. Despite those limitations, he spent as much time with Cereene as possible.

The morning he was supposed to leave for the Darian Kingdom, he prayed at the Temple of White and then trudged down the winding dirt pathway to her home.

"Cereene?" Thane called quietly as he neared her shack.

The sun had barely risen, and most of the Throatian people, scattered among the hills in their single-room stone huts, were still asleep. The trip to the Darian Kingdom was a mission in the service of Zann-Xia-Czul, so Harkbin had insisted that they abstain from a big celebration for the family. Aside from its complexity and urgency, Thane's father requested everyone treat their journey the same as any other religious task. The Asche family would quietly leave that morning and return more than a month later, depending on how the winds favored them.

"Shivanna Adul," Cereene said. "I'm ready for the hike. Do you need water before we go?"

"I'm okay for now," Thane replied. He took a

satchel from her and strapped it around his back for later.

"Do you think we can complete the entire loop of the trail within an hour? You can't be late for your journey."

"We'll move at a quick pace."

An hour wasn't long enough, and it never would be. He wished he could stay with her indefinitely and that the problem of the sorceress didn't exist. This was their last opportunity to see each other while everything was still relatively calm. Thane had a strong suspicion that once he returned to their island with the princess, the assault from the sorceress would begin. His days were numbered, and there wouldn't necessarily be an opportunity to tie up his affairs later. For now, he was living as if he had a terminal illness. He would die, and such would be his end. While Thane had accepted the purpose of his sacrifice, the enigmatic circumstances surrounding it placed a constant weight on his chest.

His heart pounded as they trekked the trails of a smaller, unnamed mountain nestled near Mount Sephorr. Unlike the snow-filled peaks of the holy mountain, the adjoining ridges retained the tropical humidity of the rest of their island. Still, the air there was thin, and the breezes that wafted from where Zann-Xia-Czul concealed himself lent a chill to the atmosphere.

"It was a direct command from our god, but none of this feels right," Thane blurted out.

Cereene's footsteps came to a halt. As she cleaned the sweat from her forehead, Thane noticed several tears cascading down her cheeks.

"I couldn't find anything in the history or lore," Cereene said. "And if I can't save you from going, I want to come with you. The Darian Kingdom's capital has a very famous library. If I could spend some time there during your wedding—"

"We've gone over this. You can't join."

"I know, I know. I just… I wish I could."

"You don't understand Common Tongue. How would you read the books there?"

"Thane…"

Cereene's lip froze in place, and Thane couldn't tell if she was angry or sad. Slowly, he stepped forward and embraced her.

"I honestly wish I were to marry you instead," he said, "but I can't disobey Zann-Xia-Czul. Even though he knows everything, he still asked me to do this. It's the only way, even though none of it feels right."

"Nobody wants you to die," she insisted. "But I… I just want us to live."

"I know."

"I've never stopped praying for another means to

fight the sorceress. And once you've returned here, I don't know how much longer—"

"You don't need to say it," Thane said, letting her go. He nudged her gently, and they resumed walking again.

As they advanced towards the summit, the snowy landscape of Mount Sephorr stared down at them from across the valley. Tiny gray huts dotted the green hills between them, and castle-like Loyalty Circles punctuated the depth of the valley every mile or so. It all seemed insignificant from so far above, and Thane couldn't help but wonder how his life was somehow powerful enough to protect all of it.

"Do you think the Darians know of Zann-Xia-Czul?" Thane asked.

"You must have forgotten they worship Asura," Cereene said. "Still, maybe you can teach them about our god while you're there."

His eyes focused far down into the valley below, where minuscule Son See'ers were lining up outside Loyalty Circle Fourteen for their contributions. There was no escaping the Reminders of Suffering and Death. Thane wondered if only Throatians bred and sacrificed their own people in the name of their religion.

"I don't think it's a good idea," Thane said. He remembered Ibiram Lionheart, the foreign man he'd killed what only seemed like days ago. "Our beliefs differ from theirs. They'd never understand Loyalty Circles or Breeding Farms. That's been a part of my recent worries."

"Why is that?"

"It strikes me as odd that our religion is confined here, and nobody really ever comes or goes from our homeland," Thane said. "One's birth is the sole means of entering our island and understanding our culture. Death is the only way out. Perhaps we're wrong about some things."

"Having these conditions is certainly by design," Cereene said. Without a doubt, her loyalty to Zann-Xia-Czul overshadowed her true feelings about Thane's destiny. "Our god chose us to be his people, and we'll expand from here when he wills it."

They continued hiking, traversing their way down the several switchbacks on the opposite side of the hill. As the temperature rose, an empty sky offered no shield from the sun's relentless rays. If they stayed out too long, their skin would not darken—it would only burn.

"It all seems like such a waste," Thane said. "Breeding Farms are no different from animal farms. We grow people only for their blood and discard the rest of what makes them human. I can't understand why we think it's right when it's obviously so wrong.

Zann-Xia-Czul needs blood to defend our island, but no other country lives as we do. Maybe our religion is why the sorceress wants to destroy us."

"You're overthinking it again," Cereene said. "It doesn't have to be so complicated. Sometimes things are simply how they're meant to be. That's the only explanation. You can't keep imagining ulterior motives, or you'll get trapped in an endless cycle of wondering what's true or false, with no way to verify any of it. You can't prove or deny the absolute intentions of a god's command."

The branches of a small, berry-filled bush reached across the trail, so Thane plucked some of its fruit. Each fuchsia berry, firm and smooth, rested in his palm as an offering. Cereene accepted one, and it crunched as she took her first bite.

"It's no different from fighting a war," she continued. "Other countries protect some of their people at the expense of others. They build armies to defend their lands or claim resources. People die for their kingdoms all the time and for many reasons. The only distinction between us and them is that Zann-Xia-Czul provides everything we need. Those who die in the Loyalty Circles serve a purpose; their deaths carry significance. We, the survivors, never forget about the deceased."

"The only differences between the Son See'ers

and cattle are that they walk on two legs, and we don't eat them," Thane chided. "Many of our people don't even have names and are forgotten from the moment we sacrifice them. People only care about remembering those they knew."

"Stop it, Thane," Cereene said. "This shouldn't be my last memory of you."

He froze. "I'm sorry."

"It's fine."

They walked in silence, and Cereene lingered behind him the entire way back. Every time Thane looked over his shoulder, she glared down at her feet. By the time they finally arrived back at her home, it was time for Thane to go to White Boar's Landing and depart on his quest.

"It won't be easy for you to marry the Darian princess, knowing what's coming next," Cereene said. "But please, promise me that, no matter what, we can talk again after your return. I want to redo our final meeting."

"I'm sorry about today, Cereene," he said. "My mind is overwhelmed, and I'm struggling with discerning right from wrong. I—"

"I know that, but promise me this," Cereene said. "Promise me that today won't be the last time we meet."

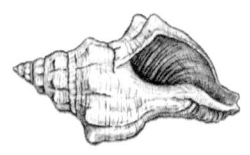

THANE'S VOMIT SPLATTERED BOTH INSIDE AND outside the small wooden bucket sitting at his feet. Sweat poured down his face as he heaved for the seventh time in the past few minutes. He must have surely lost everything from his stomach already, but somehow more bile and burning acid kept pouring out. It was no wonder Zann-Xia-Czul discouraged anyone from leaving their island—the sea was an awful place!

He sat on his bed with blurry vision. Across the cabin on the other bottom bunk, Hrodspire's faint outline was also gagging over his bucket. Only half a day had passed since they'd left home, but the dreadful fever had made every moment feel much longer. The Elder's face, ghostly pale and wrinkled, looked over at Thane.

"My prince... Are you still sick?"

"What do you think, Hrodspire?" Thane snapped. "Both of our pots are nearly full!"

"I-I'm sorry, m-my prince." The elderly man leaned down toward his feet. A minute later, he groaned and settled on his bed again.

Thane folded the cherry-red silk sheets over himself, wiping the sweat from his palms. His pale skin shined with sweat, as though someone had just pulled him from a pot of boiling water. He was tempted to order the crew to turn around and try their adventure some other day when he felt better. It would be preposterous to marry anyone in his current state!

Once more, his dry, itchy throat contracted as he gagged and leaned over the bucket. This time, nothing came from him but choking sounds—his stomach was finally void of everything else.

"Thane..." Hrodspire rasped.

"What?"

"I feel as though this illness could overtake me," the Elder moaned. "I am old. Too old to suffer like this."

"We're both ailed by the motion of the sea," Thane said. "You won't die from simply vomiting."

They remained silent for the next few moments, struggling to calm their stomachs. The ocean, a disease, or perhaps both, afflicted them in ways he'd never imagined before. Regardless of the cause, the ship continued swaying back and forth, and the tide was unforgiving.

"Thane," Hrodspire repeated. "There's something you should know."

"Old man, you won't die here," Thane hissed. "Save your wishes for another day."

"Thank you, but this isn't about me. It's about

you," Hrodspire said. "I may be the only one alive who'll tell you the truth, and if I don't survive this illness…"

Thane pushed himself up into a sitting position. "The truth about what?"

"Promise not to repeat what I reveal," the Elder said. "It's something your parents didn't want you to know, but honestly, I think you've got the right."

"What?"

"Promise me first that you'll keep this information to yourself," Hrodspire said. "It's not an easy knowledge to bear, but it will help you understand your parents' actions better."

"Fine. I promise."

Hrodspire grabbed a small canteen and took a sip of water. "Years before you were born, your parents unsuccessfully tried for a child. For nearly a decade, they were a king and queen without an heir. Twice, Urith became pregnant, but in neither case would her children find the light of life. Twice, Urith and Harkbin were nearly consumed by their anger and sorrow."

Thane could feel his head pounding—whether from his sickness or the new information, he wasn't sure. Either way, it felt the same: terrible.

"I-I've never heard of this…" Thane said. "So, I am my mother's third child."

"Not exactly," Hrodspire said. "After suffering

two miscarriages, your parents prayed to Zann-Xia-Czul every day, seeking an answer, a better outcome. Having insisted they'd endured enough suffering and loss, Harkbin and Urith declared their loyalty unbreakable. They promised Zann-Xia-Czul to do anything he wished if he'd only provide them with a child."

"And now Zann-Xia-Czul is asking for that child back," Thane said. He nodded slowly and let out a long breath. "No wonder my father would rather sacrifice a hundred thousand strangers instead of me."

"The tale goes deeper than that, my prince," Hrodspire said. "You're right that Urith eventually became pregnant. After many moons of praying and hoping, your parents' wish came true—and more, or so it seemed. Urith was with twins."

"Twins?!" Thane exclaimed. "So, I have a brother? Or a sister?"

"A sister," Hrodspire said. "After losing two children to stillbirth, being blessed with the two of you... well... it seemed like our god had repaid her for her suffering."

"Where is she—my sister?"

"Two days after you were born, your sister, Feiir Asche, died."

"Feiir..." Thane echoed.

The word meant "miracle." It was a fitting name.

His own name meant "of the ages." Their combined birthrights would have rendered them a truly majestic duo and formidable heirs to the throne. But none of it had come to pass. There were no miracles in their family, only servanthood and tragedy. Zann-Xia-Czul had robbed them of all hope for a legacy.

"Valenti had declared you were both healthy," Hrodspire said. "Feiir's untimely death was unexpected—like a blade stabbed right into the heart of your house. Harkbin and Urith hid the truth from everyone but the Elders. It was too much shame and pain to bear publicly. As the island celebrated your birth and upbringing, your mother grew to resent your father. She blamed his seed and has never been the same. Though your parents love you, you're still their own personal Reminder of Death and Suffering. They cannot look at you without also seeing Feiir and your siblings who passed before you."

Sweat dripped down Thane's face as the words sank in. "Wow... I can't—I don't know what to say."

"Sheiaa Kaaduul—above all things, this much is true," Hrodspire said. "I thought you should recognize this history. It is important to be aware of your roots and how they influence some of your parents' decisions. Never speak of it with them."

"I won't," Thane promised. "Still, I'm not sure if I should be thanking you for this information. It's so…"

"Cruel?" Hrodspire finished with a shameful nod. "And I'm sorry. I regret that now, of all times, is when you learned about this, but the truth could have died with me. None of the other Elders will break their vow of secrecy."

"I just can't believe I had a sister. If Feiir were alive now, what would she be like?"

"A good friend to you, I am sure. And powerful, surely. But now… I must rest…"

Hrodspire groaned quietly and settled back on the bed. Thane watched the candlelight of a lantern that hung on the wall, and he quickly became tired himself. A sister… How could he not have sensed it, especially after so many years of being alive without her?

"Ruik Czharr," Thane cursed, lowering down on his bed and shutting his eyes. His chest pounded as he rested there. Every few minutes, he contemplated sitting up again and holding his head over the pail. Everything spun and bobbed back and forth with such fervor that Thane worried a whirlpool had trapped their vessel. The ocean's movements never stopped, and he knew that most of it was only in his mind.

He rolled over to face the wall. A sinking feeling overwhelmed his chest, prompting him to quickly turn back and lean over his bucket. Thane's eyes closed slowly as he continued drifting up and down in rhythm with the creaking of the old, wooden ship. Lost in thought, he eventually passed out for what felt like hours, until his father woke him with a light push of his shoulder.

"Are you feeling any better now?" Harkbin asked. "It's time for dinner."

"I don't want to eat," Thane said. His collection of vomit had left a horrid stench throughout the cabin, making the thought of food repulsive. On top of that, knowing that his parents had kept such a secret from him was sickening too. Thane had a sister, yet neither Harkbin nor Urith had told him. He understood the topic was painful to address, but it was borderline disrespectful to not even mention it. Feiir was Thane's twin, after all.

"You've spent the entire afternoon down here," Harkbin said. "Come up and get some fresh air."

"Yes, Father," he sighed. Now wasn't the time to confront him about it.

On deck, as the sun dipped toward the horizon, crew members crossed blades with each other in mock battles. Harkbin required everyone aboard, except Hrodspire, to be skilled with the sword. Given the potential threat of pirates, it was essential to practice. Unfortunately, a lack of supplies from the closed port prevented them from arming their ships with ramming devices or other naval warfare add-ons.

"You should join the guards," Harkbin said. "Western culture enjoys a good tournament during major events. It helps the commoners feel involved in the celebration, since they cannot attend any actual royal weddings."

"It's only our first day at sea. We'll have plenty of time to entertain ourselves with blades later," Thane said. As he squinted into the sun, his stomach growled furiously.

"I thought you'd be eager to try out your new armor," Harkbin said.

"Perhaps not until the wedding," Thane said. Though it would function as protection, Thane wished to use his armor only as a clothing item until the craftsman back at home could paint the last seal over its surface. He'd waited this long for the suit to be finished—it wasn't worth risking unnecessary damage if he could help it. The wedding ceremony wouldn't resemble a battle, hence the risk of acquiring any scratches was minimal.

Behind them, the thud of large boots resonated against the deck. Thane and Harkbin turned around and saw Urith, who had just set down a massive war hammer. The thickness of her weapon matched that of a man's head, and it was twice as heavy. Branded into the hammer's side was the emblem of a two-headed eagle. Thane knew of only one person on the Throatian island who bore such a seal. But even without seeing it, the distinctiveness of the war hammer made its ownership unquestionable.

Harkbin's mouth fell open in disbelief. "Where did you get that?"

Urith's calloused hands tightened their grip on the metal handle as she greeted them. Thane noticed some small, dark chunks of what looked like coal caught between the crevices of the eagle decoration, and quickly averted his eyes.

"That belongs to Desaii," he said. "Did he lend it to you?"

"It's extra security," Urith said.

"But how did you—"

"Urith!" Harkbin snapped. "Does Desaii know you have his war hammer?"

"He never will."

Harkbin scowled at her, noting the dried blood dirtying her new weapon. The Elders forbade killing outside of a Loyalty Circle, as the rites within had to remain pure without losing their meaning. Personal grudges, challenging an opponent to a fight, and all other unsanctioned battles were illegal. For Urith to kill someone outside of a Loyalty Circle was even worse, and there would surely be consequences later.

Harkbin sighed before regaining his composure. "Was it at least a fair fight?"

Urith grinned, revealing her dark yellow teeth.

"It was a surprise to start, but fair once it ended. Quick too."

"Ruik Czharr, Urith," Harkbin cursed. "Who else knows about this?"

"No one will dare to question us once we return with the princess."

"Why did you do it, though?" Thane asked.

His mother's eyes flashed dangerously. "You keep playing your part to secure our island's future, and I'll keep playing mine."

"So be it," Harkbin sighed. "Indeed, no one will dare to question us. Sheiaa Kaaduul."

"Sheiaa Kaaduul," Thane and Urith echoed.

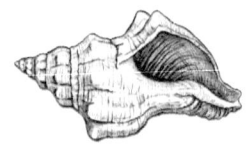

WEEKS WENT BY, AND THANE'S STOMACH GRADUALLY adjusted to the unusual atmosphere of a ship at sea. The ocean revealed itself to be nothing more than a vast blue canvas, occasionally embellished with a sequence of silvery clouds passing overhead. It wouldn't bother Thane if he returned home and never left his island ever again. The remaining journey to the Darian Kingdom was uneventful. Even Zann-Xia-Czul seemed to take a break from communicating with them—though according to Harkbin, he was still providing safe passage.

Half meditating and half snoozing, Thane rolled over in his bed. He had replaced his morning routine of prayer at the obelisks with sleeping in until well past sunrise, and his father didn't seem to mind his newfound sluggishness. Thane's willingness to sacrifice himself probably outweighed any amount of prayer he could perform in the meantime.

Even with his head buried under his pillow, he heard the creak of the stairs leading into his cabin under someone's feet. The person cleared their throat, then, a moment later, gently prodded his shoulder.

"It's time, my prince," Hrodspire whispered. "The Darian Kingdom just broke the horizon."

Thane pulled his head out from under the pillow. "The journey sure took long enough. Are you certain we've reached Starlight Beach?"

Hrodspire nodded. "Of course, I am! Their famous university stands proudly on its cliff. We'll dock soon."

"Getting off this rickety old boat is the best thing to happen to us since we boarded," Thane said, rubbing the crust from his eyes.

"I, too, yearn for solid ground," Hrodspire said, clutching his stomach. "Pardon me, my prince, but I'd like to take a brief rest before we land."

As Hrodspire returned to his own bed, Thane dressed and strolled up to the deck, where his parents awaited him. They paid no heed to the various crew members who had paused mid-chore to gaze into the distance. Thane couldn't blame them for slacking off. They were the first Throatians in several generations to see new land. Harkbin held a small wooden box in his hands as Urith carefully finished wrapping it in shiny red paper. Thane recognized the sheet as the same kind belonging to Kaelgeth. Such commodities were scarce on their island, with the Temple of White's keeper typically hoarding and reserving them for special religious occasions.

"What is in that package, Father?" Thane asked.

"A small gift for the ambassador who'll be meeting us," Harkbin said. "They will undoubtedly watch and analyze our every move, so it's best to make a good impression."

"Are you playing cautious, or do they already have a reason to suspect us?"

"We need to appear as genuine as possible," Harkbin said. "This mission is Zann-Xia-Czul's test of our abilities. I've prayed to him each day since we departed but have received no response. We're alone in this."

"I'm sure our god will intervene if anything goes wrong," Urith said, knotting a golden string around the wrapped box. "He trusts us to handle this without him in the meantime."

"I fear, in part, that something may preoccupy him, such as the sorceress or some other pressing matter," Harkbin said.

"Either way, sailing home remains our largest obstacle," Urith said. "The Darians are gullible enough to marry their princess to those they've never met. So, we'll do the wedding and leave as hurriedly as we can. Easy."

"It's not because of some foolishness that the von Stonewall family trusts us," Harkbin said. "Princess Lydia is the price they're willing to pay for a magical alliance with our island."

"And you're confident they'll believe everything without proof?" Thane said. "I know I missed a lot of the meetings with the Elders... There's just as much I don't understand."

"In my letter, I mentioned you were the only heir to our land," Harkbin said. "Fear of missing this opportunity trumps any skepticism on their end, especially since we bluffed our confidence by closing our borders. Proposals for marriage could have come from other nations too."

"Do as we say, Thane, and everything will be fine," Urith said. "Let your father and I handle the politics."

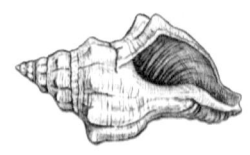

THEY SAILED FOR ANOTHER HALF HOUR BEFORE landing at Starlight Beach's harbor. As the crew secured their ropes around the dock's cleats, Thane leaped over the rail onto the moss-covered stones of dry land. His legs wobbled as they reacquainted themselves with solid ground, liberated from the sea's relentless rocking. Despite swaying from side to side like a drunkard, he made his way to where some anglers were haggling over their catch and approached discreetly to eavesdrop on their conversation.

"Why come all the way from Emil if you're not taking at least ten bags home?" the merchant exclaimed in Common Tongue. He cracked open an oyster and held the half-shell close to the other man's face. "Smell the ocean breeze inside. It doesn't get any fresher than this!"

The other man waved and shook his head. "I'm already done buying for trade. Oysters aren't that popular in Emil, so a single bag is enough."

"That's because whoever's cooking them isn't preparing them right. Add some butter, garlic, and chives. You'll have an upper-class meal at a more affordable price than beef. Tell me, my friend, have you ever tried oysters like this?"

"I haven't."

"Come on," the merchant insisted. "You'll sell these for two or three times as much as you're buying them from me. Take five or ten bags home with you. You've got room on your cart, right?"

Thane gasped quietly as he realized how well he understood their conversation. Compared to Throatian, Common Tongue was rife with inflections and complexities. When he was younger, the Elders had permitted a handful of teachers from the Silent Deserts to immigrate to the island and teach the Son See'er Vrai how to read and write in Common Tongue. The hours of studying he'd invested were paying off.

"Thane! Come back now! The ambassador is here," Harkbin called in Throatian, back at the dock.

Thane gave the merchants one last glance before turning around. Near the stone docks where Harkbin and Urith had disembarked, a great, dark-skinned Darian man dressed in silky dark blue robes waited for him. The ambassador was mostly bald, but lingering gray stubble still covered some sections of his scalp.

"Welcome to the Darian Kingdom!" the man said in Common Tongue. "You must be Prince Thane of the Throatian Kingdom. I'm Rufus Merdel, Master of Foreign Relations. It's a pleasure to meet you."

"Kingdom?" Thane blurted out in Throatian. Their island was self-contained and more of a collection of huts than a grand spectacle of various territories, cities, and towns. Appearances were essential, and nobody could be the wiser of any exaggerations on his part. He took a deep breath and then replied in the proper language. "Yes, we've sailed here from the Throatian Kingdom."

Merdel studied him from head to toe. "It will satisfy our princess when she sees you, I am certain."

"I am looking forward to meeting her as well."

"You're in for the grandest wedding our land can offer," he said. "The von Stonewall family sends their apologies that they could not greet you here in person. They—"

Merdel spoke too quickly for him to follow, leaving him to merely smile and nod as words poured from the ambassador's lips. Despite not recognizing all the vocabulary, Thane deduced that Princess Lydia's younger sister had been ill and wasn't able to travel for now.

"We understand, Master Ambassador," Thane said. "Traveling takes a lot of time and hassle. It's not worth risking one's health."

"I'm sure Princess Kira will be well again once we

arrive," Harkbin said. "We will pray for her vigor tonight."

"Ah, yes, speaking of tonight," Merdel said, "I'm bringing you to Starlight Beach's best inn, where you'll be comfortable. Tomorrow morning, we'll ride for Last Hope."

Urith stepped forward and offered the small, wrapped box. "Thank you, Master Merdel," she said. "This is a small gift that shows our appreciation for your efforts."

"Praise you, Queen Asche," Merdel replied, taking the present. The golden string bounced lightly as it changed hands. "Alas, the Oberon Memorial library lacks texts on Throatian culture. Would it be more appropriate to open this in front of you now, or should I wait until I am alone later?"

Harkbin couldn't hide the way his lips curled into a grin. "We have no such rules in our kingdom. The gift is yours to enjoy whenever you wish."

"It's considered neither greedy nor impolite to open it now," Urith added. "We only hope you admire its intricacies."

The ambassador nodded. "In that case, I'll let my curiosity overpower me."

He untied the string, tore away the paper, and removed the small wooden lid. With trembling hands, Merdel revealed a small stone plate decorated with the first twelve Throatian numbers. A silver rod protruded from its center, and a cord connected the highest point to the twelfth digit engraved on its face. Circling around the upper circumference of the sundial were the words "Shivanna Adul."

"What an elegant method of determining the time!" Merdel exclaimed. "Thank you for this wonderful clock!"

"You're welcome! We appreciate you being our escort to Last Hope," Harkbin said. "This wedding means a great deal to us. A very great deal."

6

THE CRIMSON KNIGHT

Later that evening, Merdel organized a feast for them at the inn. The chefs brought out a fully cooked boar before there was any chance to interject and request that the meat be left raw for blessing. The ambassador loved to talk and spent the greater part of the meal describing various places in the Darian Kingdom—everything from the lively markets of Last Hope to the drinks of New Ginstown. When Merdel excused himself for a moment, Harkbin quietly announced to everyone that the dinner would be an exception to the norm, and they were to keep their daily practices adjourned for now. It was best to accept their gifts gracefully and avoid risking any friction until Princess Lydia was within their grasp.

It was Thane's first time eating properly cooked

meat, let alone boar, other than jerky. Darian cuisine surpassed Throatian food in every way. The pig was smoked and sweetened with apple juices and other herbs and spices he'd never tasted before. The fact that such a meal existed rendered any plate from home insignificant. He told Hrodspire that he could eat the same dish for the rest of his life and never grow tired of its sweetness.

After dinner, Merdel bid them goodnight. He and the innkeeper led Thane, Harkbin, and Urith upstairs to their rooms, each of which was at least twice as large as the hut they shared. The prince admired the chairs most of all—the arms and legs curved smoothly, and every cushion was uphol-stered in colorful silk. Their furniture design at home was simple by comparison. Functional, yes, but simple. Though a lack of elegance went hand in hand with Throatian religious principles, he still let his envy take over.

Once alone in his room, Thane sank into the luxurious red armchair and gazed at a large painting on the wall. A great white shark, mouth wide open and baring its teeth, was about to clamp down onto a swordfish. At home, Zann-Xia-Czul forbade art other than religious works.

He drifted off for almost an hour before a knock at the door roused him. Thane jumped from his new favorite chair and opened it.

"Your father has gone to the beach to pray and meditate," his mother said. "He's worried about Zann-Xia-Czul no longer answering his prayers. You should go join him."

"This isn't worth worrying about," Thane said. "Harkbin always had to climb Mount Sephorr to speak with Zann-Xia-Czul before. With our mission defined, the emergency is over, and the old rule continues."

"No, the crisis hasn't passed until we deliver what our god asked of us. Now go check on him."

Scowling, Thane stalked off downstairs, alone and in silence. In the lobby, the innkeeper stood behind the bar, drying off a tankard. Everyone else had already gone to bed for the night. Outside, a lone Darian guard armed with a spear stood watch at the building's entrance.

"Good evening, Prince Thane," the guard said. "Councilman Merdel asked me to stay here. We stationed other patrols around the block for your security. Chances are that nobody will bother you, but the university students sometimes get rowdy as they bounce from bar to bar. So, pay them no mind. Let us know if you need anything."

The sounds from unseen parties and gatherings in the nearby streets drowned out the sound of the waves, thwarting Thane's attempt to navigate by them.

"Thanks. Which direction is the sea?" Thane asked.

"Huh? Sorry, but I can't speak your language."

Thane's face flushed red as he switched over to Common Tongue. "My apologies, sir. I asked which way the beach was."

"Oh! That's easy!" the Darian said. He pointed his finger to his left. "It's that road, sir. Would you like an escort to come with you?"

"No, but thank you," Thane replied, nodding farewell to the guard.

He strolled down the dark, empty street. The sounds of bar patrons cheering and whooping echoed in the distance, but everywhere else nearby remained void of activity. It appeared Merdel had used his authority to move a whole block's worth of people away so Thane's family would sleep peacefully.

Thane followed the road away from the noise and gravitated closer to the growing echoes of ocean waves. Darkness covered the horizon, preventing him from seeing where the tide met the sand or if their ship was anywhere near the shoreline. A half hour later, Thane gave up on figuring out where his father had gone to meditate, and turned around again, back toward the inn. His mother would be disappointed, but it was the middle of the night and their first time in an unknown land. The city blocks of Starlight Beach that remained open were well lit and easy to navigate. Harkbin could find his own path back, especially with so many guards so eager to escort them.

"Shivanna Adul," someone's voice called out from behind him.

The hairs on Thane's neck prickled as he saw that the man was a Darian, not a Throatian.

"S-Shivanna Adul," Thane replied as he switched away from Common Tongue. "You speak Throatian?"

"Vrai." It meant yes.

"That makes you the first Darian I've met who can," Thane said. "Where did you learn it?"

"I'm not Darian, and it doesn't matter where I learned your language," the man said. "You're Prince Thane, aren't you?"

He had the armor of a guard, but the color stood out in contrast to the plain steel worn by the others. His set was a full suit of crimson, though he carried no helmet. The man's neutral, simple face was covered in stubble. His dirty, sand-hued hair lay against his neck and splayed across his shoulder blades.

"I'm Thane," the prince said. "And who are you? If you're neither Throatian nor Darian, then where are you from? People outside our island don't know our language."

The man looked around for anyone who might have been passing by, then leaned closer to Thane. "I wish to make a deal with you."

Thane examined him over again for any kind of sign of where he was from, but nothing stood out for him. Everything about this stranger was plain, almost boring. The man would blend into any crowd seamlessly.

"What about this deal is so secret that you'd want nobody else to hear?"

"It's one you won't inform anyone about," the man said, ignoring Thane's question. "Follow me, and I'll tell you the rest."

Something wasn't right. Though the man dressed as a knight, the constant glances over his shoulder made him seem suspicious—more like a grifter or a thief.

"It's late. I just want to get some sleep. No deals." Thane began walking away, softening his footsteps so he'd sense if the strange man tried approaching from behind. His muscles tensed as he prepared to tackle him somewhere below the waist if need be.

"White armor won't protect you from a black storm," the stranger muttered.

Thane froze. A massive surge of adrenaline rushed through his body, and he turned to face the crimson knight again, hands forming into fists.

"What did you just say?"

"I know all about you, my dear prince," the man said. "Your impending sacrifice, the secret doubts you have about Zann-Xia-Czul, your family's mission, and, most importantly, I know about your regrets with Cereene. You're such a good Son See'er, aren't you? Obedient to the end, even though you're not getting anything you truly want out of it."

"H-how do you... How do you know all this? Who in shulkkaal are you?" Thane wished he'd brought a weapon along. The other man had a sword at his waist and confidently patted its sheath as Thane gaped back at him.

The knight grinned and waved for the prince to draw closer. "I just want to make a deal with you. And now that I've got your attention, please follow me. Time is short, and nobody can know I was here."

He led Thane down a dim alley, where various crates and boxes lined tall, indigo walls. The street led to a dead end, devoid of everything but garbage. The air was thick with the pungent stench of rotten trash and waste, causing the prince to cover his mouth to stave off the urge to gag.

"Why are we here?"

"We need privacy, somewhere away from the many ears of the sorceress." The knight pointed to the other end of the street, where there was no exit. "Go 'on, now. Walk over there and don't stop, no matter what happens. I'll be right behind you."

Thane cautiously made his way down the road as instructed, when suddenly a bright light blinded him as he stepped forward. Blasts of hot air engulfed his body, as though he'd plunged into one of the fiery rings in Loyalty Circle Nineteen. Thane instinctively threw his arms out in front of him to block whatever else was coming, but it all stopped as quickly as it had started.

He opened his eyes. The suspicious alleyway of Starlight Beach had been replaced by a cloudless, blue sky overlooking charcoal-colored sand. Endless miles of grainy dunes dominated the landscape. It was as though someone had amassed the world's supply of soot, dedicating a lifetime to grinding it into fine powder with a mortar and pestle. These were surely the Silent Deserts—there was nowhere else in the world filled with so much pure, black sand.

"Ruik Czharr," Thane muttered to himself. "He must have sent me through a World Vein."

But how? There was no stone archway in the alley, so how had he moved? This seemed different from the ancient transportation gate the Throatians had at home. Their island's gateway only opened once every several years to let fresh human sacrifices into their homeland, and there wasn't a way to control it. Kaelgeth had spent years unsuccessfully trying to open the portal. Those who came through the doorway were from another realm and could not speak the Throatian tongue—essentially, they were raw humans meant to supplement the Loyalty Circles and Breeding Farms. Sometimes, Zann-Xia-Czul even went as far as sending lightning down on the newcomers as they arrived through the invisible portal. The Elders deemed it too perilous to approach the gate or delve into its enigmatic depths.

Thane scrambled backward, so he might return to Starlight Beach, but nothing happened. This route, much like the only other pathway he'd heard of, only worked one way. Meanwhile, a foul stench wafted from the ground as the scorching black sand beneath his feet heated his leather sandals.

"It's only fun to do it the first time," the knight's voice echoed from behind.

"To do what?"

"Teleport, of course."

"How do we get back? A World Vein needs a gate, but—"

"It wasn't a World Vein that brought us here," the crimson knight interrupted. "Now, don't mind the details. Time's too short to try to understand everything. Let's make our deal."

"So, what do you want?"

"A favor from you at a time and place of my choosing."

"Get to the point."

"I'll tell you what it is when I need you to do it," the man declared.

Thane studied the knight's face but couldn't read past the calm yet inviting expression. "It's never a good idea to accept a deal without knowing the terms."

"You're already planning to do what I want you to do. I simply wish to control when and where it happens."

"Okay, what is it you want me to do, then?"

"The task loses its effectiveness if you are aware of it beforehand," the knight grinned. "That's all you need to know. In exchange for doing my favor, I'll help your family fight the sorceress."

The man seemed serious, yet there was an unsettling aura to his demeanor that struck Thane. The stranger before him beamed with confidence, but something seemed off. Even so, a single man could hardly be expected to make more of a difference than Thane and Lydia's combined blood.

"If white armor can't protect me from a black storm, then how will crimson armor do any better against the sorceress's magic?" Thane asked. "A lone knight stands no chance. Only Zann-Xia-Czul's power can defeat her."

The knight let out a single, quiet laugh, then reached to his side and unbuckled the strap of his chest plate. Slowly, he revealed a thin cotton shirt underneath. He drew his sword from its sheath and gingerly turned the hilt over toward Thane.

"Take my blade, Throatian prince," the knight said. "See how sharp the edge is? Notice how the steel emits a red hue if you reflect the sunlight just so. Tell me how it's dangerous and that it can cut deep."

Thane gripped the weapon and looked it over. It was an ordinary sword, and likely an old one too. Many chips covered its surface, but it was recently sharpened and could slice through skin, exactly as the stranger claimed.

"You'll want to get this reforged. Have you been practicing your swordplay against a brick wall?"

The crimson knight restrained his laughter. "Prince Asche, you are amusing. I enjoy making deals with the likes of you. I know you doubt me. You want proof I can hold my own against the enemy of your people, don't you?"

Thane shook his head. "Wielding a blade holds no power against magic. The sorceress—"

"Stab me with my sword," the knight interrupted, pointing at his chest.

"What?"

"Go on. Put it right through my heart."

Thane stepped back. "Why would I do that? You're crazy, but it's not worth killing you over."

The man beamed at him. "Don't forget, I'm here

to help you, my prince. Make this easier for both of us and quit asking questions. Just do it."

"It doesn't seem wise." Then again, nor was standing there in debate—the burning black sand would light his sandals ablaze at any moment.

"You've killed plenty of people in the Loyalty Circles, right? How many amongst them yearned for life? I'm telling you to stab me. This should be easy for you. Come on, now. Time is running out."

"For what? Why's it so urgent?"

"Stop asking questions, shulkkaal!"

He grabbed the sharp edge of the blade and yanked it from Thane's grasp. Then, as his fingers bled profusely onto the steel, the stranger adjusted his grip to clutch the weapon's hilt once more. Without hesitation, the knight quickly plunged the blade into his own chest.

"You're crazy!"

"I-I'm fine," he said through gritted teeth. He twisted the sword within as blood spewed onto the black sands at their feet. "Now, Thane, remove it from my heart."

Hands trembling, the Throatian prince grasped the bloody handle and pulled. The knight braced his legs and resisted as the weapon was extracted, spilling even more blood from his wound.

"Why did you do this?" Thane exclaimed. "Killing yourself to prove a point is completely idiotic!"

"I'm not dead," the crimson knight said. "Nor do I plan to be."

"It doesn't hurt?"

"The principles of your Loyalty Circles are wrong," the man replied. "Suffering is inevitable, but death is only inevitable to most. As for me, I'll be healed within an hour."

Thane stared at him. "What?"

"This is no magic. It is my very nature," the crimson knight declared. "I'll fight the sorceress and defeat her for you, but you'll have to do as I say and give me my requested favor. Do we have a deal?"

Was this man truly invulnerable to death? Even though he'd denied it, surely it was magic. No ordinary person could take a stabbing to his heart and brag about it—not even a Lucidian. The burning sun scorched his skin and had already dried the blood that covered the blade. There were no signs of civilization or water in sight. Despite removing Thane from the suspicious alleyway, the knight had trapped him in the unforgiving wilderness. Still, if this strange warrior could defeat the sorceress, there was a chance Thane wouldn't need to sacrifice himself later.

"I-I'll do whatever you ask," Thane said. "Just tell me what to do."

The knight smiled. "You've made a wise choice, good prince. For now, tell nobody that you've met me. Pretend we've never even seen each other. The sorceress has ears everywhere. Go along with your mission and do what Zann-Xia-Czul asked. Remember my face, though. When you see me again, I'll have my favor ready, and you'll do it without question."

"Okay."

"Without question. Understood?"

"Yes, without question," Thane confirmed.

The crimson knight knelt in the sand and started putting his armor back on.

"So, why do you wear armor if you can't die?" Thane asked.

"That's another question, but I'll humor you anyway," the knight said. "I wear it only because I want to. It's an elegant set, after all. Now, close your eyes, and take seven steps away from me. It's time for you to return to where you were."

Thane nodded and walked backward, keeping his eyes on the other man. The knight could create invisible portals at will... but how?

"Remember, Thane, you never met me," the stranger warned. "If you tell anyone what happened here, I'll kill your family, Cereene, and, finally, you."

Before Thane could respond to the crimson knight's threat, he had teleported around the world, back to the dark alleyway of Starlight Beach. Reorienting himself, he looked over at the invisible portal. Would the knight return as well?

He took a moment to catch his breath. A stack of boxes full of garbage tumbled nearby as a stray cat chased a mouse through the rubbish. Alone in the darkness, he waited for a few moments, but it soon became clear that the warrior would not come through. Still, it was inevitable they'd cross paths again someday. It was just a matter of when.

The strange encounter with the fighter proved the reality of magic and that all their fears about the sorceress were true. It was starting to seem more and more likely that his family's mission was only part of an ongoing series of parallel events involving the sorceress's supernatural threat. A man capable of stabbing his own heart and bragging about it afterward would be useful in the long term, as peculiar a person as he was.

The favor Thane had agreed to was both vague and concerning. He hoped it wasn't anything nefarious. Perhaps the stranger hadn't specified what he wanted because he hadn't yet decided. Still, what could an invincible, teleporting knight possibly desire?

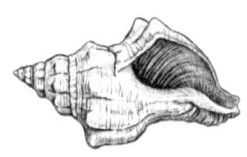

THE CHATTER AND BUSTLING OF THE BARS HAD DIED down while he was away, and the night had matured. Going to sleep would be best, for now. Besides, there was still no sign of Harkbin. Thane strolled toward the inn, listening to the calming rhythm of the ocean waves crashing back and forth. As his near-melted sandals echoed against the cobblestone streets, damp from the sea breeze, everything around him seemed darker than before. Perhaps his eyes had been overexposed in the desert's sunlight.

As he approached the inn's entrance, light leaked through the cracked entry and into the street. Suspecting that the guard had wandered off some-where to urinate, Thane let himself in. The door creaked open, revealing both of his parents and Merdel standing in the lobby's center. The light of the fireplace reflected off their concerned faces and made shadows dance along the walls.

"Where were you?" Harkbin asked.

Thane glared at his father. "Outside, looking for you. Were you hiding from me or something?"

"For three hours?" Urith exclaimed.

Thane gaped at her. She was wrong. He hadn't been gone that long... had he? Could the time differ-ence have been because of the teleportation? The crimson knight's order for secrecy echoed in his mind, so he kept quiet about what he'd seen.

"I was praying to Zann-Xia-Czul as well," he lied. "Everything is fine."

"See? There's no harm done," Merdel said. "This was an isolated incident."

"What was?" Thane looked back and forth between the three of them.

"Merely a thief in the night or a crazed beggar," the councilor replied. "We're still investigating the details. But don't worry, it's nothing to fret about. Everyone can go to sleep now."

"Someone murdered one of the Darian guards," Urith said. "Stabbed him in the heart."

"Drunk university students sometimes get in fights while they party," Merdel said apologetically. "The soldier stationed at the perimeter must have become involved. There's no sign of the attacker. We've swept the protected blocks surrounding the inn."

"Are we in danger?" Urith asked.

"You've got to be joking, mother," Thane scoffed.

"I don't want to sleep with one eye open," she said, despite being plenty more than capable of defending herself.

"Nobody even knows you're here at this inn," Merdel reassured her. "You are guests of the Darian Kingdom. The guards are here for your privacy. Starlight Beach is a very safe place. It normally has very low crime, and—"

"We appreciate your efforts, Councilman," Harkbin interjected, "and under your protection, we'll return to our rooms."

Merdel bid them good night after apologizing one more time. As Thane, Harkbin, and Urith walked upstairs, his mother grabbed his shoulder.

"Was it you?" she asked in Throatian.

"Me what?"

"Were you the one who stabbed the guard?" Urith accused. "Your tone seemed like you were lying to us."

Thane crossed his arms and grimaced at her. "I saw nothing," he insisted. "And why would I stab one of the Darians?"

"Never mind it, then," Harkbin said, waving back to the queen. "Before leaving for the capital tomorrow morning, we'll alert Hrodspire about what occurred so he can stay abreast of it while he watches the ships."

Thane leaned closer to his father. "Was he the guard standing outside the inn?"

"Yes, that one, but he died a few blocks away," Urith said. "There's no evidence that we were the targets. Still, this helps our mission. We'll use the situation to keep Merdel distracted. He can focus his attention on protecting us rather than carefully examining our every move."

"Very well, but we shouldn't present ourselves as

overly weak or in constant need of protection," Thane said. "The king needs to trust that we're capable enough to keep Princess Lydia safe."

"It doesn't matter," Harkbin said. "He's in too deep to cancel the wedding now. Turning his back on us would be scandalous. Once we get the princess home, there's nothing left to worry about."

However, the truth was a different matter—Thane knew more than they did, and plenty of other issues were exacerbating his concerns. Something about his encounter with the knight in crimson armor had left him completely unnerved. The man was invulnerable and somehow knew Throatian language. Thane couldn't help but wonder if the knight was Zann-Xia-Czul or perhaps an illusion sent on his behalf. It was likely that the inn's guard had also met his end at the hands of the knight. None of it made sense, particularly the vague agreement they'd made, and Thane couldn't shake the fear that he might have made a grievous error...

7

THE DARIAN KINGDOM

The next morning, the Throatian entourage loaded into a large carriage and set off toward Last Hope, the capital of the Darian Kingdom. Throughout the first day of their journey, Thane reflected on the unusual meeting with the crimson knight. The prince realized he hadn't fully grasped the implications of the knight's deal. However, given that few would dare to confront an evil sorceress, the pact might have more merits than reasons for skepticism. Still, the prince harbored doubts regarding his new acquaintance's motivations. The insistence on secrecy was a glaring hint that this "favor" might come with complications. He wondered whether the knight's task would be easier or harder than sacrificing his own life.

After several more days of travel, a colossal scarlet

castle loomed on the horizon, perched atop a towering hill. Surrounded by walls of the same color, the central city rested at the base of the castle. Though elegant, the royal edifice, which towered over the commoners below, showed signs of decay because of its age. Two of the four watchtowers were missing sections of bricks and seemed on the brink of collapse. Although the fortifications encircling the capital remained intact, King Ether von Stonewall's bastion appeared as though it would shatter like glass under siege.

"Behold, Serenity Keep!" Merdel exclaimed from his horse, as he drew alongside their carriage.

"Why wouldn't they repair it?" Thane muttered to his father in Throatian.

Harkbin scratched his beard thoughtfully. "Perhaps the castle's history and symbolism outweigh its defense-worthiness. The city's name, Last Hope, may describe everything in it, including the king's castle."

"Leaving it unmaintained is foolish," Urith replied.

"The distribution of resources more towards the city's defenses than protecting the royalty could work to our advantage," Thane remarked.

The carriage and its escorts ventured through the main gate and down several streets. A makeshift market crowded the square just inside the capital's border. Opportunistic merchants yelled out at them, offering water, fruits, and beef jerky for sale. Other people, dressed in torn rags, offered massages and "whatever else you need after your long journey." Thane scowled at the beggars through the small window.

"Go away! We have no interest!" Merdel yelled at the crowds. He steered his horse around and approached the royal family. "The bird I sent must not have arrived in time. A parade and party should've been waiting for us. I don't know why they're absent, but I assure you, you'll receive a grand welcome once we get to the castle."

Harkbin sneezed and brought his face nearer to the window. "It's nothing to worry about. Our arrival could never be precise. We wouldn't want to inconvenience you with anything aside from the wedding."

"Thank you for your understanding," Merdel replied. "I'm so sorry things haven't gone as planned."

They pulled into a roundabout parking area near the decaying castle's base. Various other carriages lined the stone pathway, but there seemed to be no one around. The central doorway, with twin lion statues on either side, looked quiet and abandoned from where they were. Neither guards nor any of the other staff presented themselves as their carriage approached.

"They may well have ensnared us in a trap," Harkbin whispered.

"I sense it too," Urith said. "Men at the wall or scouts should have noticed our arrival."

Sweat beaded on Merdel's forehead as he dismounted his steed. "I'll find out why there aren't any hosts tending the entrance." He stormed off to the castle's entryway, muttering about how he'd release from duty every servant in the castle for slacking off while he was away.

"The councilman's embarrassment reveals his surprise," Thane said. "I don't think he planned this."

A few minutes later, Merdel returned with four servants. All their faces were red and tense as they pushed forward with empty wooden carts. Each carrier rattled against the bumpy stone ground.

"We'll help you get unpacked and situated inside," Merdel said. "King von Stonewall and Princess Lydia are occupied at the moment but should be able to meet you soon."

The servants unloaded their belongings and guided them upstairs. They set up Harkbin and Urith in a spacious suite, while allotting Thane in his own private chamber. Between their suites were two more chambers for their escorts.

"You've had a long journey. Please make yourselves comfortable and stretch out for a few hours," Merdel said, handing them each some small metallic trinkets. "And we request you don't leave your rooms. The king plans on giving you a grand tour of everything as soon as he can. He doesn't wish for anything to be spoiled for you."

"What purpose do these serve?" Urith asked, holding up the short bronze object.

"Pardon?"

"The metal decoration," Urith said. "Is it supposed to be fastened to a weapon?"

"Oh!" Merdel exclaimed. "It's called a key. You don't use them in the Throatian Kingdom?"

The small gift had also perplexed Thane. "Key. I know this word. It is for opening a treasure box. But where is it?"

"In this context, they unlock doors," Merdel replied with an earnest grin. He led them over to the doorway and demonstrated by inserting Urith's key into a tiny hole. "We call this a doorknob. You place the key inside and turn it, then the door can open. When it's locked, you'll need the key, otherwise it won't open again. This allows you privacy while you're inside your rooms. Does it make sense?"

Thane understood the words, but not the under-lying reasoning behind them. They hadn't received keys for their doors at Starlight Beach's inn, so why now? The Darian Kingdom's nobles had privacy?

Resisting the urge to reveal his curiosity, Thane simply nodded.

"Excellent," the councilman replied. "Now, I must go help with preparations. Enjoy your time of rest, and remember, please don't leave your rooms."

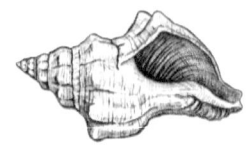

THE DARIAN SERVANTS COMPLETED THE DELIVERY OF their final crate of belongings, and Thane closed the door behind him. Now alone, he took his time examining the style of his latest accommodations in the foreign land. As with the inn at Starlight Beach, the quality and elegance here surpassed even that of the Temple of White's cathedral. The rooms at Last Hope's royal castle were smaller than the lodge they'd previously visited, likely because of the castle's age. Despite its size, the builders had spared no expense. An assortment of velvet cloths and upholsteries covered the entire chamber. Most impressively, there was a small fire pit built directly into the wall, already ablaze and radiating warmth throughout the room.

The intricacies and decorum were supreme, but there was no time to savor it. Something about the manner of the von Stonewall family didn't seem right. What was so important that they wouldn't come to introduce themselves? Councilman Merdel's request that they remain in their rooms was suspicious too.

Thane stared out the window as the crisp scent of apricots filled his nose. Though there was already a bowl of fruits on the table, the prince reached out and pulled a fresh one from the nearby tree branch. As he chewed, he gazed at his suit of white armor, which the servants had delicately mounted on a wooden mannequin. He anticipated donning it for his eventual wedding ceremony.

"Even though it's not with Cereene, I should still look my best," Thane murmured to himself as his fingers grazed the armor's smooth, unmarred surface. The prince tossed aside the apricot, then set about putting on the armor; first the breastplate, then the gauntlets, and finishing with the greaves and other leg pieces. The entire set was as perfect as the craftsman had promised, and the specialized material was featherweight and royal.

There came a knock at his door.

"Who's there?" Thane called in Common Tongue.

"It's me," Harkbin replied in Throatian. A loud creak filled the hall as Thane let his father inside. Harkbin gave him an appraising once-over, then nodded in approval.

"It appears well made," he said, caressing the

surface. "Be sure to take care of it. Don't let it rust like your old suit."

"It cannot corrode in such a manner. The armorer forged this from a special material."

"What kind?"

"I don't know, exactly, but it's the best substance the armorer could find. Very light too! I've carried books for Cereene that were heavier than this entire set."

"But you claimed it was incomplete?"

"Yes, but only for appearances," Thane said. "The armor is strong. He just needs a special coating to keep the shiny surface unscratched."

"I see," Harkbin replied, shutting the open window. "Something is amiss in the castle. Merdel's been acting odd since we arrived. Do you sense it?"

"The Darian king appears to be avoiding us too. But why?"

"It remains unclear. Will you wander around and try to gather some information? Your mother and I plan on summoning Merdel and distracting him so you can move freely about the castle."

"I understand."

"Keep your armor on for now," Harkbin said. "Until we meet the king and gauge his intentions, I don't want to trust anything for the time being, given these irregularities."

Without saying another word, Thane and his

father exited his room and went their separate ways. Thane tiptoed down a spiral stone staircase while listening for any signs of guards. The hall at the bottom was empty as well. Two possibilities presented themselves: either Merdel trusted them to remain stationary, or the staff could not enforce his directive.

Beyond the threshold, in a quaint courtyard, a towering cherry tree in full bloom stood over a modest garden. A blanket of pink petals enveloped the cobblestone path and neighboring grass. It was a sight Thane wished he could bring home with him. A young, silver-haired girl sat alone on a bench, perusing an enormous book that rested on her lap. Chances were that she was Princess Kira. Surely the servants' children weren't allowed to idle around the castle or engage in scholarly pursuits.

Thane's footsteps squished among the petals as he approached her, but the child paid him no mind. Whatever book she was reading must have been engrossing. He cleared his throat loudly.

"Excuse me, Princess Kira," he said. "I'm Prince Thane of the Throatian Kingdom. It's a pleasure to meet you. Do you know where your father is?"

"Huh?" The girl's eyes widened. She stuck a cherry blossom petal onto the page of her book and closed it.

It occurred to him that his accent might have

obscured his words, so he articulated with greater care. "I'm going to marry your sister soon, but I want to find your dad. Can you tell me where he is?"

She brushed her silvery hair. "I'm not Princess Kira."

"Oh, okay," Thane said. Perhaps this girl came from another royal family. "Which kingdom are you the princess of?"

"I'm not a princess, sorry," she said. "I'm Ursula. My aunt is Bridgette Frey."

"Who's Bridgette Frey?" Thane asked.

"She's a council member for the king," Ursula said. She gazed at his armor. "Your suit is special, is it not? Such craftsmanship is unfamiliar to me. Is it traditional Throatian attire, or reserved solely for royalty?"

Thane's lips curled into a smile. He pondered the prospect that befriending the girl might elicit some valuable insights. "My armor was custom made for me. I'm glad you—"

"Your necklace is special too," the girl said. "I've never seen dragon language inscribed on jewelry before. It's quite elegant."

"Pardon?" Thane held out Cereene's gift and pointed at the center of the cerulean amulet. "This is Throatian language, not dragon tongue. It says the name of my god, Zann-Xia-Czul."

"How fascinating," the girl said. "I recognize the character, and it's dragon language."

"What does it say, then?" She obviously didn't know what she was talking about, but she'd piqued his interest.

"I-I don't remember exactly. It was in one of my books, but I read it a long time ago."

"I wasn't aware that dragons even had a language," Thane quipped with a wry smile. "Did any of your stories tell of them taking a quill and writing their history in dragon-sized books before they all died?"

"I'm sorry, Prince Thane. I must have been mistaken." The girl's eyes began to fill with tears.

Thane shook his head. "I didn't mean to interrogate you. Sorry. Anyway, do you know where I can find King Ether von Stonewall?"

The silver-haired girl relaxed and wiped her face. "Might I suggest the throne room?"

"Good idea," he said, giving up on gleaning any useful information from her. Despite her being upper-class and naive, she didn't seem informed of the castle's current state.

"Pardon me, Prince Thane..." Ursula's voice wavered. "May I come to your wedding?"

"Of course," Thane said. "It will be everything you can dream of and more!"

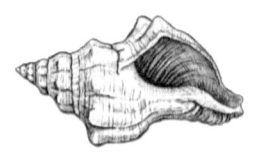

HE WENT BACK INSIDE THE CASTLE. THE SOUNDS OF chatter echoed from the staircase leading up to his chamber. Thane couldn't recognize the voices, but they were whispering in the Common Tongue. He quietly approached the stairs, ascended, and lingered behind whoever was talking.

"—antidote cured the rash on her leg too. We're so lucky she's back unharmed."

"What about the monster? Could it have been real?"

"Nah, the guy who rescued her is broke. He probably made that part up to get a higher reward."

"Either way, he saved her. I heard Frieda and Jillian weren't so fortunate."

"Really? So, they're…?"

"Yes. From the so-called monster. Only Lydia escaped. I heard it from Kenneth."

"Excuse me," Thane interjected, skipping a few stairs to catch up to the guards and reveal himself, "but the princess was in danger? How?"

The servant's face went white as he turned around. "Prince Thane! I'm sorry! Merdel told us not to tell you. He didn't want to cause any undue stress. Yes, there was a monster, but it's dead and your bride is fine. She just returned to the castle half an hour ago."

The junior servant's sweat dripped all over his maroon cardigan. Thane was well acquainted with this type of man. Many Son See'er Vrai feared those in the highest stratums of the upper class, as a single complaint could relegate them from servanthood to a life of poverty. Controlling them through fear was most effective, with their job security being a potent source of leverage.

"How long was Lydia gone?" he asked. "And why was she off somewhere dangerous?"

"Um… Um…"

"Why?" Thane snapped. He cursed in Throatian, for good measure.

"I-I can't tell you that," said the attendant. His friend stood idly by, either frozen in shock or unwilling to aid his fellow worker.

Thane revealed a small coin purse. "Do you know what this is?"

"Silver?"

"Yes, it's coin. I have two pieces in here. It's yours if you tell me everything you know. Do you want it?"

"I-I do… but I can't. Councilman Merdel will get rid of me if he finds out I told—"

"Merdel doesn't have to know."

The man cast a glance at his fellow worker, who continued to shake his head and stare at the floor.

They reeked of desperation and temptation. Their compliance would come if given the proper motivation.

"Did I say two pieces of silver?" Thane said, shaking the purse. "I meant four. And if you don't take them, I'll tell Merdel I caught you with them after I returned from relieving myself. It would be such a pity to find lowly criminals within the Darian servanthood."

He locked eyes with the two men and stared them down. Slowly, the first man extended his hand.

"Princess Lydia went missing this morning. We thought she got kidnapped, but it turns out she ran away because of the wedding. It scared her to be committed to someone she's never met. Please forgive her. She's a good person."

"I will," Thane said, broadening his chest. "And what about the monster? Tell me more about that."

The man flinched, pulling back his outstretched hand which remained empty of any reward. "Monsters aren't real. It's probably just some deformed beast that attacked the princess. A sailor merchant from the Leila Kingdom rescued her. Kaine Khalia. He's here at the castle. That's all I've heard, I swear to Asura."

Thane studied the young man in front of him, who was sweaty and trembling, and discerned he was telling the truth. Now was the time to glean information from the second servant.

"And what do you know?"

"Nothing else," the second servant said, shaking his head. "We're sorry about the hard time. Merdel is strict with us. He's always in a rush and demands perfection. Your arrival is a grand event, and he wanted to—"

"No need to ramble on about Merdel," Thane said. He tossed the pouch of silver to the two servants.

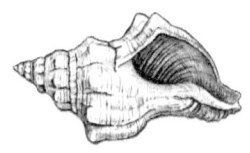

"So, we're all in agreement that the servants told me the truth?" Thane asked his parents once they'd met up in his bedroom.

Harkbin sat in the chair with his back to the desk. "Princess Lydia's disappearance explains Merdel's panicked behavior and why Ether von Stonewall has avoided meeting us so far."

"From their perspective, we've arrived here at the worst possible time," Urith said. "Concealing the drama from our view would be their top priority."

"Besides finding my bride, of course," Thane added. He began unstrapping the leggings and gauntlets of his armor and returning them to the mannequin. The skin underneath was sweaty and clammy, but it was a small compromise to make, given how effortless it was to wear the suit.

"We should keep this information to ourselves," Harkbin said, whittling a buzzard from a chunk of wood he'd pulled from the fireplace. "There's little advantage to revealing what you heard. It would also show we disobeyed Merdel's request."

Thane watched him scrape along the bird's beak, carefully refining its edge. "At least we've learned his strange behavior had nothing to do with—"

"You're both wrong about this," Urith interrupted. She sat up in the bed, where she'd been resting. "This is our chance to trick the Darians. Revealing what we know can make them think it was our magic."

Harkbin shifted in his chair, and his knife paused for a moment. "The idea is clever, but it's too risky and too late to implement it. We would have needed to act earlier, as the situation unfolded. Merdel will no doubt suspect we overheard his servants' chatter."

Meanwhile, Thane sucked in his stomach, removed his chest plate, and placed it back around the mannequin. There was a slight scuff on one side, and he polished it away with his sleeve. The suit was ready to wear again at the wedding ceremony.

Urith slammed both feet on the ground. Harkbin

gave a start and nicked his finger with the blade. He swore under his breath as blood dripped onto the floor. Then, having licked his wound, he resumed honing his knife against the wood.

"The Darians are going to ask us to display our powers eventually," Urith said. "The opportunity to trick them is already here. We only need to take advantage of it."

"Keep to the original plan," Harkbin commanded.

Urith huffed in protest.

"It's against our religion to show our magic to foreigners until after we have a ceremony at the Temple of White. Don't stray from that excuse. Understood?"

"Fine."

"Don't use that tone with me," Harkbin growled. Splinters of wood and dust floated down to his feet.

Urith marched over to him and slapped both the knife and bird from his hands. They clattered across the floor and rolled under the bed. Face red and scowling, Harkbin jumped from his chair. His index finger shook as he pointed at her, his finger positioned between her taunting eyes.

Before he could yell at her, Urith interjected. "Stop wasting time! You should spend your time praying to Zann-Xia-Czul, not crafting meaningless art."

"You've got no idea what you're talking about!

Our god gave us a mission, and we planned out the details before we left home. We're going to stay true to that plan."

He retrieved the knife and wooden bird from under the bed, dusted them off, and returned to his chair. As Thane waited to see whether their argument was over or about to escalate, he pretended to buff out more blemishes on his armor. A moment of silence went by before Urith responded.

"Perhaps Zann-Xia-Czul stopped answering your calls because of your inflexibility. We can't assume everything will go exactly as planned. We need to take every opportunity to control the situation."

Thane glowered at his mother. Their god still hadn't spoken, but there was no evidence that his father was responsible for it. Urith's harassment wasn't helping, either.

"If the plan changed, he would have stated so," Harkbin said. "Adding new ideas and tricks risks backfiring. We've come too far to change it all now."

"There's no proof of that," Urith barked. "As long as we get the princess, nothing else we do matters."

"It counts," Harkbin said. "Zann-Xia-Czul provided us with the instructions we need. It's not our place to expand upon them."

"His plan was purposefully vague, only meant to be a starting point," the Throatian queen insisted.

"Perhaps the sorceress is blocking his connection to our minds."

"Impossible," Urith said. "He reads and speaks directly into them. Magic can't prevent that. This is all your fault."

"Enough with the accusations!" Harkbin yelled. His hand shook as he carefully set the bird and knife on the desk behind him. Turning back, he folded his arms and stared at the queen. "You know we can't control any of this. We can only trust in and obey the greater good."

Urith scowled. Her mouth opened, but no words came out. Then, suddenly, she charged at him and roared like a bear protecting her cubs. She tackled Harkbin, and the heft of her muscular form sent him flying backward. The chair's leg cracked loudly as the two of them thudded to the ground and began wrestling. Thane gasped—he'd never seen them engage in physical violence with each other! Both seemed unfazed and unsurprised, so perhaps they'd hidden some past brawls from him.

"Stop it!" he yelled. "Fighting won't fix anything!"

Urith and Harkbin ignored him and continued punching each other. With her broad shoulders and muscular upper body, Urith easily pinned down her husband. Harkbin attempted to roll away from her but failed. He pounded his fist on the wooden floor in a gesture of defeat, but Urith denied his surrender.

"Mother!" Thane yelled. "The guards will hear you!"

Ignoring both their pleas, Urith relentlessly thrashed Harkbin against the ground. If someone were to walk in on them, one would assume Urith was murdering her husband. Regardless of her intent, the scene was a disgraceful sight, even within Throatian culture.

"Urith!"

The queen lifted Harkbin up by his shirt, off the floor, and charged him backward across the room. Thane leaped out of the way as his father's back collided with the armor. It tumbled over, and a crash rang throughout the suite. The prince prayed he was mistaken, that Harkbin had broken the bedroom window. But that was not the case. As Thane's suit hit the floor, thousands of white crystals scattered across the polished wood.

"No!"

He ran over to the mannequin and set it upright again. The chest and back plates were missing by almost half, and cracks had webbed their way across both gauntlets. He removed the leg pieces and found them damaged as well. In defeat, he threw them at the floor. His entire suit had turned out to be nothing more than a beautifully deceptive piece of craftsmanship.

Thane hadn't actually tested the armor's durability when he'd picked it up from the armorer. So much else was going on at the time, he'd forgotten the simple task of verifying whether the suit would protect him. Sure, he had tried it on a few times to make sure it fit, but it was sickening to know how dangerous his mistake could have been. His exemption from fighting in the Loyalty Circle was his only grace.

Urith pushed herself off her husband and glared at Harkbin's bloody nostrils. "Apparently, it's all glass that was painted white."

She was right, but it didn't matter anymore. The craftsman might as well have used seashells as his base component. Everything was ruined and useless. Thane wouldn't even be able to wear it to the wedding now.

"What in shulkkaal were you two thinking?" Thane hissed, his face aflame with anger.

"I had to beat some sense into him."

"Zaibuo..." It was unbelievable—too wild and foolish to be untrue.

Aside from Loyalty Circles, it was unlike Urith to be so casually violent. Thane wondered if being away from them for so long was causing her to look elsewhere for the thrill of a fight. Either way, assaulting her husband was inappropriate, and Thane promised himself he'd confront her about it once she'd cooled off.

Thane's father pinched his nose, while the blood still dripped down his arm. "Calm your senses. You've created enough trouble for one journey, including what you did to Desaii. If your reckless-ness ends up ruining our mission, you'll face Zann-Xia-Czul's wrath alone."

"Shut up," Urith scoffed.

"Mother!" Thane scolded. "Members of the Darian royalty surely don't behave this way. Nor should you."

The queen gave a huff and picked up the chair she had knocked over. The broken leg was irrepara-ble, so she dropped it onto the floor again. Thane shook his head in disgust as Harkbin retrieved a washcloth from a nearby table and began cleaning his face and hands.

"We should have left her at home," he whispered as Urith retreated to the bed, turning her back on them.

"There's little else we could have done about it," Thane replied. He adjusted the broken leg of the chair so it could at least stand again. It was weak but would remain stable so long as nobody sat in it.

Harkbin approached the bedroom door, struggling as he turned the doorknob the wrong way and attempted to push it open. Finally, after a moment of confusion, he pulled it ajar and peered into the hallway. A moment later, he closed it with a sigh of relief.

"It seems none of the guards heard our quarrel."

"One less thing to worry about," Thane said, as beads of sweat dripped down his body. Red scuffs covered Harkbin's face, and he prayed Urith hadn't left him with any bruises before the wedding. The less peculiar they appeared as a family, the better.

Harkbin's gaze fell upon the broken armor pieces scattered across the floor. "The fact your armor broke now is a blessing in disguise. If it had shattered while you were wearing it, the glass would have cut you and done more damage than if you'd had no protection at all. Luckily, we have other formal clothing packed for the wedding."

"True," Thane nodded. "The armorer responsible for this sham will pay dearly."

Someone knocked on the door, and Harkbin went to answer it. It was Merdel.

"My apologies for the delay. We've settled the matter at hand, and King von Stonewall can see you now." He glanced past Harkbin at the shattered shards of armor scattered about the floor. "What happened here?"

"I must also apologize," Thane said. "I was practicing my magic and momentarily lost control. I'm sorry for the mess."

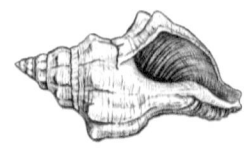

Merdel guided them into the most majestic section of the castle: the throne room. An elderly, stern-looking man gazed upon them from atop his massive crystalline chair. Cautiously, they made their way towards him across the intricately woven blue carpet. Constructed from fire-red stone that evoked memories of summer in Thane, the chamber, however, felt dishearteningly cold. He missed the flaming pit in his room.

"Welcome, my honored Throatian guests," the man said. "I am King Ether von Stonewall. You have my deepest apologies that I couldn't receive you sooner. We've had a few problems on our end. Nothing left unresolved, mind you. Everything is better now. My youngest daughter Kira was ill until a few days ago, then yesterday my eldest, Lydia, went off on her own little adventure without my permission. She's back, and all is well again."

Harkbin started by lowering himself onto one knee and bowing his head. "Shivanna Adul, King von Stonewall. It is an honor to meet you and forge an alliance between our countries." He gestured to one side, then the other. "This is my wife, Queen Urith Asche, and my heir, Prince Thane. He will make a fine son-in-law for you, I guarantee it."

Thane and his mother followed suit and bowed to the foreign king.

"Please rise. Let's get a better look at you," Ether von Stonewall said.

Thane stood and studied the king's eyes. His face, marked by wrinkles, wore a weary expression, as if each crease represented a battle fought to earn his seat on the crystal throne. Thane lacked details about the Darian Kingdom's history, but he knew their formation had come at the end of a war against the Lucidians. How the Darians had managed to survive a magical onslaught remained a mystery. Still, it would be impolite of him to ask what strategies they had used; it was likely a sensitive topic.

"Hair as dark as a crow's feathers and skin akin to a ghost," Ether von Stonewall commented. "Tall family, and respectful. It's clear I made the right choice by accepting your proposal."

As his parents rose, Thane bowed his head slightly. "Your words humble me, my king. But if I may ask, where is the princess? Am I allowed to meet her before the wedding?"

"Of course, you are!" Ether von Stonewall said. "Lydia is on her way here now. She was taking her time getting dressed to give you a good first impression."

Urith took a firm step forward. "Our first impression is that she went missing. What happened to her?"

Harkbin rested his hand on her shoulder in warning, then added, "We only pray Princess Lydia is safe and well."

Ether frowned, but quickly regained his composure. "I didn't want to worry you, but since you asked, I'll be transparent. In one of our nearby forests, there is a famously beautiful white orchid. Sought for its elegance, it only grows in the center of the forest. Legend says whoever receives it as a gift will be bound to the giver forever. Lydia went in search of that flower so she could give it to you, my prince. Unfortunately, she was naive and took two handmaidens instead of guards. A strange beast was prowling throughout the woods, but a man stopped the worst from happening. He returned my daughter to the castle unharmed. Lydia's had a busy few days, but now that you're here, I'm sure she'll soon forget her troubles."

"We're pleased to hear everything is okay in the end," Harkbin said.

Thane looked at his father, then back toward the king. "What do we know about this monster? Was it magical?" If the knight in crimson armor somehow knew Zann-Xia-Czul's plans, then it was possible the sorceress was aware of Lydia's purpose. If the witch had created the beast, perhaps the princess was still in danger.

Ether blinked and avoided eye contact as he settled his attention back to Thane. "Magical? I believe not. More likely, it was a strange abomination that came from two species mating. It's dead now, so there's nothing to worry about."

The king's nonchalant dismissal of the subject raised suspicion. Anyone else would have shown more curiosity, bragged about how it was defeated, or even aspired to study the corpse. Compelled to dig deeper into the subject, Thane foresaw the next best source of related information.

"All is well, then," he said. "I should like to personally thank the man who saved my future bride. Is he of your house?"

"Indeed, he shall be!" proclaimed the Darian king. "I've taken him on as a retainer for my other children. His name is Kaine Khalia. He'll be at the wedding too. Speaking of which, the rehearsal dinner will be tomorrow night."

"Wait, does that mean—"

"Yes, my prince. I intend to wed you and Lydia the day after next."

A relieved smile crossed Harkbin's face. "We have no objections to the speedy timeline. In fact, we also have a schedule that we must accommodate. Our religion calls for it."

"Please go on."

"The ceremony we have here proves your intentions of wedding our families, but the marriage isn't sanctioned unless we perform a small ritual at our Temple of White as well. It's in our homeland, where our god can acknowledge the union."

"I see. So… your time in the Darian Kingdom will be short," Ether von Stonewall said, frowning slightly. "Are you sure that's what you want? You've sailed a long distance and there are many places in my kingdom I'd love to show you."

"Our schedule compels us, unfortunately," Thane said. "If we don't perform the ceremony in our homeland, then our Elders consider the marriage unclean."

"Very well. Lydia and I will sail with you to your Temple of White immediately after the wedding," Ether said. "Might I inquire if you expect her to embrace your faith? As you may well know, in these lands, we are devout followers of Asura."

"We worship Zann-Xia-Czul," Harkbin said. "I have spoken to him on this matter, and he does not require Lydia to convert. However, allowing her to commit is necessary if she does so voluntarily."

"You've spoken to your god?" Ether exclaimed.

"Our god communicates with us directly through

the mind of whoever is king," Urith said. "It's irrefutable that Zann-Xia-Czul exists."

"Both of our gods are real, I'm certain of it," Ether said. "But yes, if you are okay with Lydia deciding her own religion, and that neither of us will force her in either direction, then I support the idea as well."

A loud creak echoed through the room as the main door slowly opened. Timidly and quietly, a young woman of nearly twenty years old entered and gave a low curtsy. Her long, auburn hair covered her face as she knelt, but she quickly brushed it back behind her azure dress as she rose again.

"Good evening, m-my... everyone," she said. "I'm sorry for being so late."

Thane glanced her over. Despite her royal status, she seemed as ordinary as any other girl. She was shivering, perhaps because of nervousness or the drafty air permeating the throne room. Thane, having previously encountered girls like her in the Loyalty Circles, pitied their lack of confidence and strength. The princess was slender and had likely never lifted a weapon in her life. Her small nose and well-defined jawline resembled her father's. It astonished Thane that such a delicate-looking girl possessed the magical blood that would help defeat the sorceress.

"Lydia, come up here," Ether said with a sweep of his hand.

The princess gracefully made her way up the aisle, past Thane, Harkbin, and Urith, while her father smiled proudly. Her thin fingers lifted the hem of her dress as she ascended the steps. Once beside her father, she faced them again, but avoided holding eye contact with Thane.

"Isn't she the most beautiful young woman in the country?" Ether bragged. "How about touring the kingdom tomorrow? We'll return in time for the rehearsal dinner."

"Father..." Lydia whispered.

"Yes?"

The princess leaned in close and muttered something into his ear.

"Are you serious? That old dance?"

"It's tradition," Lydia said. "Mother would have wanted it."

"No act surpasses the complexity of the Dance of the Sun and Moon," warned the king. "I'm sure our guests would rather see the best our country can offer than waste their time learning it."

Thane cleared his throat. "If it would make my bride happy, I'll learn it. My mother and father will go on the tour."

Ether von Stonewall grimaced. "Regrettably, the dance necessitates the participation of your entire family. It involves excessive twirling and partner exchanges. It's overly intricate. Lydia, are you sure you want to do this?"

"Yes."

The king rolled his eyes and sighed. "Very well. Councilwoman Thorne probably remembers all the steps and can teach them to you. It's a lot to manage in only one day, though."

Thane smiled. "My family and I will strive to uphold the tradition. After all, you have made efforts to respect ours. Shall we practice together now, Princess?"

"Hold up, hold up!" Ether von Stonewall said. "I see you're eager to get to know my daughter, but how about your father and mother? They'll need to learn it as well, and you all have had a long journey. Wouldn't it be best to wait until the morning?"

"His Highness raises a valid point," Harkbin replied. "We should begin practice at the first light tomorrow. There is much else to be accomplished before the ceremony."

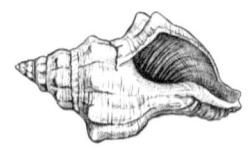

AT THE CRACK OF DAWN, THANE, HARKBIN, AND Urith re-entered the throne room for their lesson.

Lydia stood on the small platform next to the crystal throne, smoothing her violet dress by running her hands down her legs. A middle-aged woman, her narrow brow creased with several fine wrinkles, stood beside the princess. Both women, barefoot on the stone floor, braced themselves for the dance.

"Though the morning is bright, your potential to grasp this classical art burns even brighter," the woman said. Her stern voice was coarse, but also somehow calming. "I am Iris Thorne, Master of Internal Affairs. However, today I am your instructor. Are you ready to meet the Dance of the Sun and Moon?"

"The Master of Internal Affairs?" Harkbin inquired in Throatian, addressing Thane and Urith. The three of them were wearing matching red robes. "She may know where the Tears of Asura are hidden."

"Pardon?" Iris said.

"My father's Common Tongue isn't so great yet," the prince said. "He said he's nervous. The dance might be tricky to understand. In our kingdom, we don't do such things."

"Not at all," Urith added. "It's a lot of wasted time for something unproductive."

Iris's mouth fell open, and her eyebrows furrowed, but she swiftly composed herself into a smile. "Perhaps your opinion will change as I teach you everything you need for tomorrow. The Dance of the Sun and Moon is classical art, revered for its historical popularity hundreds of years ago."

Before Urith could respond, Thane gave her a sharp nudge with his elbow. Iris jumped into her teaching, pairing each of them off. Essentially, the dance called for the bride and groom to move along opposite sides of the room and spin around several times, before finally passing Lydia off to her father, Harkbin, and Urith. It was far more complicated than Thane could memorize. Moreover, Ether von Stonewall was absent from the lesson, though Iris assured them she would instruct him on his part later that morning.

Iris explained how the Dance of the Sun and Moon had gained its name, but the intricacies eluded Thane's grasp of Common Tongue. The semi-endless switching of dance partners, the twirling in either direction, and the complicated footsteps revealed why Lydia's father loathed the routine.

They exchanged partners once more, and Thane found himself again paired with Lydia. As the two of them swayed back and forth, he held onto her narrow waist. Meanwhile, Iris kept urging him to relax.

"I'm fine," Thane said.

"You're gripping her like you're afraid she's going

to run away from you," Iris commented. "Lydia, straighten your spine. You can't slump like that during the dance. Stand proud and tall! You're getting married!"

The two of them struggled to hone their stances. Iris tsked and shook her head, disappointed.

"Stop now," Iris said, striding over to them. "I excuse Prince Thane for his lack of smoothness. But Lydia, my dear, you should know better. We need to fix this."

"I'm trying!"

"Never mind it, dear." Iris sighed loudly and turned to the prince. "Prince Thane, go look down from the throne. Watch us closely. I'm going to play your part and show you how to lead Lydia."

"Sure."

Once at the top of the steps, Thane watched Iris take hold of Lydia and sway her around in circles next to Harkbin and Urith. The four of them spun repeatedly, each variation of their footsteps seemingly different from the last. Bored, Thane's eyes wandered over to the crystal throne that sat nearby.

"The chair is probably more fragile than my armor," he muttered.

He pondered the composition of the Darian throne, questioning whether it was made of glass or some frosty stone material. Faint, nearly invisible lines ran throughout the inner crevices of the chair's construction. Thane noticed rays of sunlight reflecting off the throne's side in odd directions. Light beamed in from the castle's tall, arched windows and confirmed his suspicion that mirrors hid within the royal chair. The reflective panels were arranged in such a way that made Thane idly wonder why they were there. He guessed the internal complexities somehow provided structural support.

"Prince Thane, watch over here," Iris called. "Note the synchrony between Lydia's and your mother's footsteps. Now, it's your turn."

As he hustled down the stairs, the door creaked open. A servant, hooded in a plain ebony robe, approached their group. Her pale white skin nearly matched the few strands of long blond hair that escaped her hood's concealment. She was beautiful.

"Princess Lydia," the young woman said. "You're needed elsewhere now. Please come with me."

"Who are you?" Lydia asked. "Are you a new handmaiden?"

"I am the one responsible for tailoring your wedding dress, my dear," the woman said. Her blue eyes looked over at Lydia, then lingered on the princess's hands. The tailor, likely aware that the jeweled rings shining on Lydia's fingers were beyond her means, drew Thane's sympathy for what he presumed to be her envy.

"I see. In that case, I should take my leave." Lydia turned to Iris. "Will you be okay to finish the lesson while I'm gone?"

Iris frowned. "Without you, the lesson is over. As it is now, the guests won't consider the rendition spectacular, but they'll remember it as being done properly."

"That's what counts then," Urith said. "The three of us should also leave. We have much else to prepare before tonight."

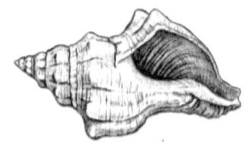

THE ASCHE FAMILY MADE THEIR WAY BACK TO THEIR chambers. The whole way, Urith grumbled about the absurdity of the dance. Thane concurred that mastering the steps was monotonous but contended that feigning interest in Darian culture was essential for the seamless execution of their ultimate plan.

"While we were spinning around in circles, do you think any of the guards found the Tears of Asura?" Urith said as they entered Thane's bedroom.

"I have not yet received any reports," Harkbin said. "Perhaps the stones are in a church somewhere, given that Asura is their god's name."

In a corner of the room, Thane settled into a new

chair. In addition to replacing the cracked furniture his parents had demolished, the Darian servants had cleaned up the broken shards of his armor. He silently prayed that his mother and father would refrain from causing any further havoc during their stay in the Darian castle. The casual destruction of the property, irrespective of the attendants' awareness of the underlying conflict, continued to be a source of sore embarrassment in the center of his mind.

"I agree the Tears are likely housed within a religious building," Thane proclaimed. "Granted, we know little about their religion, but some of their leaders must know where they're located."

"The stones are too powerful for more than a handful of people to be aware of, religious leaders or not. Chances are that only a few select elders truly know of them," Harkbin said. "If they were within a chapel or temple, the high-ranking clergy would likely safeguard them in a sanctum accessible solely to them. Locating a sacred site that remains off-limits to the general masses will lead us in the right direction."

"Then we ought to dispatch additional guards," Thane said. "We don't need them to protect us. Our time is very limited, so we should devote everyone's efforts to finding the Tears."

"I am well aware," Harkbin responded. "I've

offered prayers to Zann-Xia-Czul seeking guidance, but to no avail. He still isn't responding."

Urith parted her lips to speak, but a sharp glance from Thane silenced her. Thankfully, she held her tongue and didn't start another fight.

"We'll send out more guards, and everyone can report in after the rehearsal dinner," Harkbin said. "Our best Son See'ers came with us. We must trust they'll succeed."

"It's also worth searching the king's bedchamber," Thane added. "Aside from a vault somewhere underneath the castle, his private quarters are the most likely place he would keep them hidden. I suspect there'll be less security in those places during the rehearsal dinner too."

Harkbin gazed out the window. "Then I'll send a messenger to Hrodspire as well. Updating him should give him enough time to have the ships ready for our journey home."

"Spare the guard a trip," Urith replied. "Sending a rider now will only leave Hrodspire a day to prepare for our arrival. Ask Merdel to assign a bird to Starlight Beach instead. We don't want to show up to find the ships unprepared to leave."

"I shall seek him out and send word," Thane volunteered, rising from the chair. As he grabbed the doorknob, there was a sudden knock. Outside, the tailor stood in front of him, unperturbed by the coincidence.

"Prince Thane," the woman spoke in Common Tongue. Her visage and tone were both neutral and deep with confidence. "I came by to check on you. Does your clothing need any adjustments before the events?"

"Everything is fine with our wedding attire. Regardless, thank you for checking."

"Are you sure?"

Her insistence took him aback until he surmised that she likely received payments from the king for each alteration she made.

"Yes, we're all set."

"Very well. Then there's nothing for me to do here," the tailor replied. She looked him in the eyes. "May your wedded days with Princess Lydia be plentiful and free from sorrow."

She gave him a slight bow, then left. Thane couldn't help but suspect the woman had been listening through the door. He reassured himself that even if she had been eavesdropping, she wasn't able to speak Throatian. She wouldn't have gleaned any useful information. Still, something about the woman's bearing made it seem like she could see through any situation.

8

THE WEDDING OF THE TORN ROSE

Sundown drew near as Thane and his family concluded their preparations for the rehearsal dinner. They donned semi-formal attire of thick, ornate leather, and Merdel escorted them to the throne room. Harkbin carried a large metal scepter with him to serve as both an accessory and an intimidating display of authority. The prince sensed his father's growing nervousness about all the guards occupied with their mission and Zann-Xia-Czul's ongoing silence. The sorceress, wherever she was, was likely responsible for the lack of communication, and the monster Princess Lydia had encountered possibly involved her as well. This semi-formal banquet presented Thane with an opportunity to meet Kaine Khalia and delve into the events that had transpired in the forest.

Merdel, accompanied by a priest, led them over to the other side of the room, where the Darians were waiting for them to enter. Atop the stairs near the crystal throne, a man rang a delicate-looking silver bell. Ether von Stonewall stood by, grinning proudly at the displays of red roses and chandeliers hanging from the walls and ceilings. Lydia waited next to him, quiet and rigid, perhaps nervous about the dance they would soon have to perform.

"Welcome, everyone," the host said. "Tonight, I welcome the Throatian Kingdom's royal family. They've traveled across the ocean from their homeland to grace us with their presence tonight and for the wedding. Everyone, please pay your respects to the Throatian king, Harkbin Asche!"

Harkbin moved down the aisle, between the various groups of nobles and upper-class guests of the Darian Kingdom. Thane looked from table to table, wondering which one of them was Kaine.

"And, of course, the Throatian Kingdom's queen, Urith Asche!"

She pivoted towards him and huffed, "Must I smile for this part?"

"Try your best to enjoy your welcome, mother," Thane muttered, praying she would behave herself for the entire event. "We'll be on our way home soon."

Urith directed a scowl at him, which she

promptly morphed into a strained smile as she made her way to where Harkbin, the attendant in charge, and the king awaited her. Thane rolled his eyes as he stood by with Merdel.

"Finally, we have for you... the man of the evening, the future husband of Princess Lydia von Stonewall... Prince Thane Asche!"

He took his cue and stepped onto the crimson carpet. Smiling at the crowd, he searched for anyone with scars or who appeared like they had experience with a sword. His eye caught someone wearing purple armor at a nearby table. That must have been him. Thane made a note to go talk to him once the formalities of the rehearsal dinner were complete. For now, addressing the people and playing his part in the practice ceremony remained essential.

"Greetings, Kingdom of Daria," he said to the room. "It is an honor to visit your lands and celebrate our union of peoples."

He proceeded with his oration concerning the unification of their kingdoms, after which Harkbin took over the task of entertaining the Darians with pleasantries. His father adopted a divergent strategy, depicting their society in the most innocent light, diligently omitting any details that could jeopardize their scheme.

"Our country is a simple one," the Throatian king said. "For generations, we've limited our contact with the outside world, choosing to minimize our culture only to what's necessary. Mindfulness, loyalty to our god, inner peace, and remembering those we've lost to time are our values. Though our island is small, our dedication has no limit. Tomorrow, we join our worlds together for the greater good of all!"

Urith's speech was short and direct, and she portrayed herself as kind. To their benefit, Harkbin and Thane had written it for her, to help conceal her overall lack of poise. "I have little to say except our alliance will speak for itself as it matures. My son is the most suitable husband a woman can find, strong in both character and mind. May he and Lydia rise together as one."

As they completed the speeches, the priest led them through the logistics of the next morning's ceremony. Then Ether von Stonewall raised a toast and declared it was time for the Dance of the Sun and Moon.

Thane's gut lurched. Despite the performance only being a practice round, the thought of doing it among a crowd of strangers was daunting. Aside from praying in rituals or fighting within Loyalty Circles, he'd not performed in front of others before, and all the dance steps suddenly seemed too complicated.

"It's time already?" Thane murmured in Throatian.

"That's what he said," Urith replied. "Now go join the princess."

Forcing a smile, Thane began his dance across the room towards Lydia. He kept his eyes on her and tried his best to mimic her position and steps. Gradually, they twirled in arcs towards each other, converging at a central point. Once together, they clasped hands and slowly rotated until they'd made three complete turns. On the final spin, they separated, and Lydia joined her palms below her chest. Her fingers touched her jewelry as she pulled away from him.

Lydia sidled up to her father while Urith advanced to meet with Thane. The dance lingered on with various spins and switching of partners. Eventually, the princess rejoined Thane, but her pale, sweaty face revealed the dance's toll on her body.

"Are you okay?" Thane asked as they mirrored each other's arm movements in a crossover-like pattern.

"Yes, I just need to sit down," she whispered.

They circled a few more times and completed the dance with a bow, then Thane escorted her back to their table. Meanwhile, Ether von Stonewall announced that dinner would begin shortly as Lydia gulped down two glasses of water. While the servants brought in giant platters of bird meat, Thane wiped the sweat off her forehead.

"Are you sick, my princess?"

"No, I'm just tired. The dance was very complicated, after all. Maybe my father was right, and we could have done without it."

"We did our best, given the situation," Thane said. "Though Iris was a great instructor, there wasn't enough time to master the intricacies of it all. Truthfully, I suspect it would have taken months to perfect."

Lydia nodded as the servers set dinner plates in front of them. Though this was only the rehearsal, Ether von Stonewall had spared no expense ensuring the chicken was as extravagant as it would be at the wedding feast. The chicken's skin was well cooked, perfectly balanced between crispy and juicy. The aromas of lemon, rosemary, and thyme hovered above the plate, and Thane's mouth watered.

A few seats down from him, Harkbin was frowning at his dish while Urith stared impatiently. Ether von Stonewall appeared to have sensed their disappointment and cleared his throat.

"Is the chicken not to your liking, my king and queen? We shall make any adjustments to your liking, should the seasonings not find favor with your palates. Our chefs are renowned for their abilities, and chickens can be enjoyed in a variety of different styles."

"Father," Thane said in Throatian. "It would be rude to send the dish back to the kitchen. I'm sure Zann-Xia-Czul will forgive us eating cooked meat for the sake of our mission. Plus, you already allowed us to eat their prepared food before, at the inn."

"Don't tempt me," Harkbin retorted. "Our rules apply at home and here, even as far away from it as we are. We must resume our traditions if we want Zann-Xia-Czul to communicate with us once more."

Before Thane could call attention to his father's inconsistency, his father mustered a faint smile and pivoted toward Lydia's father. "Indeed, King von Stonewall, we have but a small request. Our religion calls for draining the blood of freshly killed animals, which is why we don't cook our food before eating them."

"All your meat?" the king asked. "You eat all your meat raw?"

"Correct," Urith added. "The blood needs sharing with our god before we can eat it. It's part of our religion."

Thane scowled at his parents as servants took their perfectly good plates away. They returned shortly after with a small cage containing three live birds. Harkbin was making a scene and seemed to have forgotten everything he'd criticized Urith for earlier.

"I'm sorry you have to see this," Thane whispered to Lydia. "This is customary for us, though I acknowledge that the world beyond does not partake in their meals in such a manner."

"Um, okay…" Her eyes wandered into the sea of tables, seeking refuge in the distance. Her hands rested demurely in her lap, and it was apparent that her appetite had disappeared. Meanwhile, Harkbin slit the chicken's throat and drained the blood into his cup. It wasn't normal for the princess, nor would it ever be.

"Have you forgotten that we need to blend in here?" Thane hissed in Throatian. "Are you trying to get these people to watch us more closely?"

Urith, who had the ears of an eagle, inserted herself into their conversation. "Thane's right about this. You're doing exactly what you told me not to do. Stay true to the plan and stop making things more complicated than they need to be."

"Every sacrifice holds weight," Harkbin said, also in Throatian. "Meditation alone won't give Zann-Xia-Czul magic. We know the real price, and there's no avoiding it. One drop could make the difference between him being able to communicate with us and not."

Lydia rose from her chair and smoothed out her dress. "I will return soon."

Thane shrugged once her back was to him, and they ate their meals in silence. A few minutes later, Lydia returned from talking to someone across the room. As she approached the table, her father asked her to address the guests. The princess elevated her wineglass as the king beckoned for the assembly's attention.

"Thank you, everyone, for coming tonight," Lydia said, clearly still trying to move past what she'd just witnessed with the chickens. "The most important day of my life is tomorrow. Tonight is a preview of the great joy we can expect. As many of you heard, I ran away from home because of my fear and uncertainty about what this marriage meant for me. Returning home, I've spent these past few days in deep reflection about my upcoming nuptials and what it means for all of us. I've realized that this wedding is not just about how I feel or what I want, it's also about serving you."

Lydia's speech continued, but Thane focused his attention on the man she'd been speaking to. The man had returned to his table and was sitting next to the knight in purple armor. Perhaps he was Kaine Khalia or would know where to find him. Thane bided his time as he waited for his future bride to finish her address and the party to continue. His eyes frequently shifted to the knight's table to ensure the duo hadn't left. He watched as they downed several glasses of wine followed by several more tankards of beer. Thane hoped this would leave them loose-lipped enough to answer his questions.

"I'll be right back," Thane said.

"Where are you going?" Urith asked.

He didn't reply. The princess was busy talking to Iris at the other end of the table about her opinion on the dance performance, leaving him the chance to talk to Kaine without interference from Lydia or her father. He marched across the room, approaching the men from behind. The other guests at the table had already left, and there were plenty of vacant seats to claim.

"Hello there," Thane said, taking a seat beside the man garbed in purple armor. "I presume one of you is Lord Khalia?"

"Yes, sir," the knight said. He lifted his fork and pointed it at the man nearby him. "That's him there: Kaine Khalia, the Boring Knight!"

Thane's eyes widened in realization. Perhaps there was more to the other man's decision to forgo armor at the banquet.

"You have my thanks, sir," said Thane. "Kaine, I've been wanting to meet you. After all, you're the one who saved my future wife."

Kaine blinked at Thane's appreciation. "You're

welcome, Prince Thane. But I'm no lord, and I got lucky when slaying the monster."

Thane glanced back at his table, making sure Ether von Stonewall was still kept occupied by conversation with his family. With nobody watching him, he took the chance to dig deeper. "You're too modest. I know it's rude of me to ask, especially since you've already helped me, but I was wondering if you could... educate me on a matter of some importance."

"Ask us anything you'd like to know," the knight in purple armor said, hiccuping as he raised his drink.

"Thank you, both of you," Thane replied. He turned his head back toward the king's table. "I've heard rumors that there is a dangerous sorceress somewhere in your country. Do you think she might be the one who summoned the monster?"

Even the slightest link between the two entities would prove she was out to murder Lydia and was fully aware of Zann-Xia-Czul's plans.

"A sorceress?" bellowed the drunk man in purple armor. "You Throatians give such fancy names to the Lucidians. They're the only ones with magic, and their Enclave is over a month's ride away from here. Plus, since the end of the war, they've all kept their tails between their legs."

Thane nodded and gave a weak smile. The tipsy

man's eyes might have possibly been deceptive, but his flushed face seemed ill-equipped for concealing any secrets. Perhaps the sorceress hadn't made herself known yet. Or maybe she was somehow, in fact, a Lucidian. It was tempting to ask the drunk man more about the war, but he feared it would inspire him to start rambling on about it, taking up Thane's time. It was best to return to his table before the king or Lydia noticed where he was.

Kaine sighed and shifted in his seat. "Please accept my apologies for our informalities tonight, Prince Thane. We've had a bit too much to drink. The monster is dead and there aren't any more of them, as far as I know. I haven't heard of a sorceress, either. Eisenbern is right that Lucidians would be the only ones who have magic."

"I see," Thane said. It was a fruitless conversation. "There'll be no more monsters for Princess Lydia to worry about then. Thank you again, Kaine. By saving her, you've done us all quite the favor. If you ever venture to our island, I'd be happy to give you the tour."

"That would be great," Kaine said. "I've been to your island before actually, but never beyond White Boar's Landing."

"Of course not," Thane said. "T-those restrictions won't be relevant anymore after the wedding."

He wished them goodnight and returned to his

seat next to Lydia. Urith leaned in and spoke to him in Throatian.

"Who were you talking to just now?"

"Kaine Khalia."

"Oh, did you meet him?" Lydia interrupted. Thane's ears went hot as he realized Lydia understood the name.

He shifted toward her and continued sipping his wine. "Yes, I wanted to give him my thanks. He saved you from the monster, after all."

The princess grimaced. "Yes, what a trouble it would have been for you if he hadn't been there."

"Without a bride, there can be no wedding," Thane chuckled.

"But it appears there can be a wedding without love," Lydia muttered.

"Pardon?"

"Nothing. I just realized there's something wrong with my dress. I need to find the tailor and have it fixed." She stood from her chair; curtsied to Thane, Harkbin, and Urith each; and left.

Thane's mother chugged the rest of her drink. "I guess the party's over."

"Father slaughtering the chicken made her sick— I'm sure of it," Thane said.

Before he could say more, the young girl named Ursula approached their table. Her silver-white hair matched the long dress she wore. Just like the first time Thane had met her, she was carrying a book that probably weighed at least half as much as she.

"Excuse me, Prince Thane," she said in a squeaky voice. "May I ask you something?"

"Who are you?" Urith demanded, as Ursula failed to conceal her widening eyes. Thane raised his hand and scowled at his mother.

"She's fine to be here," Thane stated in Common Tongue. "Young Ursula is one of the councilwomen's daughters. We met while I was exploring the castle."

"Her niece, actually," the young girl corrected.

"Sorry," Thane said. "What did you want to ask?"

Ursula heaved the book onto their dinner table and slid it over to him. It looked like some kind of encyclopedia. "This mentions your island, but it doesn't have a lot of details. I was hoping to learn more about your culture. By any chance, did you bring any Throatian books? I would love to trade some of my volumes with you and read about your history—or, even better, how to use magic."

She was too young to know the implications of what she asked. Darian adults knew better than to veer too close to the question of how the Throatians discovered magic. In Harkbin's earliest letters to Ether von Stonewall, he had requested that the topic remain taboo until after the wedding ceremony. Although the marriage between Thane and Lydia was purely political, both parties preferred not to publicly acknowledge it. Ursula, probably no older than twelve years old, wouldn't have known that the Throatians had always been a reclusive society, either. To that end, Thane couldn't fault her.

"I'm sorry, we didn't bring any books with us," he replied. "But when I return home after the wedding, I'll send you some. I might be able to provide some translations as well."

"What are you doing?" Harkbin asked in their native tongue.

Thane blinked. "I'm lying." He looked back down at Ursula. Something about her reminded him of Cereene. He hadn't known his partner when she was a child, but he imagined she had been just as inquisitive. "You really like books, don't you?"

Ursula smiled. "I try to read at least one every day, from start to finish."

"Ursula Frost!" a woman's voice rang out, both raspy and stern. "Get down from there!"

A middle-aged woman scrambled up to them and grabbed Ursula's arm. Her other hand snatched the book off the table and tucked it under her shoulder. "Your Highnesses, I'm so sorry my niece was bothering you. I swear, I left her alone for five minutes, and she ran off on one of her adventures."

Thane grinned. "It's not a bother. In fact, it is heartening to know the children of the Darian Kingdom have such a thirst for higher knowledge."

"I appreciate your kindness," Ursula's aunt replied. "Well, we'll be out of your way for now." She tugged the young girl away, back to their own table.

"Despite that strange encounter," Harkbin said once they were gone, "we have greater matters to attend to before the hour grows late and the evening is done. Come now, let's check on the other portion of our mission."

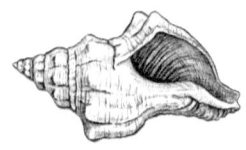

TWO HOURS BEFORE MIDNIGHT, THE REHEARSAL dinner came to an end, and Thane, Harkbin, and Urith retired to their chambers. Outside Thane's room, a Throatian man awaited them, peering out the window, as if checking that nobody had followed them. Harkbin made sure that none of King Ether's guards or servants were lingering nearby in the hallway before leading them into Thane's room and closing the door behind them.

"Shivanna Adul. Has everyone returned from their missions?"

The guard bowed so low that his forehead almost touched the floor. "We have failed you, my king. They returned undetected but found no evidence of the Tears of Asura's existence."

"What?" Urith exclaimed. "Not at all? Nothing at all? Neither the stones nor anything resembling them? Perhaps a sword embellished with the jewels?"

"We discovered various artifacts, but nothing magical. Our search included everything from pebbles to boulders," the guard reported. "Neither the king nor the Darian temples possess them."

"Ruik Czharr," Harkbin cursed. "I cannot believe this. We must find them before tomorrow's ceremony, or the mission is doomed. Dispatch everyone again, and this time, expand the search to any place conceivable."

Thane's neck tightened. "It is too risky for that now. There will be an increased presence of Darian guards around the city due to the wedding. We need to strategize on search locations. Aimless wandering elevates the risk of getting caught."

They exited the room and made their way downstairs to the garden outside, where Thane previously met Ursula. The sky was pitch black, with tiny specks of distant stars piercing through the veil of darkness. Moonlight bathed the large, pink branches of the cherry tree, enveloping them in fresh air and privacy. The guard promised to return with an update later in the evening before making his way out. With no one else nearby, the trio knelt on the grass and crossed their legs in preparation for meditation.

"And so, what other places do you propose we search for the stones, Thane?" Harkbin snapped.

"In the last place anyone would dare to touch, unless they were the king himself," Thane mused aloud.

"Don't be coy. Where?"

"Within the crystal throne," he ventured. The idea had just occurred to him, and the more he thought about it, the more sense it made to conceal the magical stones in plain sight. "There might be a secret compartment inside it."

"But isn't it made of glass?" Urith inquired. "You think they hid the Tears underneath it? But how?"

"Not beneath it, but rather inside. During our dance lesson, I observed that the chair reflects light unusually when viewed from the sides. From the front, where most people see it, the throne appears transparent. However, inside there's a set of mirrors or some other reflective material, creating an illusion. If I could have time to give the throne's surfaces a feel, I bet I could find a secret drawer or cabinet."

Harkbin stroked his beard. "A curious development…" He closed his eyes to pray for guidance but reopened them almost immediately with a glare of frustration. "We are still without instructions. If you believe you can retrieve the stones, then your mother and I will stand guard."

"The time is now," Thane announced. "However, let me handle this alone."

"Right now?" Urith exclaimed.

"The servants have been cleaning the throne room since dinner. They must be asleep by now as they need to wake up early for the wedding. I shall return shortly."

"Well done, Thane," Harkbin said as he situated his body to meditate. "If the stones are there, as you suspect, you've saved our homeland. Zann-Xia-Czul will be most pleased with your achievement."

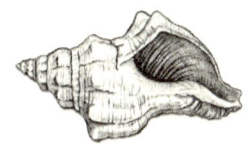

FLICKERING LIGHTS OF ORANGE TORCHES BATHED THE hallway as Thane edged closer to the entrance of the throne room. Outside, crickets chirped in a predictable rhythm, and Thane timed his breaths to their cadence, moving as stealthily as possible. Although the lobby appeared deserted at this late hour, Thane considered the possibility that a servant or two might linger, still tidying up after the rehearsal dinner.

He peered through the cracked doorway and confirmed that everything was dark on the other side. A high-pitched creak resonated as he leaned into the ancient wood, but it was likely that no one else was around to hear it.

"Zann-Xia-Czul," Thane whispered, "if you can hear me, please let the Tears of Asura be where I think they are."

He slipped through the entrance and surveyed the dining tables, already set for the following morning. Every place setting was decorated with roses and fresh wine glasses, and even in the darkness, the decor's grandeur surpassed that of any event he had ever witnessed. He wanted to admire everything more closely in the light, but recognized he should wait until the next day. However, there were more pressing matters at hand.

Holding his breath, he approached the crystal throne. He lifted the tattered red cushion and ran his hands along the base of the seat. The polished surface was smooth, revealing no signs of seams or gaps.

The edges of the giant chair, near where he'd seen the mirrors, were also smooth as glass. It was only when he searched the back of the throne that his fingers scraped across a thin dividing line. Slowly, his thumb traced the path, forming a rectangle. He grinned and tried lodging his fingernails into the crack. Though he was sure the hidden compartment was there, his hands couldn't get a solid grip on the drawer. He descended the stairs with purpose and snatched a butter knife from one of the tables. With his new tool, he resumed prying open the secret area of the throne.

Unfortunately, the crystal proved to be more resilient than his blade, which yielded and bent. Thane cursed under his breath and flung the deformed silverware across the room. Out of frustration, he delivered a punch to the rectangle, his fist landing near its edge. A click sounded. Thane's eyes widened in surprise as he traced the edges anew, realizing it still hadn't budged. Regardless, something had definitely happened, so he pounded his fist against the throne's rear once more.

A second click came from where he'd hit, but again, the drawer didn't open. This time, he pressed his palms against it and gradually applied more pressure until it moved inward. He let go, and the shelf slid out on its own.

"What kind of contraption is this?" Thane whispered. It seemed mechanical rather than magical, and unlike anything he had ever encountered. Ether von Stonewall must have hired some of the world's most intelligent craftsmen to make the throne.

Moonlight streamed through the open window, bathing the spherical stones resting in the drawer in its glow. Each stone reflected a different color: green, blue, black, and silver. The Tears of Asura were so small, yet somehow, they yielded magic powerful enough to rival a sorceress.

Thane lifted them, one by one; they were as light and unremarkable as any common pebble. He didn't feel any surge of power or any change within him, leading him to surmise that something else was required to activate them—perhaps an incantation or a ritual. Nevertheless, he'd found them—his parents, along with Zann-Xia-Czul, would respect his success.

He slipped the stones into his pocket and made his way back to the lobby. Confident that he was still alone, he quietly closed the door behind him, a grin spreading across his face as he retreated to his bedchamber.

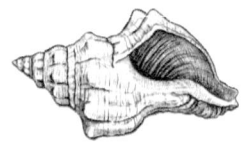

"PRINCE THANE," THE PRIEST SAID AS THEY STOOD IN the throne room the next morning. "Do you take Lydia von Stonewall, the first daughter of Ether and Lily von Stonewall, to be your lawfully wedded wife?"

"I do," said the prince, fixing his gaze on Lydia's forehead instead of her eyes. His heart ached for Cereene, and the knowledge that the young woman before him now would be sacrificed upon their return to his homeland filled him with overwhelming guilt. Though Thane was ready to die protecting his people, Lydia lacked any knowledge for what fate had in store for her.

"And Princess Lydia, do you take Thane Asche, the first and only son of Harkbin and Urith Asche, to be your lawfully wedded husband?"

"I-I do." Lydia's lips quivered, and her fingers trembled at her sides. She mustered a smile, striving to mask her sadness.

She had no greater desire to marry Thane than he had to bind himself to her in matrimony. Even in the absence of future magic, for now, they were strangers who had only engaged in the most superficial conversations. Likely, only he and the nearby-standing priest could perceive their uneasiness and discomfort.

As Lydia glanced towards Thane, her gaze evading his, the priest raised his imposing scepter high, casting a shadow over them. "As the Darian Kingdom and the watchful eyes of Asura bear witness, I urge you both to solemnize your union by making the Everlasting Wish."

"Honorable Priest and Prince Thane, my soon-to-be lawfully wedded husband," Lydia recited. "I would like to be the first of us to make the vow."

"Proceed," intoned the priest, as he lowered his scepter.

Thane stared at Lydia's azure eyes, suddenly burning with fire. He sensed a shift in her emotions, from fear to fierce determination. Her father, standing behind her, couldn't see her face, but it was probably better that way.

"Today, not only does this marriage bind our families together, but also it intertwines our destinies," said Lydia. "The Dance of the Sun and Moon that you witnessed dates back generations. It symbolizes our shared trajectories in the universe and how life is a cycle of comings and goings. Today, our kingdoms have united for eternity. We must continue to do what's best for the common people, no matter the cost."

Her words enraptured the crowd. The applause she got afterward was deafening—the nation truly loved Lydia.

"And Prince Thane," the priest said. "What will you promise in your Everlasting Wish?"

Thane cleared his throat. "Lydia, I know we haven't known each other very long or very well, but I promise that this marriage is not only what's best for our kingdoms, but for the entire world. I promise to stay by your side for the rest of our lives and do my best to make you happy during that time. Our circumstances are unique, but I'll do my best to ensure we care for you as much as possible."

Close to half of the crowd applauded as his speech concluded. Although Thane could not see his parents, he suspected that Urith was casting a glare at those who did not applaud his vow. Whatever was happening behind his back didn't matter—he just needed to focus on making it through the ceremony and leaving for Starlight Beach. The sooner they could get home, the sooner they could start their preparations to defeat the sorceress.

"Thank you," the priest replied. "With the Everlasting Wishes made, I decree by the power vested in me, you are now husband and wife."

Unlike with Thane's speech, the entire crowd cheered for the sanction of their marriage. As expected of them, Thane embraced the princess and kissed her.

"They rejoice in your happiness," he said to Lydia as he let her go.

"Let them have their party. Let them smile, drink, dance, and sing. Give it to them today, for not all their days can be filled with such light."

Her words made him suspect she knew something she shouldn't. Her clever quip was suspiciously accurate, and it was important he figure out whether he was overly nervous because of the ceremony or if Lydia had already realized the truth about her fate.

"Indeed, we'll be leaving this afternoon, so the party won't last as long as I'd hoped," Thane said, hoping to provoke her. "Once we've sailed to my island, the second part of the wedding will begin, and it will be my people's turn to celebrate our marriage. Are you looking forward to seeing my homeland and the ceremony there too?"

It was sufficient. If Lydia had somehow become privy to their plan, then her emotions would inevitably betray her and reveal whatever she knew.

She spoke, all traces of her nervousness having vanished. "Yes, I'm eager to learn more about your island's history and culture."

Thane felt his shoulders lower in relief. Perhaps she knew nothing after all.

"There's plenty on my island to show you."

He turned his attention to the crowd and saw Ursula staring back at him from one of the frontmost tables. Her silver hair was styled into a bun, and Thane noticed the tint of her blue eyes was almost a shade of violet. The young girl smiled in awe of the wedding. Thane pitied her, though, for Ursula would eventually hear the story of how Lydia died in a sailing accident while traveling to the Throatian island.

The fate awaiting Lydia once she reached Thane's homeland wasn't fair—she was innocent in all this. Regardless of whether she was aware of the circumstances, he wanted to give her the choice to sacrifice herself... but there was no way Harkbin and Urith would allow it. Zann-Xia-Czul had called for their blood, and Thane's alone would not suffice. It was all the sorceress's fault, and Thane wished he could tell his bride how awful a predicament they were in because of the foreign magical threat.

Instead, he turned back to her with a faint smile. "You're right about all the partying and celebrations happening on our account. Happiness is an illusion."

"Then we should embrace the illusion as long as we can," Lydia said, biting her lip.

Ether von Stonewall interrupted them by running up and embracing his daughter. "She's married!" he yelled. "My first child is married and will become a queen someday!"

Harkbin met them in the middle of the platform, smiling. "My son and your daughter are the perfect complement to each other. They'll do great things in the future, I'm sure of it."

"A powerful alliance," Urith commented. She raised her wineglass. "To Thane and Lydia!"

Harkbin leaned in close to Thane and whispered in Throatian, "Our carriage back to the ship is ready, along with our escorts. Merely another hour or so, and we shall be on our way."

"Thank you, Father," Thane said loudly in

Common Tongue. "You needn't hide that your daughter-in-law is the most beautiful woman here!"

"Besides your mother, of course," Harkbin laughed, looking over his shoulder. Urith was engrossed in her drink and, thankfully, hadn't heard him.

Merdel approached and informed them that breakfast was ready to be served.

"Let us not delay then!" declared the king with a clap of his hands. "Bring out those chickens!" He turned to Thane. "Don't worry, my son. We've got the raw ones prepared for you too."

"And not just that," Merdel said. "We have the finest baked goods in our kingdom, including the famous mooncakes from the markets of the Leila Kingdom."

"Councilman Merdel," Ether said, grabbing the ambassador's shoulder. "I haven't had the chance to say it, among the chaos of the past week, but it's really thanks to your efforts that today's wedding was a tremendous success. We couldn't have pulled this off without you. Thank you!" He raised his glass and took a large gulp.

The aging man smiled and gave a bow. "It pleases me to serve your house and unite it with the others. The chicken and other delicacies should be out shortly." He excused himself and made way toward the kitchens.

Thane looked over at his new father-in-law. "Someday, before I grow old and die, I'd like to try a cooked bird from your chefs. Perhaps my god will permit it once we've sanctioned the marriage in our homeland."

Ether slapped him on the back. "I pray to Asura that your god allows it too. You have no idea what you're missing out on! Darian barbecued chicken is amazing!"

"I'm sure," Thane said. "My people and I must continue to trust and obey that our traditions are what's best for everyone."

"Everything will play out how it's meant to be." Ether von Stonewall gestured toward the reception table, where they would all eat near the crowds of attendees. "After you, my son. We'll enjoy what we can while we can."

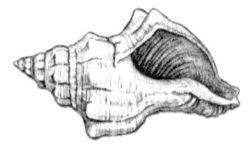

NEARLY AN HOUR AND A HALF LATER, THE ASCHE family, along with Princess Lydia, were seated inside a spacious carriage. Ether von Stonewall had adamantly insisted on accompanying them on their journey to Starlight Beach. He had arranged for escorts from Wargonne to rendezvous with him there for his return journey to Last Hope. Despite Harkbin and Urith's insistence that Ether shouldn't join them, Thane reminded them that he would only go as far as the coast and his presence wouldn't affect their subsequent plans. Though a minor inconvenience, it served as a last gesture of goodwill before their permanent departure from the Darian Kingdom.

"We've succeeded against all odds," Thane had told Harkbin as they boarded the carriage. "Lydia and the Tears of Asura are in our hands, and nobody has raised any suspicions."

"I just wish I knew why Zann-Xia-Czul hasn't talked to us the entire time."

"It'll all make sense once we are back home. There had to have been some reason. I still bet it's because of the sorceress."

As their carriage trundled along the dirt road, departing from Last Hope, they were escorted by four Throatian guards mounted on borrowed horses. Thane wished he could trot with them, but he imagined there was an unspoken Darian custom that he should remain inside with Lydia.

"In your land, is it customary for women to learn the art of horseback riding?" he inquired, as they were half an hour into their journey.

"Sometimes."

"Horses are rare on our island," Thane explained.

"They're mostly for transporting goods, not so much for leisure. I hope I can practice someday."

"They have some upkeep, yes, but a good stableboy will keep them healthy and ready anytime, for both labor and recreation," Ether interjected. "I'll tell you what—these stallions are yours if they fit on your ship. If not, I'll bring them along when I come to your homeland for the first time. You're going to love horseback riding, my son."

Thane forced himself to grin. "Yes, how could I not? They're horses!"

The moment the king turned away from him, the Throatian prince frowned.

"Harkbin, have you ever ridden before?" Ether asked merrily.

"No, I haven't."

Urith looked up from her feet, suddenly interested in their conversation. "Is it true that the Darian Kingdom has tournaments where warriors fight from their mounts?"

"It is!" Ether smiled. "I wish we had more time here, so I could host one for your enjoyment. Such matches are prime entertainment."

"Watch?" Urith asked, revealing a wide grin. "No, I'd want to compete."

"Ha! Now that's the sort of indomitable spirit that secures victory!"

"It must be a costly event," Urith added, "with all the horses that will inevitably die."

"Oh, we have a rule that everyone should only aim for the rider, or else you're right, it would get expensive quick."

"You can't attack the horse? It's such a sound strategy. Why not put armor on it?"

"That would reduce the game to just kicking the other person off their mount and then fighting on foot," Ether explained. "Putting the horses in harm's way adds a pointless step that only endangers the animals."

"But in a war, you'd aim for them, right?"

"Of course."

"So why not in the contest?"

Thane's shoulders tensed. Now wasn't the time for his mother to cause an argument. He prayed that she'd back down and move on to another topic.

"It's just the way we do things here." Ether sighed, his face somewhat scowling. "We want the spectacle of the tournament without the cost of cleaning up bodies. There aren't enough farms to meet that demand, even if it were moral."

Harkbin put a hand on Urith's shoulder. "The Darian king makes a fair point. Horses require a lot of investment to breed. Killing them for entertainment is a waste."

"I see." Urith said. She sat back in her chair and held her breath. Thane sighed in relief.

They journeyed in silence for several more minutes before halting in an expansive open field. Ether opened the carriage window and called out to ask the Darian driver what was going on.

"Naught of significance, sire," the chauffeur announced. "Merely a drunk man on the road. Might someone tell the Throatian guards to give him some water or the like? The sun is relentless this day, and I fear he may suffer from dehydration."

"How'd he wander this far away from the bar?" the king wondered aloud. He turned to Harkbin. "Did you get that?"

"I'll have them take care of it," declared the Throatian king. He ordered the escorts to allow the drunkard a swig of their canteen and a muffin from their carriage.

Ether cleared his throat. "My apologies for this. I've not heard of anyone getting so inebriated to go so far as leaving Last Hope. Perhaps his friends played a cruel joke on him."

They continued sitting and waited a few minutes for the guards to deal with the drunkard before a knock rattled the carriage door.

"Yes?" Ether asked.

"Something is strange," the escort replied in Throatian.

"Oh, I think it's for you," Ether said. He pulled on a lever-like handle, unlocking the door.

"What seems to be the matter?" Harkbin asked in their mother tongue.

"The man isn't drunk. He's asking for Prince Thane."

"Did he walk all the way here from Starlight Beach?" Urith said.

"He's not Throatian," the guard said. "You may wish to talk with him."

Thane's stomach lurched as though he were once again at sea, throwing up into buckets next to Hrodspire.

"Let's find out what this stranger wants," Harkbin said. He calmly turned to Ether and Lydia. "The man outside asked to speak with us. We'll be just a moment."

The three of them disembarked from the carriage, leaving the von Stonewall family inside. As he stepped around the carriage, the stranger in crimson armor grinned wider than Thane ever thought possible, confirming his suspicions.

"Shivanna Adul, Prince Thane," the knight said. "Your mother and father must be so proud of you—married to Princess Lydia and all. Everything's going splendidly, isn't it?"

"Have we met?" Harkbin said. "Your Throatian is

excellent, but I don't remember seeing you at White Boar's Landing."

Thane stuck an arm out between his parents and the man. "Let me handle this."

"You know this man?" his mother asked.

He glared at the knight. "We've met. Now, what do you want?"

"The plan from Zann-Xia-Czul has changed. You're to give me the Tears of Asura now."

"Who are you?" Harkbin interrupted. "And how could you know anything about that?"

The knight ran a hand through his dark, golden hair. "I've talked to him. Haven't you?"

Harkbin stared him down. "I don't believe you. Zann-Xia-Czul won't converse with anyone but a king, especially not a foreigner."

"It's the truth, regardless of whether you like it. You're just going to have to trust and obey." The knight gave a jovial wink.

"Why would our god want you to have them?" Thane asked. "We're on the way home already."

"If you have to ask, then you're not entitled to know," he leered. "Now hand them over. I'm certain they're in your pocket."

"Who in shulkkaal is this person?" Urith said. "And how is he aware of our plan?"

Thane shrugged. "I met him at Starlight Beach. He knows everything, but promised he'd help us fight the sorceress. He's got magic—I've seen it myself."

"Well, I don't trust him," Harkbin said. "The more we learn of him, the more he goes against everything we know."

His father was right, but the situation was too bizarre to be a lie. The crimson knight knew so much that his supposed conversation with Zann-Xia-Czul may truly have happened. Perhaps the sorceress was already approaching their island, and the knight, with his teleportation magic, was the only way to get the Tears of Asura there in time.

"You're doing all this to help us fight the sorceress, right?" Thane asked. "And you're taking the stones to Zann-Xia-Czul?"

"All this?" the knight said. "There's nothing spectacular about my being here. You should have expected me. It's Zann-Xia-Czul's plan."

"So be it." He delved into his pocket, his fingers grazing the supple leather pouch within. "As long as this helps us battle the sorceress."

"Defeating her has always been the goal," the knight replied. "Now please, stop wasting time and give them to me."

"Thane," Harkbin warned, "should this man's words prove false, it will ruin our mission. Our people will suffer the consequences if you're wrong."

The door to the carriage creaked open and Ether

von Stonewall stuck his head out. "Is everything okay out there?"

"He's an old friend," the prince called back in Common Tongue. "We're just telling him about the wedding."

"So how about it?" the crimson knight urged, holding his palm out.

"Don't give him the stones," Urith barked. "I smell filth all over this one."

"A man cannot be trustworthy until he proves it," Harkbin said. "Don't let him—"

"Trust and obey," Thane reminded them, placing the purse into the outstretched palm. "Zann-Xia-Czul wouldn't have allowed him to reach us if it weren't meant to be."

The knight could not hide his grin for even a moment. Once the stones were in his hand, he peeked inside the bag and placed it into his pocket. He gave the group a nod.

"Excellent work, young prince. You've made the right choice. Now, about that favor…"

"That wasn't the favor?"

"No, not at all," the strange man laughed. "Giving me the stones was Zann-Xia-Czul's request. For me, you'll kill the princess. Now."

"What?!" Harkbin yelled.

The crimson knight raised his palms in the air as he shrugged. "Thane agreed to do whatever

I asked of him, without question. Isn't that right?"

"Yes, but not to this," Thane said. "We can't kill Lydia until we're back on our island for the sacrifice."

"You don't want to murder her now, but I'm telling you to do it anyway," the man commanded. "Without question."

"You intended to destroy our mission all along, didn't you?" Harkbin said. "Return the stones and shulkkaal off! Guards!"

One escort drew his blade and stepped toward the knight.

"Don't even try it," the stranger advised. "Needlessly spilling blood outside your Loyalty Circles will disappoint Zann-Xia-Czul. You wouldn't want to do that, now, would you?"

Harkbin looked back at the guard, who was ready to attack. He shook his head, and the guard eased off. Meanwhile, the powerful stranger smiled and waved jovially at them, then turned his attention to Thane.

"We agreed that you'd grant me my favor without question," the knight said. "So, are you going to ask me one?"

Thane stared at the man's borderline-maniacal eyes. Although he had many questions, he couldn't find the words to demand answers, even if it was allowed.

"Why?" was all he could muster.

"Because that's the way it needs to be," the crimson knight replied. "I get the feeling you're not quite convinced yet. Come with me, Thane. I want to show you something."

"He's not going anywhere with you," Urith hissed.

"Oh, but he will. Turning one's back on an agreement yields a certain weight. We cannot ignore it. Come over here, Thane—closer to me. I want to whisper a special secret into your ear…"

Thane's skin prickled as he nodded hesitantly at his parents. "I have to do this."

He stepped toward the knight, but something enveloped him in a sudden coldness. Before he could blink, a gray sky towered above him, and cold, white ash drifted down from overhead. For a moment, he didn't understand what was happening. He turned to look for his parents or the carriage, but they weren't there anymore. Instead, there was only more ash and a silvery sky. Standing alone in a bleak new world, he shuddered as an unforgiving wind whipped him with a chill more desolate than anything he had ever conceived.

9

THE BLOOD OF ROYALS

Thane clutched his arms to his chest, shivering in the face of the shocking, unruly climate. Tiny white crystals speckled his bare skin, left vulnerable by his sandals. He'd been teleported somewhere far away once again, but this time, he did not know where he was. Nearby, shrouded by the falling snow, stone ruins stood abandoned, lifeless and broken—ravaged by the icy climate or perhaps by war. Whoever had inhabited the buildings was long gone, maybe even generations ago.

"Hello?" Thane yelled into the wind, hoping the crimson knight would materialize and retort with something arrogant or unnerving, but there was no response.

Guided by his instincts, he ran toward the largest

of the broken walls enclosing the abandoned village. Climbing the steps carved into the barrier, he made a disheartening discovery: he was trapped. Though the wall itself was short and easily scalable, the other side was at least a two-mile drop to white snowy plains below. Somehow, the land on which he stood was an airborne platform, and there was no way down.

"Welcome to my dungeon in the sky, Prince Thane," the knight's voice bellowed in the wind behind him. "There are some wire cables nearby you can use to slide down to the surface, if you dare. Though I must warn you, it's a fruitless endeavor."

"Here to punish me?" Thane muttered, breath creating steam in front of him.

"I merely wished to speak with you in private once more," the man said, seemingly unbothered by the cold. "I won't bore you with the history, but this is my favorite place in the universe. If I leave someone here, not only will they die, but they will cease to exist. Staying here too long will erase you. No heart, body, or soul left behind."

From high on the wall, Thane stared down at the man. "It sounds like a lot of trouble when you could just kill Lydia and me. Last I checked, we'll die if you stab us. So why go through the hassle?"

The knight's smile broke. "I have no intention of

killing you today. But I am going to make you choose between your wife and Cereene."

Thane's face became hot. "You stay away from her!"

"As you wish, young prince," the knight said. "But you should know that Cereene's already here. If I abandon her now, she'll... you know." He resumed his terrible grin.

"Where is she?" Thane yelled, jumping from the wall and rolling himself upright again.

The knight pointed to one of the collapsed buildings. "Over there. This will teach you how to do things without question. You have a choice, you can either—"

Thane stopped listening; he was already sprinting toward the building. There, almost hidden from view behind the wall, Cereene rested on the white, cold ground. Her eyes were closed and her face blue, but she was alive. Her skin was colder than the Temple of White's floor, but he could still feel her breath against his cheeks.

"Cereene!" he yelled. "Wake up!"

Her lip quivered, but she wouldn't wake from her slumber. How long had she been out in the cold?

It was at that moment he realized how powerless he was against the crimson knight, Zann-Xia-Czul, and the sorceress alike. All his years of praying, performing sacrifices in the Loyalty Circles, and doing as he was told were for nothing. He was a prince of his people, but it was pointless if he wasn't powerful enough to stand his ground.

"Crimson Knight!" Thane cried out. "I... I don't even know your name! Please, keep Cereene alive and take her home! Leave her out of this—she's innocent!"

The knight's boots squished against the snow as he approached. "So, you'll do as I ask without question? You'll kill the Darian princess?"

Thane lowered his head toward Cereene. "Yes, I'll do it. Without question."

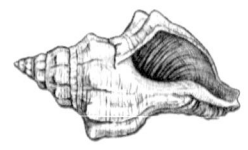

BEFORE THANE COULD EVEN TURN AROUND, HE found himself back on the warm, sunny road of the Darian Kingdom. His body relaxed instantly, liberated from the biting cold of the floating ruins, though his toes retained some of the chill. The crimson knight stood before him, smirking.

"Cereene is safely back home and will be fine," he assured. "Now, it's your turn to make a move."

Thane grimaced as he pivoted toward Harkbin and reached out his hand. "Father, I need your knife."

"Thane!" his father uttered. "Killing Lydia too

soon ruins everything we've worked for. Zann-Xia-Czul ordered that we bring her to the island. We must obey."

"I-I understand, but this man possesses immense power. He wields magic and is seemingly immortal. He even stabbed himself with his own sword as proof—I witnessed it myself."

"He's not trustworthy," Urith said. "Don't fall for his illusions and tricks."

Thane furrowed his brow. "The only one deceiving us is Zann-Xia-Czul! He hides on Mount Sephorr and forces everyone on our island to kill each other for nothing. Yes, he possesses magic, but he doesn't care about his worshippers. And if I'm wrong, I pray he proves it with his lightning now!"

The carriage door screeched open again as Ether von Stonewall teetered outside. "What's going on? Is our visitor causing concern? We can have the guards remove him if need be."

There was no turning back. Thane paid no heed to the Darian king and continued speaking in Throatian.

"Like it or not, Zann-Xia-Czul is either a false god or an evil one." He stepped in Harkbin's direction. "Either way, I believe he commands it. Give me your knife."

His father shook silently. With a trembling hand, he slid his knife from its sheath and cast a forlorn gaze at the red jewels on the handle. He tossed it aside, and the blade clattered against the dirt. Thane understood why his father didn't want to hand him the weapon; he was absolved from much of the guilt, if killing Lydia so soon truly was a mistake.

"Place your trust in me, Father," Thane said, picking up the knife and brushing it off. He cast a glance at the carriage escorts. "Bring the princess here and assemble as we would in a Loyalty Circle. We shall make amends with Zann-Xia-Czul too."

The guards dismounted their horses and approached the carriage. Ether von Stonewall sensed something was wrong and demanded they stand back, but even if the escorts had understood him, they wouldn't have listened. The driver bolted from the carriage, but before he could support his king, one of the soldiers knocked him over the head from behind. The man collapsed, out cold.

The other Throatians pulled Lydia and her father out of the carriage and surrounded them. Lydia was crying; they knew what was about to happen.

"Please, don't kill Lydia," Ether said. "If you're trying to overthrow my kingdom, you can have it, but don't hurt her. Please."

Thane glared at the crimson knight. "What of the Darian king?"

"Kill him, too, if you wish. I don't care."

Thane nodded. "The Darian king will live. Move him aside."

The coachman regained consciousness and pushed himself up from the ground. He charged at one of the Throatian guards but failed to take his sword. One quick movement later, he dropped to the ground, dead.

"Sheiaa Kaaduul," the guard muttered as he removed the driver's body from their circle.

"There's a bucket in the carriage," Urith said.

Another escort hustled over to retrieve it, then worked on draining the driver's blood just outside the circle. Meanwhile, one of the other guards seized the Darian king and tugged him over to the edge of the ring.

"No!" Ether yelled. "Take me instead! Don't hurt her!"

"I'm sorry," Harkbin said in Common Tongue. "We only needed your daughter. You should turn away."

As a guard restrained Ether, Thane stared into Lydia's teary, red eyes. "I'm sorry about this, Lydia. I didn't mean for it to happen this way."

She sniffled. "You're not like the others."

"Kneel, please," he said, uncertain of what she meant.

He nudged her onto her knees and squatted down close to her. After telling his family to move

243

away from them, he clasped her shoulder and whispered into her ear: "I didn't want any of this."

"I-I know," she mumbled back. "Remember, white armor cannot protect you from a black storm."

The hair on his neck prickled. "I had a feeling you somehow knew our situation. Perhaps this storm is almost over."

"But the real storm hasn't even begun…"

There was no way she could have known what the future would bring, but some part of Thane believed her. The plan had already deviated too far from what it was supposed to be. Every ounce of his soul knew that killing Lydia was wrong, especially before returning home to Zann-Xia-Czul, but the situation had trapped him. The strange knight bearing crimson armor had demonstrable power, greater than anything that had ever come from blood sacrifices. Whether he'd lied about the command coming from Zann-Xia-Czul didn't matter. Either way, the crimson knight wanted Lydia gone now.

"I-I'm sorry. I have to do this," Thane said, unable to take any more of her words. He plunged the knife into Lydia's stomach.

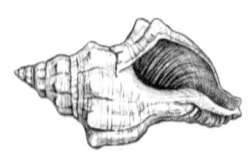

"WE'RE FINISHED," HARKBIN PROCLAIMED AFTER A short while as they journeyed on in their carriage. "Our island will be caught between the wrath of the sorceress and the Darian Kingdom. I hope you realize the gravity of your actions, Thane. You've ignited a war."

"I saved us!" Thane protested. "The knight could have massacred everyone, seized the stones, and left unscathed. Instead of plundering us, he pledged his aid in battling the sorceress. We should count ourselves fortunate to be alive!"

"You're a fool," Urith said. "He manipulated you too easily with his illusions and tricks. We needed those stones for our mission!"

"It was all real," Thane insisted. "The knight knew too much for it to have been otherwise."

Though Harkbin was stroking his beard in contemplation, his scowl hadn't disappeared. "Even if the magic were legitimate, it's no coincidence that Zann-Xia-Czul couldn't communicate with us. The crimson knight must have been blocking our minds."

"You really think that's how it was?" Urith asked. "Not the sorceress?"

"What?" Thane said.

"Yes. The knight has magic, knows our intentions, and struck a deal with you to ruin our plans," Harkbin said. "If he wasn't the sorceress, then it's likely he was working for her."

"No, it couldn't be," Thane said, shifting in his chair. "Why would he promise to help fight her, then?"

Harkbin gave him a slap on the back of his head. "Because he's a liar and you're a fool!"

The crimson knight had quietly teleported away from the scene as soon as Lydia was dead. There had to be some higher purpose for why things had turned out for the worse. Thane couldn't imagine any possibility other than Harkbin's, yet he was still sure there had to be something else happening that they were all unaware of.

"I-I don't know what's going on anymore," Thane admitted. He stared down at the dried blood on his hands. "Earlier, I acted based on what I believed was right. I was not in favor of it, but it seemed rational."

"That's the end of you doing what you think is reasonable then," Urith said. "You clearly lost all judgment and foresight when you made a deal with that suspicious foreigner. From now on, I forbid you from making any more decisions, actions, or choices on our behalf. Your father and I will oversee bringing us home, not you. Understood?"

"Yes," Thane mumbled, clenching his fist.

"And when we return to the ships, you'll be confined to your cabin," Harkbin added. "What you did is treasonous. I may be able to protect you from the Elders, but I cannot control Zann-Xia-Czul's judgment. Hopefully, he understands your point of view."

"I know, I know. And I'm sorry."

"And why'd you stab her in the stomach?" Urith asked. "You should have just slit her throat and made it easier to remove the blood. You know this."

She was right, but Thane ignored her. Everything was already done. Even if it were possible to turn back time and kill Lydia "better," he still wanted no part in it.

"Now, we must meditate and listen carefully for his call," his father instructed. "Close your eyes."

Thirty minutes went by without another word. Although Thane kept his head bowed throughout, he didn't engage in prayer. Everything seemed like a pointless endeavor now that Lydia was dead and their god couldn't read their minds anymore. He could force his brow into a tight scowl until it became as red as the sun, but that wouldn't render his thoughts any more decipherable. Furthermore, the evidence that Zann-Xia-Czul was misleading them seemed more compelling than ever.

A true god would have been aware of an invincible, magic-wielding knight—regardless of whether he was friend or foe. He should have informed them about the knight in some way, either through a warning or with a command to recruit the man to their cause. The strange, unnamed man, as elusive as he was, seemed more like a god, anyway. The knight knew more, had proven his powers, and wasn't afraid to show his face to them. Though Thane wanted to bring that point up with his family, he knew they'd never consider the possibility that their religion was mistaken.

"Stop the carriage," Harkbin commanded.

Thane opened his eyes to see his father drenched in sweat. "What's wrong?"

"I've just realized why Zann-Xia-Czul cannot communicate with my mind anymore," Harkbin said.

"And?"

"We haven't made any sacrifices recently, aside from the princess. Weeks have passed since our last participation in a Loyalty Circle."

"I've been itching for a kill," Urith said. "But wouldn't Lydia have been enough, despite how unplanned and untimely her death was?"

"Killing her the traditional way may not have properly unlocked the magic inside her," Harkbin answered. "Therefore, we need to sacrifice more. With enough blood, we might allow Zann-Xia-Czul to communicate with us."

Thane took a moment to consider his words before revealing his thoughts. "I'm sure the Son See'ers at home haven't stopped the Reminders of Suffering. Even without Lydia, he's still been getting the usual blood. I don't think a lack of sacrifices is the reason."

"But what if it is?" inquired Harkbin. "We need to sacrifice as much as possible. Overabundance is better than too little."

"And whom do you propose can we slay?" Urith asked. "People of Starlight Beach?"

"Absolutely," Harkbin said. "And I realize the stallions are viable too. It's not human blood, but there's a lot. Everything might count now."

"Wait!" Thane said. "If we kill our horses, we won't travel as quickly. We need to return with Lydia's body as fast as we can. We can't let her decay while Zann-Xia-Czul could still do something with it."

"Remember, you're done deciding anything," his mother warned.

"But you know it's illogical to butcher them," Thane said. "The horses help us travel. It took days to reach Last Hope from the coast. On foot, we might move faster at first, but we don't have the stamina for—"

"Shut up, Thane!" Urith growled. "Stop talking."

"Fine."

Their stubbornness only helped prove he was correct. Lydia's death had shocked them into a reality that was tough to face, but it was already done. Pride and fear aside, the fastest way home was the horses.

He wanted to tell Urith and Harkbin to let him have one horse and meet them later in Starlight Beach but knew better than to speak up now. To fix their sudden stubbornness, Harkbin and Urith would need to discover the futility of blood sacrifices and the facade of Zann-Xia-Czul on their own. Nothing was clear yet, but it would be once they returned home.

"The horses it is then," Urith said. "Shall we do it?"

"Yes," Harkbin replied. "Order the guards to lead them one by one into the nearby forest. Sacrifice one at a time and dig a hole in the ground for the blood. Make a Loyalty Circle."

"All eight of them, right?"

"All eight—and cover their eyes."

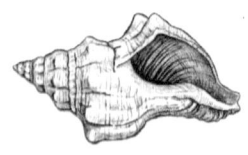

AFTER SACRIFICING ALL THEIR HORSES TO ZANN-XIA-Czul to no avail, Harkbin whittled a short wooden stick into a dowel and used it in conjunction with the sun to estimate the direction of Starlight Beach. Their party proceeded southeastward on foot, bearing their supplies as well as Lydia's blood and remains. For two straight days, they marched almost nonstop, resting only for six hours at the start of the third day. Harkbin insisted they move as swiftly as possible—once they reached their ships, they could rest.

"Maybe the horses' blood wasn't suitable enough," Harkbin admitted. "Regardless, the nearer we are to home, the more plausible it is that Zann-Xia-Czul can resume communication with me."

For the greater part of the week, Thane remained quiet and gave up on challenging his parents' immoral behaviors and broken logic. Ether von Stonewall would eventually return to Last Hope with news of what had happened. Also, guards or a bird would be on their way toward Starlight Beach with news of what they had done. It would be best if they were long gone from the port before anyone local became wiser of the situation. Starting an argument with Harkbin and Urith would only make the return trip home more stressful.

On the seventh day, the familiar seashell archway of Starlight Beach welcomed them back to the coastal town. Aside from the bustling of the market just inside the entrance, the people there still seemed unaware of the events that had followed the wedding.

"Hey!" someone yelled out. "Who are you?"

A man clad in an elaborate green uniform approached them. "You need a permit to sell things here."

"What do you mean?" Harkbin inquired in Common Tongue.

"A permit for the farmers' market," he clarified. "You can't set up shop here without one. I can tell you're not from around here because of your accent."

"Oh…"

As Harkbin hesitated, the man meandered over to the guard and cast a glance at Lydia's body, which was tightly enshrouded in cloth. "What is it you've got there?" he asked. Then he saw the almost-full bucket. "What's that in there? Cherry-flavored jelly?"

The man assumed they were merchants, but something about him seemed strict and knowledge-able about everything and everyone that moved through the streets. To tell the truth and say they were just passing through would appear more suspicious than providing a lie that would complement the context. Plus, it was better that Thane said something before his mother caused a scene.

"How much is a permit?" Thane asked quickly. "We're from the Silent Deserts and have another cart coming in an hour. We mostly have deer meat—this is only the sample. The blood in the bucket is a nutritious jelly we baked. I'm sorry for any issues—

we've been behind schedule. Just tell us what we're supposed to do so we can get set up."

"It's fifteen silvers, including the late processing fee."

"Right away," Harkbin said. Thane exhaled in relief as his father began pulling the coins from his pocket.

The market organizer looked them over. "Thank you. You can have stall twenty-one. Someone sells tea and coffee at number ten. You all seem like you need it."

"Thanks for your help," Thane said. "We'll come back after we prepare the meat in our friend's house."

The man sneered at them. "Note that the seller's permit is non-refundable, and the market closes at sundown."

Harkbin gave Thane an approving nod and guided their party through the alleyways and streets towards the docks. Off in the distance, the university's castle towered above the city, observing everything in its midst. Aside from the initial man's inquisitiveness and eagerness to make money, none seemed to take any notice of them. Thane and his family had gotten lucky. News of the Throatians returning home so soon had apparently not reached Starlight Beach yet. Even better, they'd also arrived ahead of the news of what happened with Lydia and her father.

Ten minutes later, they saw their familiar ships along the dock, unchanged since their initial docking some days prior.

"I hope Hrodspire got our bird," Urith said, staring down at her bloody, dirty feet. She used one to scratch an itch on the other leg.

"Much has changed since we wrote that letter," Thane remarked.

"It doesn't matter. Assemble the troops," Harkbin commanded. "We shall bring additional sacrifices with us."

"What?!" Thane cried out in disbelief.

His mother's eyes lit up with a malicious glee. "An excellent consolation prize. But why transport them when we could execute them here?"

"Our ships need Zann-Xia-Czul's blessing for better winds," his father said. "Without his magic, we risk moving too slowly. The sacrifices must be performed at sea."

If Zann-Xia-Czul hadn't shown his power outside the island so far, it seemed improbable that he would wield it now. The sole prospect of magic was the Tears of Asura, but they were in the posses-sion of the crimson knight. Thane wished the crazed knight would have just used his magic and tele-ported them home, saving them from the trouble of sailing. Still, if their god's plans had indeed changed, perhaps it was destiny that they take the longer journey. The prince found himself ensnared in confusion, unable to reconcile his belief and doubts toward Zann-Xia-Czul's abilities. Moreover, bringing Darian hostages would prove itself as pointless as killing their horses. Hrodspire was the one chance at changing his parents' minds.

"We should first check with Hrodspire," Thane said. "There might not be enough supplies for hostages."

Urith scoffed dismissively. "As though we'd give them any."

Thane's eyes sharply shifted in her direction. At their island, even those born solely for the purpose of sacrifice were accorded some respect and provided with fundamental necessities. While foreigners were by no means Son See'ers, they were still people. To deprive someone of their livelihood was one thing, but it was unjust to treat them as subhuman.

"We're buried too deeply in this predicament to do anything less," Harkbin said. "We'll take everything we can, whatever is necessary. If so, it enables the restoration of our bond with Zann-Xia-Czul."

"So, you intend to starve the Darians?" The prince's face contorted into a scowl. "I object to taking hostages, especially under those circumstances."

"This is not your decision to make, and you shall obey my command," Harkbin warned. "Blood is the currency of magic, and Zann-Xia-Czul demands it—this isn't negotiable."

"You've screwed up enough already, remember?" Urith interjected, giving his shoulder a contemptuous slap.

Thane's cheeks flushed pink with humiliation at her words. Persuading them to make their way homeward without further incident seemed an insurmountable task. Thane found himself at a loss to discern whether the severity of their situation had made Harkbin and Urith cruel, or if such ruthlessness had been intrinsic to their nature all along. Their devout worship of Zann-Xia-Czul furnished plenty of reasons to kill in the name of their religion, but now he realized his mother seemed to relish the violence. Regardless of their traditional views, who they were now wasn't acceptable. His disappointment with them mirrored their own disillusionment with him.

"Fine."

They advanced along the pier to where their ships awaited and relayed to Hrodspire the events that had unfolded since the wedding ceremony. Despite Thane's objections, Harkbin and Urith insisted on capturing whoever they could find in the town. Hrodspire's wrinkled face cringed at the idea of withholding food from prisoners, but he stated they would have enough fresh water to keep everyone alive.

"I'm planning on sacrificing two people a day, if we have the numbers," the king announced. "This will provide a steady stream of blood for Zann-Xia-Czul."

"Very well," Hrodspire said, a hint of dryness in his tone. "There're no beds for them, so they'll have to sleep on the deck. Perhaps we can use some blankets to provide them shade from the sun and warmth when—"

"Stop right there," Urith said. "When they arrive, tie the prisoners up and lay them face down until they're needed."

"Um, o-okay," the Elder stuttered. His eyes met Thane's, who silently shook his head. Without saying a word, Hrodspire revealed that there was little chance of him changing Harkbin and Urith's minds on the matter either.

As Urith seized her war hammer, a Son See'er Vrai presented Harkbin with his sword. The king examined it for a moment, as if he'd longed to be back in combat, before addressing everyone nearby. "Be ready for the prisoners soon. It's going to get dangerous, so prepare to launch the moment Urith and I return."

"It'll be done as you request," Hrodspire promised. "The winds are in our favor, for now."

"And lock Thane below deck," Urith said.

"What?" exclaimed both Hrodspire and Thane in unison.

"You will not interfere," his mother said, pointing her dry, calloused finger at the Elder. She then shifted it toward her son. "If we had time, I'd gather seashells and make you kneel for how much trouble you've caused us."

Thane wanted to call her out on the amount of strain she'd created on their journey, but decided it was better to go quietly. Two guards escorted him to his bed below deck and bound his arms and legs with silver rope. As Thane lay restless, he contemplated whether any of his actions warranted getting treated as a common prisoner. Footsteps creaked down the stairs as the escorts returned, carrying Princess Lydia's body, still wrapped in cotton.

"Urith requested we lay her next to you," the guard said apologetically. "She said it was for your protection and so you'd learn your lesson, whatever that's supposed to mean. What's gotten into her?"

They carefully set Lydia's body on the bed. The cloth did a fair job of concealing the awful smell, but it had already been a week since she'd died. The situation that arose from Zann-Xia-Czul's need for magic had developed in the worst ways imaginable. Only Cereene might understand why Thane had made the choices he had.

"My mother and father only have Zann-Xia-Czul left to lean on," Thane said, "and even that seems lost. They're clinging to what they've known their whole lives, despite it all falling apart."

"If you need food, water, or anything, call us," one guard offered. "It isn't right to do this to you, regardless of what happened with the mission."

"You must follow your orders. I understand," Thane said.

The only way he could redeem himself to his parents was by sacrificing his own life if that still counted. Unfortunately, without Lydia's fresh blood and the Tears of Asura, Thane's blood alone might be insignificant. If that was the case, chances were that everyone would demand he die anyway for treason. The Elders would have the greatest weight in the decision, aside from Zann-Xia-Czul himself.

The two Son See'ers bowed and returned upstairs, leaving Thane by himself. He stared at the wall and took a deep breath for what felt like the first time in days. As he rested, he breathed softly, but couldn't come close to a meditative state. Instead, the roof of his mouth trembled as the muscles in his face contracted. A single tear ran down his cheek to the pillow below. Thane hadn't cried in years, nor did he want to admit it to himself, but that was the reality of it. With a sniff, he turned away from Lydia's body and drifted off to sleep.

Sometime later, there was a hard pounding against the deck above him, startling him awake. After the second thud, he pushed his elbows against the mattress, forcing himself up. Something was amiss upstairs. Shouting echoed above and the creaky wood ceiling shook as people ran across the old flooring. Thane stood and bounced himself over to the stairway to peer up, but he couldn't see anything. Suddenly, the entire room moved, and Thane lost his balance and thudded to the ground. The ship was leaving the Darian Kingdom.

"Hello?" he called, as he struggled to right himself.

Moments passed without a response, until Hrodspire's raspy voice emanated from above.

"My prince," the Elder said. "We've launched toward home, but the Darians will soon be in pursuit."

He quickly hobbled down the stairs and grabbed Thane's shoulder to help him up.

"How do you know?" Thane asked, pushing his knees against the ground.

"The Darian king and his soldiers arrived earlier than we expected, prompting our ships to depart the port. Numerous of their citizens died, and we apprehended only half the number that the king and queen had desired."

"How much of a lead on them will we have?"

"Less than an hour," Hrodspire said. "My apologies, but I need to go. Your parents are above, and they need me."

"I understand," Thane said. He went back to his bed and sat down. "Thanks for helping me up."

Hrodspire stepped back up the stairs but turned around again halfway up. "Before we get home, I want to hear your side of the story of what happened to Princess Lydia."

"There's not much else to disclose," Thane said. "I bear the blame for her death, and the Tears now reside with an immortal individual."

Hrodspire shook his head. "I can tell you're keeping us in the dark about some of the reasons behind your decisions. Whatever they are, you're better off letting them out before we get home."

"They say Zann-Xia-Czul sees all," Thane said. "If that holds true, then he'll be the one to pass judgment upon me."

The Elder glanced back up the stairs, then advanced a few steps toward Thane. "That's precisely my concern. The conflict with the sorceress might have begun the instant we departed from our island. If Zann-Xia-Czul was defeated or otherwise preoccupied in battle, it would account for his sustained silence."

Thane's eyes lit up. "You're right, Hrodspire! That would explain everything! If the crimson knight is truly on our side, then he might have taken the Tears of Asura from us to deliver them to Zann-Xia-Czul faster. Your theory would explain the urgency. I hope that's what's going on."

"Oh?" Hrodspire said. "I must admit, I don't grasp the full context. If he were our ally, what motive could the knight have for forcing you to kill Lydia?"

"Because he…" Thane's voice trailed off, unable to fathom the purpose. "I'm not sure."

Hrodspire scratched his head. "There must be an underlying rationale why everything happened the way it did. It's possible that it's connected to her blood in some way, but if that's the case, why would the knight have slain her and yet spared you?"

"Obedience," Thane said. "For one reason or another, my obedience and loyalty to Zann-Xia-Czul has to be why."

THE WHISPER OF ZANN-XIA-CZUL

S everal hours later, the guards reappeared at Thane's cabin, announcing that his parents had summoned him. Having been instructed not to unbind him, the duo heaved their prince up the stairs where Hrodspire, Harkbin, and Urith were engaged in debate. It was unclear why the three of them hadn't just moved downstairs, but Thane was happy to be out in the fresh air and away from Lydia's body. Once the guards dropped him off, he could stand, but remained unable to freely move. Neither his father nor his mother gave orders to cut the ropes binding his ankles and wrists. Nonetheless, it became evident rather swiftly that Hrodspire was advocating for the prince's release.

"It may very well be that Zann-Xia-Czul's plan has changed since we left home," the Elder said.

"Your communications with him stopped long before Thane's encounter with the knight at Starlight Beach. I don't claim it was our god's intention, though I believe it's a possibility. If it is, then Thane has done nothing wrong, and we should free him."

"Absolutely not," Urith growled. "He may be my son, but he willingly gave up the Tears of Asura and murdered our very purpose in venturing here."

In contrast to Urith, Harkbin appeared more open to the Elder's line of reasoning. "There must have been some reason the knight wanted Thane left alive. It makes me wonder what influence he may still have over him."

Urith's hand curled into a fist. "I still say keeping him locked up is best. If he's innocent, then we'll certainly know when we return. No harm will come to our son by confining him here."

Their conversation was strange; he'd been standing there for a while, but neither of his parents had acknowledged him. Hrodspire had given him a brief glance, but it seemed the three of them were in such an intense debate that none could let their guard down. So, why had he been summoned?

"Speaking of no harm done…" the Elder added. "Aside from the Darians pursuing us in their ships, we're isolated out here on the ocean. Releasing the prince to meander the ship won't cause any trouble. What could he possibly do?"

Urith scowled. Harkbin stroked his beard and rubbed a hand along the stairway's railing.

"I agree with Hrodspire," the king said, finally. "Locking our son up may have been an overreaction. We'll let him walk free for now, but the moment that we reach ground, we'll put him on trial." He turned to Thane. "Is that agreeable?"

"Yes," the prince spoke up. "I'll avoid causing—"

"He can't interfere with anything—*anything*—we say or do," Urith interrupted, pointing at Thane, and glaring at her husband. "He needs to follow our orders, not issue them. It's for everyone's protection. Is that clear?"

"Fine," Thane growled. Being treated like a convict had exhausted him.

"Fine," Urith said.

Harkbin cut the ropes binding Thane's body. The prince massaged the red imprints they had left and conveyed a discreet nod of gratitude to Hrodspire.

"What course of action have we devised for handling the Darians?" Thane added. "Are we prepared to fight? Our ships lack weapons."

"If everything goes right with the prisoners, we should be able to avoid a fight," Harkbin said.

"And the purpose of the prisoners is…?"

"Sheiaa Kaaduul Drakkar Fayyte," the king said solemnly.

Urith's eyes widened, but Thane wasn't sure what the phrase "Drakkar Fayyte," meant.

"The practice stopped generations ago," his mother said.

"What is this?" Thane blurted.

"It's how our family earned our name," Harkbin said. "Before there were Loyalty Circles, our ancestors did the ritual with specially selected Son See'ers."

"You're a shame to our house for not knowing it," Urith said. She turned back to her husband and muttered just loud enough for them to hear, "Sacrificing this way leaves no blood left for Zann-Xia-Czul. Only ash."

"Sheiaa Kaaduul Drakkar Fayyte is to be sacrificed by fire," Hrodspire explained.

"As a person's body disintegrates, their soul fades into the planet and sky," Harkbin said. "Their soul can no longer reincarnate, but it invariably enters Zann-Xia-Czul's grasp, no matter how far away. The essence of life trapped inside permanent death is more valuable than blood."

Thane swallowed. "So, you'll burn the hostages."

"It's necessary," Harkbin said. "Once the soul reaches Zann-Xia-Czul, he'll provide us favorable winds."

"I thought he needed blood for magic," Thane said. "Perhaps that's why it's outdated now—souls don't work."

"Sheiaa Kaaduul Drakkar Fayyte is an old practice, but viable," Harkbin insisted.

"Sure."

He sensed Harkbin was lying. Their flawed logic would end with the pointless deaths of innocent people either way. Disagreeing and debating with Harkbin and Urith was only going to get himself tied up again.

"However, igniting flames on our wooden deck seems unwise," Hrodspire said. "Does a Loyalty Circle genuinely fall short in this situation?"

Harkbin nodded. "Everyone will follow the rites as our ancestors performed them. One prisoner per ship every hour. We'll suspend them from the metal rods used for our sails—we have spares."

"But the prisoners include children," Thane interjected. "What is to become of them?"

"They, too, shall face the flames. Every sacrifice counts now."

"Spare the children," Thane said, aghast. "We shouldn't end their lives while they're so young."

Urith snorted. "Who are you to tell your father what to do?"

Thane stepped forward. "If this is what Zann-

Xia-Czul wants, it's wrong. I pray you don't truly want to do this."

"My faith is immeasurable. I'd burn every child in the world if it meant giving Zann-Xia-Czul what he needs."

Thane's face turned red, and for the first time, he felt the same rage within him that his mother harbored on an almost daily basis. His fists were tense, ready to strike his father until he called off the sacrifices. He was relieved that his arms were no longer bound, but perhaps they had erred in freeing him before revealing their intentions. Just as he was about to make his punch, the thought of his sister came to his mind.

"Would you have burned Feiir like this if she were alive?" Thane blurted out. He instantly knew he'd overstepped, but it was too late.

"What did you say?!" Urith screamed. Before Thane could react, she struck him in the jaw, sending him sprawling. The bottom row of his teeth seemed looser, and there was no telling how far his mother might go.

Thankfully, Harkbin stepped between him and Urith, raising an arm to shield him. "You weren't supposed to know about her," he said. "It's our family's greatest wound. Who revealed this to you?"

From the ground, Thane cast a glance at Hrodspire before turning his attention back to his father.

"A long time ago, Desaii Egon told me the truth," he responded, his jaw aching with each word. Thane prayed his lie would be believed. Desaii was dead. There was no way to prove anything, for better or worse.

Harkbin let his arm drop. "You weren't supposed to find out... but since your cousin is no more, there's not much we can do. Feiir was the hardest lesson for us to learn. Sheiaa Kaaduul. Never speak of her again, to anyone."

"Ruik Czharr," Urith cursed as tears streamed down her face.

"Now please," Thane pleaded, "don't burn the children."

Harkbin shook his head, his gaze fixed on a point beyond his son. "My faith is unwavering. I would sacrifice every man, woman, and child in the world, including Feiir, if it were Zann-Xia-Czul's command. It would be neither easy nor enjoyable, but it would be done. We must trust and obey our god's will for the better of all."

Before Thane responded, Hrodspire gripped his shoulder.

"Then, let us pray that the souls of the prisoners grant us a swift journey home," said the Elder. He gave Thane a gentle tug. "Come, my prince, you need to rest for a while before the sea makes you ill."

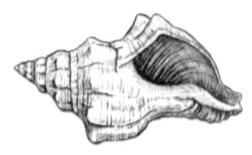

THE SMELL OF BURNING FLESH AND HAIR PLAGUED THE decks of all three ships that night. At the start of each hour, Harkbin and Urith initiated the ritual by dousing a prisoner in oils. The prisoners were strung up by their legs and suspended upside-down from the stern of the vessels. In the final steps, Harkbin led the remaining Son See'ers in a chant, praying loudly enough for everyone to hear over the screams of the victims.

Meanwhile, Thane quickly retreated and hid behind some barrels. Burning hostages in an ancient rite was something he wanted no role in. As was the case when the king ordered them to slaughter their horses, the bloodshed proved ineffective. Their speed remained the same, and they heard nothing from their god. Likely, the silence would continue until they reached home. Although Thane's predictions came true, and the winds stayed calm, Harkbin and Urith persisted in performing the ritual every hour. They were desperate—their god had never forsaken them before.

A torch crackled menacingly as Harkbin lowered it below the ship's railing, close to the latest Darian prisoner—a young girl. He prodded her with his torch, allowing the oil to ignite. Every hour, they randomly selected a hostage and repeated the round of prayers and sacrifices.

"Zann-Xia-Czul, we know the enemy you face," he bellowed into the wind, for the fourth time on the seventh night. Beneath him, orange flames erupted, and screams echoed against the evening's winds. "Your strife intertwines our fates. Save us from our pursuers and free us of their turmoil! We give you our souls so that you might help us return to the Temple of White. We spare nothing in our sacrifices to remain Son See'er Vrai!"

As the girl's screams echoed into the darkness, Thane could hear another man similarly yell from the ship nearest theirs. During the raid on Starlight Beach, Harkbin and Urith had claimed a diverse set of men, women, and children and divided them among the three vessels. None of it was right, and Hrodspire knew it too. As the first round of killings concluded for the night, the Elder feigned chest pains and abstained from the remaining sacrifices.

Hour after hour went by, as the same cycle of prayer and sacrifice continued. Finally, unable to stomach being so close to so much pointless death, Thane retreated below deck. Hrodspire lay on his bunk, facing the wall. The smell of Lydia's body dominated the room, making every moment insufferable. Still, it was better than what was happening above them.

"Hrodspire," Thane whispered, covering his nose with his sleeve. "How's your chest?"

"Better now."

"Better since moving away from Drakkar Fayyte?"

"I haven't the slightest idea what you mean," Hrodspire said, pausing for a moment. "Thank you for covering for me earlier. Still, you weren't supposed to let your parents know what I told you."

"Let's be honest with each other," Thane said. "We both recognize the horror of sacrificing hostages, even if it appeases our god. We're aware these rituals align with Zann-Xia-Czul's wishes, but... what if he's wrong?"

The old man sat up and stared Thane in the eyes. "For weeks, I remained here and waited at the docks for your family to return with Princess Lydia. I don't speak Common Tongue, but you needn't understand the Darian's language to see their way of life. The ports of Starlight Beach aren't much different from White Boar's Landing, and their people are naturally similar to us. Every country has its share of war and conflict, but—"

"What's your point?" Thane asked.

Hrodspire cleared his throat. "Our religion has always advocated inner peace and mindfulness for the individual, but what about within the community? Violence. Though they contrast each other, the concepts co-existed, perfectly balanced for generations. Observing the Darians made me believe that killings and reminders of pain aren't needed to maintain harmony."

Thane covered his mouth, blocking some of the smell as he shifted Lydia's body a bit closer to the wall, then sat down on his bed. "It seems logical to me. But it goes against the teachings of Zann-Xia-Czul. People aren't willing to give that up yet—look at what's happening above us now."

"That's why this whole situation confuses me," Hrodspire said. "Blood may link the physical world with whatever spiritual processes create magic, but how can a lone sorceress rival a god? And if what the crimson knight showed you is truly as you saw it, then how could the warrior and the sorceress not be such entities as well?"

"Right. Between Zann-Xia-Czul, the knight, and the sorceress, they're either all gods or none of them. It must be the latter," he said, "because despite being powerful, nobody seems adept enough to do whatever they want."

"Maybe, but how could you know for sure?"

Thane stood and moved to the bottommost stair. He stared at the small, burning light of the lantern that hung on the opposite side of the room, and it only reminded him of the atrocities happening above them.

"Perhaps the term 'god' merely refers to an entity so powerful and beyond our understanding that we can have no other name for it," Thane said.

"But that would, by definition, make it a god," Hrodspire replied. "I can't quite put my thoughts into words, but I know something's wrong with the way we've done things. The vulnerable always serve the strong."

"I've thought about that, too, ever since my father lingered on Mount Sephorr that day," Thane said. "He hasn't been the same since then. My father led our people for so long... He was the most powerful Son See'er on our island, but then Zann-Xia-Czul demanded everything from him."

"His greatest secret right now is how shaken his faith has become. Between sacrificing a hundred thousand more people and his only son, the decision alone infested him with guilt—he told me so," Hrodspire said. "One thing our king won't admit to anyone, including me, is that he feels Zann-Xia-Czul has turned his back on us because of his hesitation."

"I'm more convinced that he isn't truly a god. Why does his power manifest solely on our island?"

"Regardless of the truth, be wary of your thoughts upon our return home," Hrodspire cautioned. "I assume he will regain the ability to hear our thoughts once we're back."

The deck overhead creaked as Urith entered, huffing, her breaths labored.

"The princess," she said. "Give me her body."

Thane turned around and stood. "No, you won't burn her too!"

"This isn't your choice."

"Urith!" a voice called from above. It was Harkbin. He quickly arrived behind her in the doorway, escorted by four Son See'ers armed with blades.

"Fine," Urith retorted with a snort. Her war hammer was nowhere in sight; otherwise, Thane suspected she would have posed a greater challenge. "We won't sacrifice her, but who'll be next?"

"What's the meaning of this?" Hrodspire blurted out.

"We're out of hostages," Urith said. "The princess's corpse could be worth something."

"Absolutely not," Harkbin said. "We don't even know if her soul is still here. We should sacrifice our own people first before her. Zann-Xia-Czul may demand her body."

"How about we start with the men next to you?" Urith said.

"Calm down, both of you," the Elder urged. "These are troubling times, so it's important we keep our composure."

"Survival is our key priority," Harkbin retorted. "Sacrifices are indispensable in granting Zann-Xia-Czul with the power he requires. Come with me, Hrodspire. We'll first take volunteers. If no Son See'ers give their lives, we'll choose from them ourselves."

"Yes, of course. We'll keep Drakkar Fayyte going every hour for the rest of the night." The Elder hurried up the stairs and followed behind Harkbin.

Thane stepped toward the exit as well, but Urith raised her thick arm to block him.

"I know you want to interfere, but you won't." Before he could protest, she summoned guards. "My son must remain down here. It's for everyone's safety that he's constrained. Tie him up again."

As the Son See'ers reluctantly approached, Thane held his silence. Their sluggish handling of the ropes and the loosely tied knots around his wrists and ankles suggested they recognized her unreasonableness and sympathized with him. Still, nobody dared speak up, for compliance was easier than debate.

After they left, Thane untied himself and slid the ropes under his pillow. Screams echoed from above as another victim burned alive. Powerless, he tried his best to ignore the sounds as he lapsed into a deep slumber.

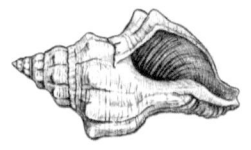

A LOUD CRASH WOKE HIM THE NEXT MORNING, AND its force threw him off the bed and onto the floor. Before he could even comprehend what had happened, he heard the sound of feet stomping down the stairway.

"Thane!" Hrodspire yelled. "The Darians caught up to us!"

"What?!"

"They rammed the ship! We're sinking!"

"How did they—never mind. We need to leave. Now." He pushed himself off the ground and ran toward Hrodspire.

"You must carry the princess," the Elder said. "There's no point in trying to survive if we don't bring her home too."

Thane rushed back to his bed and lifted the princess's body. Though the white cloth remained tightly wrapped around her, something about her seemed more delicate than before.

"I'm sorry, again, Lydia," Thane whispered as he heaved her over his back.

They moved to the deck, and Thane discovered the crash had been from one of the Darian ships lodging itself into theirs. Son See'ers were already crossing over onto the other vessel and engaging in battle. It all seemed pointless if the ocean floor was destined to claim both vessels. Endless plains of sea surrounded them—to stay onboard their compromised craft guaranteed death.

"Where's my family?" Thane bellowed at whoever could hear him.

"On the other ship, there! Look!" a Son See'er responded, pointing across the deck. Thane recognized him as one of the guards who had tied him up, but it hardly mattered.

Harkbin and the purple-armored man from the rehearsal dinner were engaged in a duel. Urith was nowhere to be seen, likely off massacring people nearby. Meanwhile, the other two Throatian ships were on their way over to rescue them. Despite the chaos of the fight, it was easy to see the Darians outnumbered them. There was no way the Throatians would win the battle.

"Get ready! The other ship is coming for us!" Thane yelled. "Transfer everything you can! We're abandoning this one!"

But nobody seemed to hear him. Everyone was busy battling the Darians or already evacuating to the other vessel. He froze. It wasn't clear whether they were more likely to survive by fighting or fleeing. The ship was listing and would soon be vertical in the waves.

"Thane!" Hrodspire said, lightly slapping his back. "Even if they heard you, they wouldn't disobey Harkbin. We need to take care of ourselves! Come on!" He guided Thane to the front of the ship, which was quickly becoming the vessel's highest point. At the other end, water filled the crevices where the other ship had punctured the hull. Moment by moment, everything became heavier.

"If we can hold out for a few minutes, they'll make it here," the Elder said.

There was a crash, and they jerked sideways, causing Thane to drop Lydia onto the floor. Hrodspire quickly grabbed a railing and saved himself from almost falling as well. One of the Darian ships had freed the two lodged vessels from each other by ramming them both. Now, the ship they were on was sinking faster than ever—it would submerge in minutes!

"Ruik Czharr!" Thane yelled as he scrambled to save Lydia's rolling body.

"Hold on just a little longer," Hrodspire said. "Once we get away from this, we're almost home—I can see it."

"You can?" Thane said. The Elder pointed off in the distance and sure enough, beyond a thin veil of fog, the small outline of Mount Sephorr greeted them from the horizon. It was much too far to swim, but sailing there would take less than an hour.

"Zann-Xia-Czul doesn't seem interested in saving us, it appears," Hrodspire said.

"As you said, we'll have to save ourselves," Thane replied, still scowling over having dropped Lydia. Suddenly, he remembered the time he'd prayed at the Temple of White, and how irritating the Elder had been on the day Thane ascended Mount Sephorr.

"Hrodspire, there's something I need to say," he added. "I'm sorry about the times I've been rude and arrogant to you throughout the years. All of them."

The Elder took a moment to ponder, before giving a slight grin. "Apology accepted, my young prince. But don't count on dying just yet."

One of the allied vessels approached and they jumped over to it. Once aboard the intact ship, Thane carried Lydia below deck and carefully laid her on a bed. Satisfied her body was safely stored within the rescue ship, he asked a guard to lend him a sword, then made his way back above deck.

"Thane," Hrodspire said. "My apologies, but the battle is over. We've lost."

"What?" Thane's grip loosened, and his newly acquired blade dropped to the floor.

As the weapon clanged against the deck, he looked over at the Darians. They had captured Harkbin and were forcing him to kneel before Ether von Stonewall. Urith was still nowhere in sight but was likely in their clutches too. It was up to Thane to negotiate their release. Meanwhile, the ship from which he had escaped had already disappeared beneath the ocean's surface.

"I'll fix this," Thane whispered to Hrodspire as he moved over to where the enemy would see him.

"You've bested us for today," he called out in the Common Tongue across the water. "We'll pay you an appropriate amount of gold for my father and mother."

King von Stonewall shot a glare back at him from the other ship. "We don't want money. Give me my daughter's body along with all your food and supplies."

"Done," Thane replied. Lydia's body was a small price to pay for the release of his parents. Still, there was no sign of Urith. "But where is my mother?"

"We don't know," Ether said. "I haven't seen her since you threw me out of your carriage." The Darian king seemed to be lying, but surely Urith would have announced herself if she were free. It was highly unlikely she'd died in the battle.

"She boarded your ship, I'm sure of it."

"If neither of us sees her, then she's not here," Ether said. "Even if we bested her, we would have kept her alive as leverage."

He made a valid point. Holding two royal hostages alive was infinitely more valuable than if they were dead. However, his tone seemed suspicious. He was hiding something, but what? Provoking his father-in-law would be a chance to get the truth out.

"Fine," Thane said. "My wife for my father, and my men's lives for our supplies."

"I want Lydia and the supplies first," the king barked. "I'm sure you'll understand that I don't find your people trustworthy."

"Okay, then."

It seemed Ether von Stonewall didn't know Urith's location, after all.

"Give them everything. And his daughter's body," Thane commanded in Throatian. "We're trading them for my father and the Son See'ers."

As the remaining crew ferried crates and barrels over to the Darian's ships, Hrodspire rested his hand on Thane's shoulder.

"You got lucky in the negotiations, my young prince," the Elder whispered. "You've made the right choice. Despite our own needs, allowing them to bury their princess is the least we can do to mend the tension. They're in a position to kill us all."

"War is still inevitable," Thane said. "I don't like this, but we get to live another day."

Someone shouting across the ships' gap interrupted their conversation.

"Burn in the black sands of Tornaa," the man

nearby Harkbin and Ether said. "Lydia was worth more than your entire family combined."

It took Thane a moment to realize it was Kaine Khalia. Apparently, he'd traveled all this way to save Lydia again, but this time in vain. Thane understood his pain, but it was too late to change the outcome.

"Kaine," Ether ordered. "Check if it's her."

Kaine cautiously crossed the plank connecting the Darian's ship and theirs. He gently unwrapped the upper flap of the cloth covering her body. Shocked at the state of the princess's body, he quickly closed the cloth again.

"It's her," Kaine announced, barely above a whisper. His face trembled at the sight.

"Okay," Ether muttered. "Guards, bring me my daughter."

Another group of soldiers carried Lydia's body over to the Darian ship. Carefully, they set her down on the deck and took a few steps back.

Thane wanted to apologize, to explain that everything that had happened was only because of the sorceress's threat. But just as he was about to speak, the Darians began butchering all the Son See'ers they'd captured. Before Thane could react, the knight who was holding Harkbin hostage switched places with Ether von Stonewall, allowing the king to hold a knife to Harkbin's neck.

"You needlessly took my people captive and

burned them aboard your ships," Ether said. "Your crew paid their price. Now, since you killed Lydia, it's only fair I take someone important from you too."

Kaine and his purple-armored friend protested, but despite their objections, the Darian king wouldn't yield.

"I need to protect my children," Ether von Stonewall said. "Can't you see it? The war started when they murdered Lydia."

Thane's heart pounded as the knight again urged the king to stop, but von Stonewall continued holding the blade to Harkbin's neck. Regardless of whether he was bluffing, there wouldn't be enough time for him to run over to the other ship and rescue his father.

"They didn't allow Lydia to change her fate," Ether von Stonewall declared, and stabbed Harkbin in the throat.

Thane's vision went blurry as his father gagged on his own blood and fell to the ground. There was no room for doubt—his family was dead. He realized the battle had likely consumed Urith too, otherwise, she would have already taken her revenge. With the Darian king's betrayal, Thane was now the last surviving member of the Asche family.

Time slowed down, yet he remained unmoving. Harkbin's bloody corpse neither surprised nor saddened him, but he knew he should have felt something. Not this... nothingness. He couldn't tell whether the numbness was due to shock or if the two sensations were the same. His mouth hung open despite being unable to release any words.

Meanwhile, the Darian king retired below deck on his ship, leaving the purple-armored knight and Kaine to clean up the mess.

"Guards, return the Throatian king to his ship," the knight ordered. "It's the least we can do."

"Do the same for the Throatian queen," Kaine said. "She's by the stairs below deck. Bring her carefully and respectfully."

Four Darians worked together to carry Urith's body into view. Hrodspire turned white at the sight of their strongest warrior, felled.

"I-I can't believe this," the Elder stammered. Thane understood his shock but couldn't feel the same way. Instead, a lulling void continued dominating his consciousness.

Before anything else could happen, several black clouds coalesced in the sky, giving rise to a massive thunderstorm that plagued the entire area. The raindrops were sharp and solid, cutting Thane's skin like tiny, vicious knives. He hadn't felt such intensity from rainfall before, but he'd heard the Elders mention it many times in the past: it was Zann-Xia-Czul's magic! It had arrived, but far too late.

The howling storm danced around the ships, forcing them apart. A gust of wind, heavier and stronger than the rest, shoved Thane's vessel closer to their island. He seized the ship's railing to avoid being thrown overboard, struggling to maintain his balance as the deck turned slippery.

"It's so strong!" Thane yelled toward the sky. "Zann-Xia-Czul, your magic is too powerful."

The prince and his people dropped to the floor in the sudden storm. As rain dominated all in sight and wind pushed their ships closer to their homeland, Thane couldn't help but let his mind wander. His thoughts looped back and forth between the sinking reality of his parents' deaths and his lack of reaction to it. A part of him had always suspected they'd die in battle, but he'd imagined it would be when they were older—in a Loyalty Circle, maybe.

The storm and its darkness rolled them toward Mount Sephorr, then faded away completely. The two Throatian ships were likely less than half an hour from White Boar's Landing now. Despite the loss of Harkbin and Urith to the Darians, the sight of their homeland again brought a sense of calm to Thane's heart. Best of all, the Darian vessel was nowhere in sight.

He pushed himself up from the floor, his clothes dripping as if he had just emerged from the ocean.

Despite the storm, their ship remained fully unharmed.

"We're saved!" a Son See'er yelled. Thane couldn't understand their happiness—were they also numb to the fact that their king and queen had just died?

"All hail Thane Asche, the new Throatian king!" Hrodspire announced to the remaining crew.

"King Thane! King Thane Asche!" a Son See'er yelled. The group repeated the cheers several times over, with no sign that Harkbin and Urith's absences were a problem.

"Don't celebrate so soon," Thane replied. "We still have a war against the sorceress to win! I don't know what will happen when we arrive—our people may already battle against her as we speak. We won't learn the truth until later, but I vow to you this: you are all my Son See'er Vrai! Zann-Xia-Czul called on me to sacrifice myself for you, but our plan has changed. I cannot see what's needed of us until we reach White Boar's Landing, but whether I live or die, I'll continue serving you however I can!"

The Son See'ers cheered at his speech. Many of them began pounding their chests and chanting. Their support took him by surprise, as it seemed that nobody held him accountable for the premature death of Princess Lydia. Or perhaps they all simply disagreed with Urith's sanctions against him. Either way, they now acknowledged him as their new king.

"My father and mother... they changed in their last days," Thane continued. "The pressures they faced were immeasurable. They relied on what they knew rather than what we, as a society, could become. This trial, and the journey along with it, challenged all our beliefs. When we reach home and return to normal life, we're going to make some changes with the Loyalty Circles and Breeding Farms. I don't know what those changes are yet, but I want fewer pointless deaths."

The Son See'ers continued chanting in the background, but their intensity was rising. Some even began yelling at the top of their lungs, fully dedicating themselves to Thane's cause. The recent events had opened their eyes to the fallacy of their religion, and Thane wondered if the old ways were on their way out.

"We've lost the battle at sea, along with many of our brothers and sisters," he said. "Sheiaa Kaaduul. Never forget them as we press forward and secure our homeland from the sorceress! Never forget that one day, the violence plaguing our home will end!"

The chanting stopped, and everyone became quiet. They were staring at him, wide-eyed and fearful.

"Did I say something wrong?" he quietly asked Hrodspire. He'd seemed to have everyone's favor a moment ago. Why had they changed their opinions?

"Look behind you, my king," the Elder said.

Off in the distance, at White Boar's Landing, crowds of people lined up along the piers, armed with swords, spears, and every other weapon Thane could imagine. At their head, a broad man he barely recognized watched them approach.

"Zann-Xia-Czul must have alerted them about our battle with the Darians," Thane said to his crew, relieved. "It's good we had backup just in case Ether von Stonewall followed us the rest of the way home."

"Indeed..." the Elder murmured, his voice weary as if he were ready to rest for the day.

Thane was also eager to take a break from the excitement. Everything that had happened—from the seasickness on the journey from his homeland to the last battle upon the ocean—left him weary. Thankfully, there were no indications that the sorceress had launched her attack, and the island seemed to await their return. Nothing had gone as expected during the mission, but at least they were home now, and that provided Thane with a long-awaited comfort.

THE FIRST LOYALTY CIRCLE

T he two ships glided into the docks at White Boar's Landing, where some of the Son See'ers, who had been waiting, helped secure them. Once the ropes were secured, Thane and Hrodspire were the first to disembark, eager to be home but dreading the announcement that they hadn't been able to return with the princess alive.

As soon as their feet touched the wooden planks, a seasoned warrior in his mid-forties approached them. He stood nearly as tall as Thane's mother and was clad in chain mail armor, covered with a silvery, ankle-length cape. His coarse, short beard complemented the colors of his clothing.

"Shivanna Adul, Thane Asche," greeted the Loyalty Circle veteran.

"Grimm Kathaar, Shivanna Adul," Thane replied.

Thane couldn't remember his exact relation to Urith, but Grimm was a family member—most likely a cousin or half-cousin. Years had passed since he last spoke to Grimm. "It's been a long time since we've crossed paths. I hope you've been well. Thank you for providing the extra defenses. How fares the island?"

"The sorceress has not yet made an appearance; thus, we remain unscathed," responded Grimm. "Is it true that both Urith and Harkbin perished by Darian blades? Zann-Xia-Czul told me this, but I couldn't truly believe it unless I heard it from you."

With a solemn nod, Thane forced his face into a neutral expression to mask his surprise. "They passed. My mother died in a fair fight during the battle, but the Darian king betrayed Harkbin."

"I see. Then everything is as Zann-Xia-Czul explained to me."

Hrodspire cleared his throat. "The Asche family's absence would have left the Elders in charge of the homeland. I'm surprised our god spoke to you rather than them. Is something wrong?"

"The king leads and serves as the vessel through whom Zann-Xia-Czul speaks," Grimm declared.

Thane's stomach gave a lurch. How could Grimm possibly claim kingship? "Your power and title were temporary, I assume. The Elders only transfer such authority when the rightful king remains unreachable."

"With Harkbin and Urith Asche gone, Thane is next in line," Hrodspire said. "Since King Thane has returned, whatever powers you may have had are now expired. The Elders explained this, no?"

"That is the norm, but not this time," countered Grimm. "Thane's royal title is void."

"Impossible," Hrodspire said. "While it's true Thane will probably be sacrificed, he's still alive today and, therefore, that makes him the rightful king. Where are the other Elders? They should all be familiar with the law!"

Grimm nodded nonchalantly. "They're on their way here, and as you mentioned, they are well-versed in the procedures and rules. Foremost, Zann-Xia-Czul stands with me. You'll need to accept that I'm in charge now. Please understand, I'm not self-ishly grasping for power. This was my calling, and there's nothing any of us can do."

Thane exchanged a nervous glance with the Elder. It was certainly possible Grimm was legiti-mately the next in line after him, but Hrodspire had a point—Thane wasn't dead yet. He was the last of the royal family, yes, but still alive. Why would Zann-Xia-Czul circumvent his own laws?

"Perhaps my family made some mistakes while

we were abroad," Thane admitted. "Still, it wouldn't void my birthright."

"It doesn't matter," a familiar voice called from behind Grimm.

The crowd of Son See'ers on the dock moved out of the way, revealing the crimson knight standing among them.

"You!" Thane exclaimed. "We did as you asked! Why are you here?"

The mysterious, invulnerable warrior tsked at him. "You failed your mission, that's why. Zann-Xia-Czul sent you to collect Princess Lydia and—"

"We did everything right, and it's all done! My parents paid the price with their lives!"

The crimson knight shrugged and drew a rusty blade from his waist. Grinning, he pointed at some Son See'ers and motioned toward Thane's vessel. "Search the ships. Kill anyone who resists. You know what you're looking for."

"Ruik Czharr! What the shulkkaal is this?" Thane exclaimed, stepping sideways to block the guards.

"The Tears of Asura," the knight said. "You tried to deceive me, didn't you?"

"I gave you the stones. The small satchel!"

"You provided me with fakes. Ether von Stonewall had the real ones—I could sense their power," the knight said. "You switched them after the wedding somehow. You want their powers for yourself!" He shoved Thane out of the way, into the knee-deep water alongside the dock. Meanwhile, the guards passed by and entered the ships.

"You've lost your mind," said Thane as he hoisted himself up. Why hadn't the knight recognized the stones were counterfeit right away? It wasn't clear if he was lying or delusional. "I gave you the Tears. It's not my fault if you can't activate them or something. They're real!"

Water dripped from his face and clothes as Thane glared at the knight. Before he could make a move, Grimm charged forward, blade drawn. "Regardless of the issues surrounding your mission, I place you under arrest, Thane Asche!" he declared.

"You haven't the right!" Hrodspire yelled.

"Hrodspire Svekk, I don't expect you to believe anything until the other Elders have enlightened you. But if you side with Thane Asche, then consider yourself arrested as well."

"This is utter zaibuo," Hrodspire spat out. "Of course, I choose my rightful king."

"So, Thane or me?" Grimm asked.

"Thane Asche!" the Elder said. "The true Throatian king!"

Grimm frowned. "So be it. Take them both."

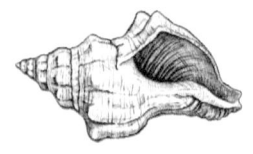

THAT EVENING, THANE AND HRODSPIRE SHARED AN isolated cell, separated from the other prisoners. As soon as the guards locked them behind bars, they both collapsed into a deep, defeated slumber, exhausted from the recent battle and events. As the sun rose the next morning, the familiar bells of the Loyalty Circles rang in the distance, awakening Thane and reminding him he was home again.

Hrodspire continued sleeping undisturbed, and Thane stared through the bars of his window at the Temple of White. It stood ominously on the horizon. So much had changed since he last set foot there and partook in worship. He couldn't help wondering why Zann-Xia-Czul had dethroned him.

His knees made a crackling sound as he settled onto the floor to meditate. He prayed for a response to the ongoing events—anything that would satisfy his thirst for reason, to show him why everything had turned out this way. Aside from the strange, massive storm that had freed his ship from the Darians' grasp, Zann-Xia-Czul seemed to have abandoned him. For the first time, the people who Thane relied on were gone, and those who were still alive remained just as secluded from the truth as he was.

Everything had spiraled out of control from the moment the wedding had concluded. They'd murdered Lydia prematurely, both of his parents had fallen to Ether von Stonewall, and the Tears of Asura were supposedly missing.

"How could they have been fake?" Thane whispered to the empty cell across from theirs. Ether von Stonewall had gone to such great lengths to hide the magical stones inside his crystal throne. The drawer hidden among the array of mirrors was a genius idea, too good a design to waste on decoys. No, more likely the satchel he'd grabbed was legitimate—it was the crimson knight's fault for not knowing how to properly use the powers within the gems.

Three weeks passed with Thane and Hrodspire idling in their cells, devoid of answers and uncertain of their eventual release. Hrodspire claimed the dubious honor of being the first Elder in Throatian history to be arrested. As the days crawled by, Thane's face grew a dark, wiry beard that strongly resembled his late father's.

Over his time in solitude, he concluded that Zann-Xia-Czul, regardless of whether he was truly a god, needed to be worshipped as one—he was simply too powerful to have as an enemy. Perhaps Grimm Kathaar had acknowledged that fact, and that was why he had suddenly been appointed king. Thane and Hrodspire had both had their doubts over the past months, and now they were paying the price for their lack of faith.

As the deposed prince meditated, the echoing footsteps of someone approaching their cell reverberated through the corridor. Thane quickly broke from his trance-like state and stood, facing the shadow that slowly crawled along the prison's stone hallway.

"Shivanna Adul." It was Valenti, accompanied by Kaelgeth.

"Wake up, Hrodspire," Thane said as he squatted down to nudge the old man awake.

The two Elders looked behind them to check whether anyone had followed.

"Isola, why am I here?" the prince demanded. "You know I'm the rightful king."

"It's your mother's fault," Valenti said. "Right after you set sail for the Darian Kingdom, Zann-Xia-Czul spoke into the minds of the Elders. He told us that Urith was the one who had murdered Desaii Egon and stolen his war hammer. Aside from Loyalty Circles, murder is a violation of law—you know this."

"It was wrong of my mother to do that. My father and I decried her immensely for her sins."

"We agree with you on that end," Kaelgeth continued, "but the law is clear about this situation. If she were still alive, the punishment is that we would have stripped her title as queen from her name."

Hrodspire quickly approached the cell's bars, getting inches away from the other Elders. "You already know Thane had nothing to do with it. There's no motivation for him to manipulate who'll succeed him once he dies."

Valenti nodded solemnly. "We acknowledge Thane's innocence in the matter, but you realize the law."

"What law?" Thane asked.

"If a Son See'er commits a crime and, for any reason, cannot receive the corresponding punishment, the responsibility is passed on to the next of kin," Kaelgeth explained.

"That law doesn't extend to the royal family," Hrodspire hissed. "And even if it did, the responsibility should have been transferred to Harkbin, not Thane. The discipline can't be re-assigned twice! You can't—"

"We admit there the law is somewhat vague about royalty, but Zann-Xia-Czul already commanded that Grimm Kathaar assume a permanent role as king," Valenti muttered. "We don't like the result either—Thane should be our king as long as he's alive."

"You understand we cannot take this into our

own hands by directly contradicting what our god asks," Kaelgeth added.

"B-but..." Hrodspire was out of words.

"So, if I'm not the king, you're all okay with Grimm Kathaar assuming leadership?" Thane asked. "In some ways, he's worse than my mother was."

Valenti shook her head. "Respectfully, so far, he's upholding our traditions better than we expected. He's outlined a plan to build more Breeding Farms and gather more resources for them as well. Same for the Loyalty Circles."

"I would have done the same!" Thane lied.

"Maybe so, but our hands are tied," Kaelgeth said. "Therefore, the Elders acknowledge Grimm as the rightful king. Do you comply with the consensus, Hrodspire?"

The Elder frowned at Thane. "I... I must uphold the law and Zann-Xia-Czul's words, even though it's wrong. So be it. Grimm Kathaar is our lawful king. But what of Thane? Must he still die to fight the sorceress?"

Valenti sighed in relief and unlocked the cell. "We don't know what's happening with her threat or how the events from abroad affected the overall plan."

"Why was I imprisoned for so long if I committed no crime?" Thane asked.

"Grimm wanted you there for now, so you'd have the chance to settle down," Valenti said. "Officially, you're being tried for contempt of Zann-Xia-Czul. Today, to prove your devotion to him, you're to take part in a Loyalty Circle. Perform three rounds of the Reminder of Suffering, and then we can set you free."

"Though he won't be a prince or king, he'll be a Son See'er Vrai, at the highest rank below Elder or royalty," Kaelgeth said. "Grimm told us he understands your position and doesn't blame you for anything—he just wants the formalities out of the way, so we might refocus our combined efforts against the lingering threat."

If it was still Thane's destiny to sacrifice himself, then fighting to keep his royal title was a meaningless endeavor. He could appease the laws and live on until the sorceress came. Kaelgeth's tip that the trial by Loyalty Circle was merely a formality hinted that whomever they'd pit against him would be an easy victory.

"So, complete three rounds and I'm free? I can do that."

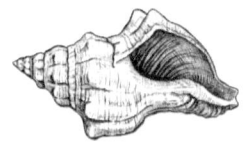

LATER THAT MORNING, THANE AND HRODSPIRE WERE escorted by guards and Elders through the valley to

Loyalty Circle One. This was the oldest of all the sacrificial arenas. Unlike its successors, this monument was a lone, giant pit dug into the center of an open field. Large stone benches ran along the lip of the crater, from which observers could watch the battles. Otherwise, Loyalty Circle One maintained its integrity as originally imagined generations ago. At the bottom of the pit, two Son See'ers would fight to the death. A rope would lower from the top only once a single person remained standing.

"Who chose Loyalty Circle One?" Thane asked Valenti as they approached the stone benches.

"King Kathaar," Valenti replied.

"And who will be my three opponents?"

"We don't know yet," Kaelgeth replied. "Grimm currently prays to Zann-Xia-Czul for guidance on the trial. He'll be here shortly."

"It won't be the foreigner in the crimson armor though, right?"

Valenti asked, "Why does it matter?"

"Never mind… It really doesn't."

While they waited for Grimm to arrive from the Temple of White, Thane gazed down into the pit. To safely reach the bottom, he would need to tuck in his neck and arms and roll as he landed. An assortment of swords, spears, and shields from previous battles lay scattered about in the mud. Many of them were rusty and broken, but they would serve well against whoever he faced.

A few minutes later, the newly crowned Throatian king arrived, dressed in black leather armor and a dark red cape. Grimm appeared stern and focused, ready to obey whatever Zann-Xia-Czul had asked of him.

"Are you the opponent?" Hrodspire blurted.

Grimm offered a faint smile. "That would be quite symbolic, wouldn't it? The past and future of our island, fighting for who'll control everything. But no—we won't be dueling each other today."

"Do we know when they'll arrive?" Thane asked. "I'm eager to settle this and clear my name."

His cousin nodded, though his facial expression remained neutral. "Zann-Xia-Czul just selected your first opponent a little while ago. Son See'ers are retrieving them now. Unless you have any last words, please wait at the bottom of the Loyalty Circle."

"Great," Thane said. "At least I'll have my choice of weapon."

Thane sat on the ground beside the lowest stone bench and slung his legs over the side of the pit. It was quite a distance down, but the muck at the bottom was soft enough to minimize his chances of injury. He confidently shifted himself off the edge and rolled down the soggy crater wall.

Upon landing in the heart of the First Loyalty Circle, he wiped some of the sludge off his clothes. Browsing the collection of relics, he settled on a somewhat rusty sword and a dented metal shield. Examining the blade, he confirmed its sharpness. Satisfied he'd gotten the best choice of the weapons, he sat down on a large boulder and waited for his opponent to arrive.

Several minutes later, two Son See'ers escorted a hooded prisoner to the mouth of the pit and rang a bell to announce the imminent start of the fight. They unbound the person's hands and pushed them over the cliff. The man, still unable to see, tumbled helplessly down to Thane's level. By the time he slammed into the muddy ground at the bottom, the fall had twisted both of his legs in the wrong directions.

Moaning, the prisoner struggled to remove the black hood from his face. When he finally finished, Thane recognized him as the armorer from White Boar's Landing. Although Thane knew he would have to kill him, he couldn't help but allow his curiosity to momentarily take over.

Thane called out, "Shivanna Adul. You're the one who crafted my white armor for me. Were you aware that it would shatter like glass?" He pointed his blade at the man.

"My prince, I apologize. I was aware of it—I had

planned for your armor to break." The armorer pushed his hands into the mud, lifting his chest off the ground and turning his upper body toward Thane. He attempted to stand but yelped in pain as his broken legs refused to carry him.

"Why?" Thane growled. "You clearly wanted me dead, but what had I done to you? I paid you handsomely for your work."

The armorer hung his head. His arms shook in their struggle to hold his weight. "It wasn't I who wished for your death, my prince. It was Desaii Egon. Desaii and his followers discovered I was making you a suit of armor. They forced me to make it fragile, threatening to kill my family otherwise. I apologize, Prince Thane. Zann-Xia-Czul knew I had no choice. Who else but he would have believed me?"

Thane scoffed at the man's accusations. He couldn't be lying—there was no point for the armorer to twist the truth anymore. Being in the Loyalty Circle was a death sentence, but perhaps such an inevitability had prompted him to clear his conscience. Desaii, on the other hand, had pressured Thane to enter the Reminder of Suffering, maybe to increase the chances he'd die. If Zann-Xia-Czul hadn't swept Thane and his family away to the Darian Kingdom, the prince would eventually have worn his white armor inside the Loyalty Circle, fully vulnerable. If Thane had died, Desaii would have been next in line to lead the Throatians, after Harkbin and Urith. Now, Grimm had the role dropped onto him instead.

The blade in Thane's hand shook ever so slightly as he approached the broken man lying on the ground. Desaii ceased to be a concern because Urith had murdered him, but now it appeared his mother had done so with a purpose. Had she known that Desaii, and possibly Grimm, aspired to rise in power by backstabbing their way through their family? The thought that she might have been protecting him all along was overwhelming. He yearned to delve into the past once more to unearth the connections between his mother, Desaii, and the white armor; however, with both of them gone now, nothing could be proven. Only Grimm, closer in blood to Desaii, might know those details.

Thane fixed his gaze on the armorer, who was still trembling at his feet. "You're correct in that few would have believed you," he murmured, "but I forgive you for what you've done."

"Thank you, my prince," the elderly man said. He looked down at his legs. "Please, end this quick. The First Loyalty Circle hasn't been kind to me."

Thane nodded, tightening his grip on the rusty blade. "I'm sorry it has to end this way."

"I as well, but this is a bittersweet means for me

to die. After you sailed to the Darian Kingdom, the guilt of what I'd done tormented me every day afterward. It brings me peace to step aside now, so that you might live on."

The prince bit his lip, then managed a half-smile. "Free yourself from your guilt—you're forgiven, and freed, from all this. Sheiaa Kaaduul."

Thane thrust the blade into the old man's heart. The ceremony ended as the armorer collapsed in the mud. A bell rang from above them, confirming Thane's victory—though he didn't consider it one.

"Sheiaa Kaaduul!" he shouted to the spectators above. "I've proven my worth this round! Who shall be my next opponent?"

The faint outline of Grimm waved at him in a request for patience. Moments passed by in silence, then Hrodspire slid down the muddy incline of Loyalty Circle One. Unlike the armorer, the Elder deftly maneuvered down to the pit's bottom, remaining uninjured.

"Shivanna Adul," he began. "It seems my title no longer grants me exemption from the Loyalty Circles. They have chosen me as your second trial."

Grimm selecting Hrodspire wasn't just a trial of loyalty to their god—it was an illegal political cleansing. In the past, Zann-Xia-Czul wouldn't have tolerated his ulterior motive, so why now? Thane held every advantage against the wrinkled old man if they were truly to fight each other. The underlying purpose must have been to assess the loyalties of both men. It was a simple and obvious conclusion, but he couldn't help but wonder in what other ways the selections of his opponents were being influenced.

"What crime could they have possibly accused you of?" questioned Thane. Hrodspire was innocent; unless Grimm intended on instating a new Elder in the Temple of White, there was no need to slay him.

The old man shrugged. "My outburst earlier was how they justified it. At least this will be another easy victory for you."

"I don't want to do this—especially not to you."

"Who could doubt it?" Hrodspire said. "However, we both know that you must be the one to walk away from all this. I've done enough in my time here—I only hope you'll someday reclaim your rightful place as king and correct the errors in our island's ways. Your soul is awake now, though the others remain asleep. Awaken them, Thane. Today isn't your day to die—it's only your time to suffer."

"I promise I won't let your sacrifice be in vain... King or not, I'll set things right."

The elderly man smiled and lifted his chin. His jaw trembled slightly, perhaps because of his advanced age or the realization that he had finally reached life's end, attaining freedom from Zann-Xia-Czul's grasp.

"Since you were a child," he said, "I've taught you everything I know. You've experienced all there is to know about suffering and death, but more importantly, you've also learned the value of a life. Shivanna Adul, my king. None of my efforts with you were in vain."

With tears streaming down his face, Thane charged forward and impaled the man who had been like a second father to him. Hrodspire gasped in his last moment, then dropped to the ground, bleeding. Thane's fingers gripped the blade as he pulled it back toward himself. Only Zann-Xia-Czul could be cruel enough to orchestrate all this. When the bell above them rang, Thane closed his eyes to avoid gazing upon the body of the great man he had just slain.

Undoubtedly, the crimson knight would be next in line to face Thane—two mock challenges, foes who never posed a true threat, made little sense unless they intended to surprise him in the third trial. Zann-Xia-Czul had lost all use and regard for him—Grimm Kathaar was proof of that. Thane was disposable now, regardless of his loyalty. His death would serve as an example to the other Son See'ers, and that would be his ultimate purpose.

He took a deep breath and cast his eyes over the bodies of Hrodspire and the armorer. The two of them, unfortunately, were just instruments—their god had used and discarded them once they were no longer useful. Thane was the same, a means to retrieve the Tears of Asura and kill Princess Lydia. Now that he'd fulfilled his tasks, his time had also come.

A full ten minutes passed before Grimm announced the arrival of the final challenger. A bell rang from observation benches above and Cereene rolled down the cliff, screaming hysterically. Caught unprepared by the fall, she slid to the bottom, her body covered in cuts and smeared with mud.

"She's a Son See'er Vrai!" Thane yelled to the top of the pit. "She's exempt from the Loyalty Circles!" There wasn't anything she could have done that would have called her loyalty into question—Cereene was certainly innocent.

"This is his chosen one," replied the new Throatian king. "I'm sorry, but the commands of Zann-Xia-Czul overrule the laws."

Slowly, Cereene pushed herself off the ground. She appeared frailer than the last time Thane had met her, in the icy land where the crimson knight had teleported them. He wondered what had happened to her since the last time they'd met.

"Thane," she said, and her voice broke. "I tried to find a way to save you from this, but I couldn't do it. I'm so sorry."

Abandoning his sword in the mud, he ran over to her. They had first met in a Loyalty Circle. He'd refused to kill her then, and he would do it all over again.

"You have nothing to apologize for, Cereene," Thane said, enveloping her in his embrace. "It's me who should say sorry. It's because of me they keep using you."

"Is this the last time we'll meet?"

"I-I don't know. But I hope not." Thane held her tightly. If Zann-Xia-Czul were so cruel as to make them kill each other, then he'd have to kill them both.

Tears cascaded down her pale cheeks. "Thane. Do you remember what I said about the future?"

"What?"

"The future. None of us can stop what's meant to be and what's coming," Cereene repeated. "Life and death are natural states. We have only what we can control. It's a sacrifice by definition. It's about giving up something that you'd rather keep. We mustn't forget that suffering is inevitable in life, as it is death. Sheiaa Kaaduul."

"No," Thane said. "I'm done with sacrificing. All I do is give myself up and hurt others for nothing— I'm so tired of it. If this means throwing away my loyalty to Zann-Xia-Czul, then so be it. We need to live for ourselves."

"You already know why we can't do that," she whispered. "You must do this if you're going to move forward."

"I don't have to do anything, and even if I did, I'd still refuse it," Thane yelled. "They can't kill me so long as they need me to fight the sorceress."

"You know the truth. As long as I breathe, they can wield me as a means to control you."

He scowled. "I-I know—it's because I love you."

"I love you too," Cereene said. "But we're in a Loyalty Circle. Only one of us, the person most loyal to Zann-Xia-Czul, can leave today. You need to be the one who goes."

"I can't do this…"

"Just finish it, Thane. You have to move on. I don't think I can do this myself… And even if I could, it doesn't prove that you're loyal."

"Cereene, I won't hurt you!" He knelt in the mud. "I-I need to pray."

Thane closed his eyes and meditated. He breathed and silently pleaded for a way out of the situation, but Zann-Xia-Czul wouldn't reply to his calls.

"Thane!" Cereene cried. Thane opened his eyes.

The crimson knight was standing next to her.

"Let her go!" the former prince yelled, grabbing the nearest weapon, a spear.

The clouds overhead darkened to a brooding

gray, as tendrils of fog descended from the sky, dense yet intangible. Clusters of white filled the pit's depths, piling up to the top and blocking the view. No longer able to see Grimm or the Elders back up at the surface, it was clear the sudden change in weather was being orchestrated.

"It's your lucky day, Thane Asche," the crimson knight said, wrapping his arm around Cereene's neck and holding her close. "I just finished proposing a deal to your god, and he accepted. We'll give you another way to prove yourself and leave your woman unharmed. Interested?"

The knight, in collusion with Zann-Xia-Czul, had orchestrated this scenario from the beginning. Everyone knew Cereene was his weak point. As long as they had her, he'd have to do whatever they asked.

"You searched my ship, hoping I'd stolen the Tears of Asura for myself," Thane said, twirling his new spear. "But the jewels I gave you were real. I know they were. Don't send me out looking for them again—I don't know where they are."

The knight's brow furrowed. "Lucky for you, Zann-Xia-Czul believes you aren't trying to deceive us. Still, the fact remains that the stones you brought back failed to work. But that's not why I'm here. I want you to—"

"Stop controlling me. You manipulate me at every turn, forcing me to—"

"No, Thane," the crimson knight said. "This whole time, you've been making your own choices. We've always given you the options, but you've always been the one deciding which to choose. You've been a good Son See'er, Thane. Despite your occasional lack of faith, you've obeyed Zann-Xia-Czul well. You can't blame us for the outcomes of your own decisions."

"Let Cereene go," Thane pleaded. "She's got nothing to do with this."

Rain descended from the sky, its drops gentler than the needle-like onslaught he had witnessed at sea. Part of him knew that Zann-Xia-Czul had designed every aspect of what he was experiencing. The rain was a warning of the black storm still to come.

"We both know that's not true," the knight replied. "A Son See'er always needs their hope for a better life. Otherwise, why else would they remain motivated to keep going? Breeding Farms and Loyalty Circles run on the smallest slivers of wishes and possibilities. Remove their hope, and the whole system falls apart."

"It… it's not right—none of it is! Let her go!"

The crimson knight smirked. "As if you have the power to command me. Now, are you going to listen to my deal, or not?"

Beads of sweat trickled down Thane's fingers,

dampening the wooden handle of his weapon. Cereene was correct: for whatever reason, they needed Thane alive to fight the sorceress. Using that to his advantage was the only way out.

"I'm done with this." He threw his spear into the ground, for it was too long for what he wanted to do. He glanced at all the other weapons lying scattered about in the mud. "I don't want to be a Son See'er anymore. Let Cereene and I leave this island— we'll go peacefully."

His gaze settled on a rusty short sword embedded in the muck. It would suffice.

"It's funny that you mention exiling yourselves," the knight said. "That's part of the deal. Zann-Xia-Czul and I want—"

Thane dove toward the ground, grabbed the dirty blade, then held its tip against his chest—right above his heart.

"No more deals!" he thundered. "Without me, you stand no chance against the sorceress!"

The knight threw Cereene down, abandoning her to the mud. "Stay there," he told her, then looked back up at Thane and smiled. "Here's the truth: of the two of you, only Lydia was special. Your blood is as ordinary as any other person's. If you kill yourself now, that's fine. I've no objections—we don't need you."

"Liar!" Thane moved the sword to his neck.

"Do it then," the knight said. "We knew there was only one way you'd sacrifice Lydia. You would only find the courage to kill her if you were willing to die for the cause yourself. The princess could wield the Tears' magic—that's why I wanted her dead. That was the point of everything. She had the ability. You don't."

As the words sank in, Thane's blade quivered, slicing into his flesh. From the beginning, he'd questioned how his blood was special, but it seemed his suspicions may have been right all along. From being spared at the top of Mount Sephorr to now, every step of the way, Zann-Xia-Czul had kept him alive—but why? If Thane's blood was normal, was he only alive so that he could kill Lydia? No, there had to be something else, some other reason.

"You, along with Zann-Xia-Czul, wanted the magic and eliminated anyone else with the ability to harness the stones. That much is clear," Thane said, lowering the blade. "You forced my father into arranging the wedding for that purpose. But is there even a sorceress? Or is that all a lie too?"

The knight strolled over to the spear Thane had previously abandoned and picked it up. He examined it casually, then beamed at Thane. "I'd say this weapon is over three hundred years old, by the looks of it. It's interesting that it's survived this long without degrading."

"Answer me!"

"The sorceress is indeed real, and as I vowed, I shall fight her in battle once we cross paths again," the knight affirmed. "None of that was a lie. Everything we've done so far is for that purpose. You just never had all the facts."

He threw the spear at Thane, nearly impaling him. The prince sidestepped the attack and pointed his blade back at the crazed foe in front of him.

The knight smiled. "So, you were bluffing about killing yourself. I knew you wanted to continue living. But unless you or Cereene commit to the opposite, the two of you are going to stay here until one of you dies. That's how your Loyalty Circles work, after all."

"Shut up!"

"My deal is the only way out of this situation that will leave you both alive. Don't forget, the point of being here is to prove yourself. Shouldn't you hear the third option?"

"Fine," Thane said, squeezing the handle of his blade so hard his knuckles turned white. He couldn't kill his foe, but it made him feel better to have something to hold. "What do you want?"

"Prove your loyalty by assassinating the sorceress. Do that, and we'll let you and Cereene leave the island. Permanently. No catch," the knight explained. "Under certain conditions, the sorceress and I can sense each other—I'll know when she's defeated."

"Don't do it, Thane!" Cereene yelled. "It can't be that simple."

Thane narrowed his eyes at the knight. "Suppose I agree... How am I supposed to kill her? As you said, my blood isn't magical, and she possesses tons of power, correct?"

"Both are true, but we possess the element of surprise," the knight said. "I'll teleport you right behind her. One quick thrust, and your job is done. The sorceress is vulnerable to a blade, unlike me."

"If it's so easy to kill her, why don't you do it yourself? Also, how do I return here afterward?"

The knight smirked. "I'm not the one who needs to prove my loyalty to Zann-Xia-Czul. By doing this, you'll become a hero among your people, and the two of you can live happily ever after." He pointed at Cereene.

The whole affair was suspicious. Defeating the sorceress could not be such a trivial task, but if Zann-Xia-Czul and the knight had truly wanted him dead, they'd have killed him already. Unless their only purpose was to torture him, perhaps there was a glimmer of truth to the knight's words. Still, he couldn't comprehend why a knight so powerful would insist Thane do his dirty work.

"Do we have any better weapons than what's here?"

"No, Thane!" Cereene pleaded. "This has to be a trap! You can't kill her on your own! Don't agree to this."

"I have to obey Zann-Xia-Czul one last time. I'm sorry," Thane said. "It's the only way we'll free ourselves from all this pain."

The knight disappeared through one of his invisible portals. Before Thane could react, he felt a knife against his neck. The knight had suddenly reappeared behind him.

"You'll murder the sorceress just like this. You'll slit her throat—just like how your father died." He lowered his weapon and offered the red-jeweled knife to him. Thane instantly recognized it as Harkbin's.

As he cautiously took the blade, Thane considered the implications of the deal one last time. "So, once I kill the sorceress, you'll let Cereene and me go. We'll start new lives elsewhere. Do you and Zann-Xia-Czul agree with these terms?"

"Don't do it!" Cereene screamed. "It has to be a trap—you're going to die! They're toying with you!"

Thane lowered his head and stared back at her. "This won't be the last time we meet. I promise."

The knight smiled and motioned toward the

invisible portal. "The deal is finalized. Step forward whenever you're ready to save your kingdom, Thane Asche."

SOMNIUS

Thane's limbs trembled as he stepped through the invisible portal. This time, it seemed the knight had teleported him to a quaint clothing shop. Dresses in every hue and style covered the walls from the floor to the ceiling. Many boasted floral patterns, while others had bold colors accented with gold sequins. Thane gaped at the number of brightly colored textile variations, confused.

Perhaps the crimson knight had made a mistake. There was no sign of the sorceress. This couldn't be the right location. He needed to figure out why he was here, of all places. He tiptoed toward a set of windows and opened them.

Peering outside into the city, Thane recognized Serenity Keep resting off in the distance. He was back in Last Hope. There was a high likelihood that if anyone identified him, he would be arrested and executed on the spot. Last Hope was the worst place he could be right now. Ether von Stonewall was likely still on his way home from the battle, but news of Lydia and the incident at sea had probably already reached this far by birds. Thane quickly closed the window again and rummaged through the nearby cupboards, searching for some clothing he could use to hide his identity, but it was all dresses.

Shuffling through the drawers and shelves, he only found large, uncut sheets of fabric and threads. He chose a shiny black silk and used Harkbin's blade to try cutting himself a suitably sized garment that would cover every part of his face below the eyes. It ripped instead of dividing evenly, and he spread the sheet along the table's surface to start over. Before he could make any more progress, however, a creak sounded from the room's rear.

Thane froze as a young, blonde woman entered the boutique—presumably its owner. She donned a sleeveless white dress, covered in intricate laces on the front. Her attire, like the other items in the shop, was likely very difficult and time-consuming to make.

Appearing unfazed by his intrusion and the disarray he had caused on her table, she fixed her blue eyes on him before giving a single, solemn nod.

He could sense something powerfully unnatural about her, reclusive and magical—a feeling he hadn't felt since ascending Mount Sephorr and standing outside of Zann-Xia-Czul's cave. She was, without doubt, the sorceress, and it was his destiny to kill her.

But something was wrong.

"I cannot say welcome to you, Thane Asche, for we both know you've received no invitation to come here," she said in Common Tongue.

Her voice was dominant and full of authority, causing him to drop his blade. His eyes widened as he gawked at her, his hand trembling, causing Harkbin's knife to clang against the table.

"Whatever your reasons for coming," the sorceress continued, "the fact that you've arrived is an ominous sign of what's still to come. This reveals that Bios Auras has already made his next move."

Thane retrieved the blade and pointed it at her, conceding he'd lost the element of surprise. Something about her was unnerving. She seemed familiar, like they'd met before... but no, it must have been her magic at work. He knew he stood no chance of defeating her. Still, he wouldn't go down without a fight.

"You may set down your father's knife. We both know you don't want to use it," she said, "nor can such a weapon defeat me."

Cereene was right; everything was a trap.

"Just get it over with," Thane said. "We're both aware I can't do what they've sent me to."

"By delivering you here, Zann-Xia-Czul committed to discarding you, while Bios Auras only wanted to exploit you one last time," the sorceress declared. "Despite their plans for us, you don't need to die here today, Thane."

"What?"

"The only reason they sent you was to show me they know where I'm hiding. Now, they expect me to kill you and start running again. But it doesn't have to happen that way." Her eyes flicked to his knife, then back up to his face. "Do you like tea?"

"What? Tea?" Thane stammered. "I don't understand. What's happening here?"

It had to be a trick. Maybe she wanted to poison him instead of wasting her magic. The eerie calm that enveloped her made the back of his neck prickle, as though with a wave of her hand she could cast a spell and obliterate him without a second thought. He still couldn't shake the feeling that he'd seen her somewhere before. Something about their conversation seemed odd, almost like the times he'd encountered the knight in crimson armor.

She gave him a light smile. "We needn't be enemies, Thane Asche. Let's share a drink, and I'll explain why. For the moment, we're safe here."

For now, hearing her out was the only way to stay alive.

"Um… okay."

"I knew you wouldn't resist such an offering," the sorceress said.

She led him to the front of her store—a delicate tearoom brimming with so many pink blossoms it could have been mistaken for a flower shop. She told him to take a seat at the smallest of the tables as she moved behind the counter to prepare their drinks. A pot of water sat, already boiling, on her stove. Above it, shelves on the wall were covered with jars filled with various leaves. The sorceress selected one of them, then changed her mind and put it back. She skimmed her massive collection until choosing another, smaller container. Her latest choice was almost empty of its emerald-green leaves.

"I hope a smoky blend is okay for you," the sorceress said. "This is from a farm in the Tornaa area of the Silent Deserts. Producing the tea is a very delicate process, you know. There's a serious chance the entire basket will catch fire and disintegrate while it's absorbing the smoke, with all that black sand."

Tornaa: the place the crimson knight had tele-ported him the first time—it was the only place he'd seen with sand so dark and hot. They had to be the same location. Despite his curiosity for more details, he kept his silence as she poured water into a white ceramic teapot. Delicately pinching the leaves from the tiny, almost empty jar, she placed some of them inside. While the tea steeped, she laid out their teacups, some napkins, a bowl of sugar, and silver spoons on a wooden tray. Satisfied with the arrangement, she positioned the kettle at the center of the tray and carried everything over to him.

"Give it five minutes," she said, sitting down across from him.

"I know I've encountered you before," Thane said. "But where?"

"We've met, though it was brief," the sorceress replied. "I wouldn't expect you to remember me. I was hiding in plain sight, after all."

He looked over at her face again. Her skin was pale as the Temple of White, with wavy long hair intricately woven in braids. She was familiar, yet still a stranger. He couldn't think of a name that paired with her face, either. The woman seemed to be in her mid-thirties and spoke as if she were well-educated.

"Perhaps you were at the wedding?" Thane said. "Or were you a Darian Council member? I can't remember."

"You saw me as the tailor. It was the only way for me to assist Lydia while remaining hidden. There's your proof that I have no intention of killing you."

She was indeed the woman who'd first appeared when they'd practiced the Dance of the Sun and Moon. The times he'd encountered her were so brief and so vague, but apparently, they were significant. Why, then, had the sorceress been helping the princess instead of murdering her?

"We've met twice already," Thane said. "However, if you were with Lydia, why didn't you kill me?"

"More than twice, but I wouldn't expect you to know the rest of them," she replied. "More importantly, the princess told me everything she knew about your character."

"What? She talked to you about me? But we barely knew each other. What could she possibly have told you?"

"Plenty. That's why I didn't kill you when you turned up in my shop." The sorceress knew of her advantage over him—that Thane had traveled through the portal directly into what was probably her home. It was strange for a sorceress to live in a clothing and tea shop, but perhaps not everything was as it appeared. Hiding in plain sight and concealing her true powers was her strategy. The real question was why she would set herself up in Last Hope and involve herself with the Darian princess's affairs.

"But I thought Lydia's blood had enough magic to defeat you. Why did you help her instead?"

With a smirk, the sorceress poured tea into their cups. Though the leaves had been green, the liquid now before them was reddish-brown. Carefully, she set the teapot back onto the table and slid a cup over to him. Fingers trembling, he gripped the hot drink but restrained himself from taking a sip.

"Zann-Xia-Czul wove a simple lie from a complicated truth," the sorceress said. "Using that lie, he and Bios Auras manipulated your family into bringing them the God Stones. You've realized this by now, right?"

Thane stared at his steaming cup. "I knew all along something was wrong on our island, but I couldn't understand what. So, you had no plans to attack my homeland?"

"Your people have their complications, but I had no intention of directly interfering. I planned on arriving someday, but only to fight Zann-Xia-Czul and Bios Auras—they are the greatest issue. The three of us remain at war, and I am at a disadvantage."

She appeared to know about Throatian Loyalty Circles and Breeding Farms, as though she had visited their island before.

"Why would a sorceress risk her life fighting a god?" Thane asked. "As cruel as Zann-Xia-Czul is, he's equally magical."

She nearly choked on her tea. "Haven't you

figured it out yet? Zann-Xia-Czul is a dragon, not a god."

"What?"

She wiped her lips daintily with her gold-embroidered napkin. "He is perhaps the last of his kind, within this realm anyway," she replied. "The others all died at the hands of the Black Moon Tribe, north of the Darian Kingdom in central Yaenia. We'll save that history lesson for another day. What matters is that Zann-Xia-Czul is the last of the dragon slavers. Your people are his servants by design. Like all dragons, he's brilliant and manipulative. He wields powerful magic too."

Thane's jaw hung open, yet no words could spill from it. Could it be that what the Throatians considered their religion was, in fact, a psychological cage that constrained and manipulated their entire way of life? If Zann-Xia-Czul was a dragon, then it was no surprise why he had hidden himself away in the cave of Mount Sephorr. Even without magic, Zann-Xia-Czul could kill everyone. Why did he have to hide? How he had survived as the last dragon was...

Thane could only let out one of the many thoughts racing through his mind. "He has magic, but he can only use it when he's close by..."

"Pardon?"

It had been a mystery why Zann-Xia-Czul ignored Harkbin's prayers, along with everyone else's, after their ship departed the island. Their god's magic was powerful but seemed confined to the areas surrounding Mount Sephorr.

"But how could he be a dragon?" Thane asked.

"Dragons can breathe fire and have some control over the weather," she said, taking another sip of her tea. "They lack vocal cords, so telepathy is a must. It's how they communicate with each other. The more skilled among them can also read minds. The stronger the dragon, the greater the range of its magic; however, none are powerful enough to absorb the thoughts of the entire world. Your religion forbade leaving your island and socializing with foreign nations. That's why your people never learned of this."

Thane was taken aback to learn that there were once other beings like Zann-Xia-Czul. If a single dragon could control and rule a nation, how had the Black Moon Tribe defeated them all?

"Your world is complex with a lot of moving pieces," the sorceress continued. "Dragons are no easy foe, and a steep price was paid to defeat them in the past. Though Zann-Xia-Czul is but one dragon, there'll be a heavy cost to overcome him."

"But among the three, who is the most powerful?" Thane asked. "Zann-Xia-Czul, the crimson armored knight, or you, a sorceress?"

She sighed. "There isn't a straightforward answer

to that question—and please, stop calling me a sorceress."

"What are you then? A witch?"

"I am a goddess."

Thane stared at her. She was joking—she had to be. The woman had an odd demeanor, so perhaps her statement was sarcastic or there was a cultural gap between the two of them. She appeared as human as any other person. Still, nothing since he'd teleported from the Loyalty Circle had gone as expected so far.

"A goddess—that's a bold claim," Thane replied, his eyes narrowing.

"My name is Somnius and I'm a goddess of another world. Asura, your world's one true god, asked me to make everything right again in his place after he died. I don't expect you to believe me or understand all this, but that's my purpose for being here."

He'd never thought the Yaenian god was even real, not to mention somehow deceased. "Asura... died? But how can a god die? It shouldn't be possible, right?"

She shook her head and took a sip of tea as she gathered her thoughts. "When gods of various worlds are in strife, everything becomes complicated, to the point where even I am still learning those details. For now, it matters not to you. My point is, the one whom this world calls Asura is dead, and I am Somnius, the goddess of a neighboring world. I've been among your people for a long time now."

"Somnius?" Thane repeated. "Are you well known? Perhaps you've got a different name? I've never heard of you."

"I'm unknown to all except my enemies," she replied, not affronted by his statement. "The struggle between Bios Auras, Zann-Xia-Czul, and I is but a small part of something greater. Everything depends on stopping them from gathering the God Stones."

Thane remembered the conversation he'd had with Hrodspire as they sailed home from the Darian Kingdom. Back then, Thane had concluded that being a god meant having unmatchable power and existing beyond understanding. Still, he needed to know whether Somnius's claim was true, for Thane knew he'd been deceived too many times already.

"Can you prove you are who you say you are? Zann-Xia-Czul never would do that for me, so I always suspected something was wrong."

"Yes, I will," Somnius said. "Once we're done with our tea."

Her promise wasn't proof, but it was more than what his former god had ever offered him.

"So, the crimson knight, Bios Auras—what happens if he collects all the Tears of Asura?"

"He will possess the full powers of a god and aid Zann-Xia-Czul in reopening the gate to his world—the Dragon World. Trapped here, the false god of your homeland remains isolated from his allies. It's all thanks to Asura's sacrifice. But Bios Auras can undo all of it. I can't allow that to happen."

"A gate to another world…" Thane said. Like the ancient stone archway under the Temple of White that even the Elders could never figure out how to use. "You mean a World Vein gateway, right? But we can't use the gateway because—"

"They only let you travel within this world?" she finished. He hadn't known that, but it was too fascinating to interrupt her. "Yes, that's how they are now, rare and finite. Asura's sacrifice limited them in that respect. Nothing else can physically come or leave your realm, including me. Coincidentally, my powers here are limited because I'm a goddess of a different world."

"This is a lot to take in... but how does Lydia fit into all of this? Why did you allow me—or rather, the crimson knight—to kill her?"

"Whenever someone uses a stone, both Bios Auras and I can sense its general location. Bios Auras already has the one he stole from me—the Teleportation Stone. Like Bios Auras, Lydia could wield the God Stones."

If Lydia could wield the magic, then just how

different were they from each other? Was it a God Stone that allowed Bios Auras to stay invulnerable, even when stabbing himself with a sword?

Before Thane could ask that question, Somnius replied to his first. "When the princess initially discovered the God Stones, Bios Auras and I both sensed they were in Last Hope. Such began Zann-Xia-Czul's plot to use your family to find them."

"But how did you know it was Lydia who used them?" Thane asked. "It could have been Bios Auras. Or better yet, how did you know Ether von Stonewall had them in the first place?"

"For generations, Bios Auras and I raced in our search for them," Somnius said. "I had some pieces of the puzzle, many of which were unconfirmed rumors. Nothing was clear until we sensed the stones' activation in Last Hope."

Thane gazed at his tea. All along, he'd known his family was being used as tools to bring Zann-Xia-Czul more magic, but the implications of their role only dawned on him now. He hadn't even considered Zann-Xia-Czul's long-term plans or what else he could do with that power beyond protecting their island. The Tears of Asura were a source of great magic, not merely limited to war. With Zann-Xia-Czul and Bios Auras working together all along, they made formidable opponents. Meanwhile, the Darian king had everything they wanted; it was likely that unlimited power and the ability to wield the Tears ran through the royal bloodline.

"It strikes me as odd that Ether von Stonewall didn't use the Tears of Asura himself," Thane said. "If both Lydia and Ether had the ability, how did they not succumb to corruption? Couldn't they have conquered the world?"

"I don't have solid proof of this, but in the previous war, evidence hinted that Princess Zelia of the Lucidian Enclave entrusted Ether von Stonewall with protecting the God Stones," Somnius said. "Ether's mission was to hide them. He's unable to use their power, so when they activated, it was clear someone else close to him must have done it."

What Somnius said contradicted history. The Lucidians were at war with the von Stonewall family. Why would the Lucidian Princess have given their enemy such a powerful weapon? There had to be a treason involved, if not a misunderstanding. Regardless of the reason, it made sense that anyone hungry for power would want the God Stones.

"So, Zann-Xia-Czul was uncertain whether Lydia or Ether could wield the magic," Thane concluded, "but by having my family bring her to him, he could confirm. If it turned out she couldn't use the stones, she'd still serve as a hostage that would force Ether to trade whoever actually had the ability."

"Exactly. When the princess used the Transformation Stone on her handmaiden in the forest, I had already moved to Last Hope and sensed the stone's activation once more. From there, the tale of Kaine Khalia and the monster spread. This revealed to me that Lydia was the one who used the God Stones."

Thane was unaware of the handmaiden's involvement in the story, but the timing aligned with what he already knew from before the wedding. Somnius was correct: the world had so many moving pieces and complications, yet the goddess had mingled among the secret chaos all along.

"I understand now. You approached the princess by posing as her wedding dress tailor," Thane said. "That's why she didn't recognize you as one of her servants when we were practicing the Dance of the Sun and Moon."

"I instructed her to use the Memories Stone on me. It was a risk I had to take, especially since Bios Auras might have already figured out Lydia was the one who had used the magic in the forest. Letting her read and experience my memories helped her trust me and understand my cause. From there, she read your family's minds at the rehearsal dinner. This revealed Zann-Xia-Czul's assignment for your family. It also showed us that Bios Auras had met you at Starlight Beach. I pieced everything else together from there."

"The first time I met the crimson knight—Bios

Auras—he knew he wanted me to murder someone at a moment's notice, someone close to the von Stonewall family. He just wasn't sure who it would be yet," Thane said. "But sometime later, probably from the story of Kaine Khalia, he figured out it was Lydia and had me kill her right after the wedding."

"You're correct, and Bios Auras cannot kill or harm anyone directly due to a safeguard built into the God Stones," Somnius said. "The magic won't activate for someone with a long trail of sins behind them. He desires the power, but his nature renders him ineligible. That's why he went to such lengths to force you to murder Lydia instead of doing it himself. It's a fatal loophole in the design of the God Stones."

Thane noticed the steam had stopped flowing upward from his teacup. It now seemed clear that Somnius didn't intend to kill him. She would likely make a request of him later—yet he couldn't shake off the feeling that something was off, preventing him from trusting the tea she'd given him.

"But what made Lydia special?" Thane asked. "And why didn't you save her? Couldn't you have used the Tears of Asura? With them, you'd be able to turn the tides against Zann-Xia-Czul and Bios Auras instead."

"To answer your first question, I don't yet understand why they activate only for some people,"

Somnius said. "Yes, it involves blood, but there's another factor that remains unclear to me. As for Lydia's death, we both agreed beforehand that her sacrifice was necessary to keep the God Stones hidden from Bios Auras."

Thane remembered Lydia's speech at the wedding, and how she'd urged that they do what was best for the common people, no matter the cost. The princess also implied destiny would weave their kingdoms together for an eternity. The proclamation made more sense now that Thane knew Lydia had intended to sacrifice herself by that point. But why had she done it so willingly, without even a protest or a fight?

"Lydia and I needed to let Bios Auras and Zann-Xia-Czul think they'd won," Somnius continued. "What happened with your family and Lydia was extreme, and Bios Auras will suspect he's unable to use his newly gained stones because of his sins. Plus, he'll still be able to use the legitimate Teleportation Stone he already had—this will keep him busy. He'll eventually understand that the stones he took from you are fakes, but for now, I just need more time. I'm… saddened that Lydia paid the price for it, but also thankful."

"There's one problem, Somnius," Thane said. "Bios Auras has already realized that the God Stones I brought him are not real. Were you aware?"

"He accused you of bringing him fake stones," the goddess corrected. "He doesn't know for certain yet, and that's our advantage. I've hidden my involvement in this, for if I had revealed myself earlier, it would have confirmed the truth to him."

"So, the only reason Lydia died was to keep Bios Auras from knowing whether the stones he got from me were legitimate?" Thane asked. "And there's no way for him to verify the truth because he might have accidentally activated the safeguard that will prevent him from using the magic. That's it?"

"Bios Auras's suspicion doesn't diminish Lydia's sacrifice," Somnius replied. "He made you murder Lydia, and because I didn't step in and save her—as normally I would have—he doesn't know whether I had influence in this. The relationship we share has always been... complicated. We both need to secure the God Stones, all while avoiding each other. His sending you here was a warning for me to stay away."

"Stay away from what?" Thane asked. "My homeland?"

"From the God Stones. Kaine Khalia must have already informed Ether von Stonewall about your theft of the counterfeit stones. Lydia and I gave Kaine the information he needed to know, and he passed it along to the king," Somnius said. "In public, Ether von Stonewall will have to play along and pretend your family succeeded. In reality, the God Stones will remain hidden in his care."

"So, the objective of all these actions was to delay your unavoidable confrontation with Zann-Xia-Czul and Bios Auras?"

"Yes."

There had to be more reasons for it. What else was Somnius not saying?

"But the actual stones are probably back in the crystal throne. You know where they are—so why don't you use them?"

"If I use them, I'll…" she faltered, brushing her hair back. "Touching them scares me, honestly. I'm a goddess, and the Tears of Asura are his essence. If I were to use them, I might become something worse than Bios Auras. I can't let that happen."

"I understand your fear, but I don't follow what you're saying," Thane said. "I still don't understand how a god can die."

"It's complicated to explain, but he did it to save this world—his world. Bios Auras is the only person who can undo his sacrifice. It's my mission to ensure that it doesn't happen. Will you help me, Thane?"

"What could I possibly do?" Thane asked. "The past few months only showed me how incapable I really am. My blood isn't magical at all, is it?"

"Royal, yes, however, not magical. One day, the light will reclaim its rightful place on your island, overturning the darkness that plagues it. That light is within your heart, Thane—your people will need you for it someday."

Her words were inspiring, yet the reality surrounding their island was far more intricate than he'd ever suspected. His family, and all the Son See'ers, were pawns in a war between magical beings.

"Even if that's true, what role can I serve?" Thane said. "I can't fight Bios Auras, and unless I know how the Black Moon Tribe defeated the other dragons, Zann-Xia-Czul won't die either."

"You're right—you cannot confront them directly," Somnius said. "Still, you'll have a part to play in gathering the means of their defeat."

"I'll help you, but can you save Cereene?" Thane asked. "She's in danger. The crimson knight loves making deals. Is there anything we could trade for her?"

"You've already seen the consequences of bargaining with him," Somnius replied. "Short of something that will put him closer to getting the God Stones, we have nothing he'd desire."

"Is there nothing we can do?"

"Unfortunately, we won't be able to learn Cereene's fate for years to come," Somnius said. "Unlike Bios Auras, I cannot teleport throughout the world. Otherwise, I'd have already rescued her for you. Until we're ready for the last battle, we cannot sail to your island. But when the time is right, I will help you save her if the opportunity arises."

Somnius was right; without magical means to free Cereene from the grasp of Bios Auras and Zann-Xia-Czul, the task was infeasible. Yet Thane still felt there must be a way. The two of them would just have to find it.

"By the way," Somnius added. "You wanted proof that I am truly a goddess, not a false deity like Zann-Xia-Czul. To that end, I'll provide you with that, along with a gift. Please rise."

The chair screeched against the floor as he shifted it back from the table and rose.

"Just a few feet away from there is fine," Somnius instructed. "Now, stay still."

After setting down her tea, she held her palm out toward Thane's chest, almost as if to push him away. For a moment, he thought she was about to cast a spell on him, but before his fears could fully materialize, a calming warmth engulfed his body. He remembered a time long ago when he was a child. A simpler age, when he could meditate on the sands near White Boar's Landing, and the sun's purity had vanquished every hint of cold inside him. Now, his body glowed brighter than the Temple of White's polished stone walls. The sunlight consumed him, then disappeared as quickly as it had appeared.

However, a faint glow of jade remained behind, and he sensed hope from within it.

"White armor cannot protect you from a black storm," Somnius said. "I learned of your situation from Princess Lydia. So, this is my gift to you, Thane Asche. Though white armor cannot protect you from a black storm, armor of light will help you defeat the darkness."

He looked down at himself, now clad in material so magnificent it put his former white suit to shame. Somnius's gift consisted of ebony metal, except for the glowing jade trim that bordered every edge of the suit. The green lights mesmerized him; he knew of no substance, material, or paint capable of emitting such a glow. Surely, magic was embedded within it all.

"What you have now is the same protection my holy knights once wore," Somnius explained. "Do not be alarmed by what comes next."

She held her hand out once more, and another burst of light overtook him. This time, she created a helmet. A transparent visor left his vision unhindered as he ran his fingers along the helmet's smooth surfaces.

Before he could finish admiring it, a bright golden spear ejected from Somnius's hand directly at him. There was no time to react—the spear shot directly into his chest, rocketing Thane into the tea shop's wall. Framed works of art fell from the wall where he collapsed, bashing against his head, and debris from a nearby shelf piled atop him. He should have been dead, or at least knocked unconscious with several broken bones. However, though he'd felt the impact of the spear, it hardly seemed to hurt, and the armor's surface was undamaged.

"See? There's nothing to worry about," Somnius said. "The armor is legitimate. It's yours now, regardless of whether you choose to help me."

It was better than legitimate. There was no armor in the world that could have better protected him from the impact of the magical light spear and subsequent crash into the wall. Thane brushed the debris off himself and approached the goddess, unscathed.

"Thank you for this. I will proudly wear this armor in your service. But what should we do now?"

She motioned for him to take his seat again and returned to her place at the table. She took another drink of her tea before responding.

"We shall journey together to the land where the Black Moon Tribe resides. There, I'll resume living in the shadows until the proper time. As for you, you'll journey even farther to meet those who can speak like the dragons."

The idea of a person communicating solely through their thoughts was both intriguing and somewhat terrifying. How could a human learn to do such things? Were the people Somnius referred to Lucidians?

"Wait a minute," Thane said. "Why are you going back into hiding? Isn't there more you need to do?"

She lowered her arm beneath the table and rested her hand on her stomach. "My powers are limited for now. There is a prophecy of one who will defeat Zann-Xia-Czul and Bios Auras once and for all. We need only prepare for it."

"A prophecy?"

"When my child is born, he will fulfill the destiny foretold by Asura. For now, until he comes of age, we must prepare ourselves for the war that's yet to come—a greater conflict that will follow the current one. That's the reason I cannot act now—I need more time."

Thane took hold of his teacup and raised it from the table. Even through the armor, his hands could still feel its warmth. Gently, he took a sip, and it instantly filled his sinuses with the smoky scent Somnius had referenced. If he'd only drunk the tea earlier, it would have put him at ease.

He gazed down at the goddess's stomach, his curiosity unabated, and realized he had an endless number of questions he could ask her. There would be time to learn more details about the mission entrusted to Somnius. For now, though, helping her finish what Princess Lydia had started mattered more.

"There's still so much I don't understand, but I pledge myself to you and your mission. We can't let Zann-Xia-Czul and Bios Auras roam freely anymore."

"You have my deepest gratitude, Thane Asche," she said. "Whatever I may ask of you in the future will be for a greater light—I promise. You'll no longer feel the gravity of obedience."

EPILOGUE

"There is still one matter I must attend to before we leave Last Hope behind," Somnius added, her chair scraping softly against the floor as she rose suddenly.

Thane's eyes shot up in surprise. "Do you have other business here?" he asked.

Why were they leaving so early? He followed her across the room, watching her graceful fingers pluck small canisters from the shelves. Each container appeared ancient, some decorated with symbols, others weathered by time. The scent of dried herbs wafted in the air as she gently tucked them into a satchel. It wasn't clear why she needed them, but it seemed she knew something about them he didn't.

"I must visit Serenity Keep one last time to run an errand," Somnius said. "I didn't expect you to arrive in my home today, but as it is, the fact that Bios Auras sent you here means he knows where to find me. He could arrive at any time now. Therefore, we must handle the last of my affairs and leave."

"And he'll likely expect to find my dead body when he arrives," Thane replied with a hint of scorn. His hand formed into a fist at the thought. Maybe Bios Auras, with his arrogant gaze, wouldn't even notice his favorite tool was gone. Still, the shelves he'd knocked over in Somnius's shop would at least lead him to believe there had been a struggle.

The goddess halted, her hands stilling on a canister. She gazed comfortingly at him, though he could not help but sense a secret dread behind her wavering smile. "In our current situation, it's impossible for either of us to know what the future holds. That leaves us with the burden of imagining every possibility, and we simply can't do that."

"You can't know the future? Not even as a goddess?"

"Not even as a goddess," she confirmed.

"It's surprising there are some things even a goddess cannot do," Thane said. "So, what must we do at Serenity Keep?"

"We need our allies for when Bios Auras eventually brings himself out into the open. Kaine Khalia can be one of them. That's my errand. I know you have little reason to fully trust me about everything yet, Thane, after how much you've been used before, but our fates are intertwined. Give it time."

"I can agree with your reasoning so far," Thane said.

"Kaine's loyalty to the von Stonewall family, particularly Xander and Kira, grows stronger," Somnius explained, "but in the future, we will all be on the same side. Strong-willed knights are what we'll need in the darker times yet to come."

When they had spoken briefly at the rehearsal dinner, Kaine seemed excessively formal and tense, especially compared to his companion who'd donned purple armor. To him, Kaine resembled young men who were on the brink of entering the Loyalty Circles to fight for the first time. They were ready, but anxious that they might have missed something important that they were unaware of. Kaine had held such an essence, but perhaps he'd only been nervous about meeting him as a prince. Disregarding their first interaction, Kaine had a long list of brave acts on his shoulder.

"He did save Lydia from the monster, after all. He also came out to sea to retrieve her body. But why recruit him specifically? He's unlikely to ally himself with me, not after what I did. He doesn't even know who you are yet, does he?"

"He still needs time to grow after everything he's experienced," she said, seemingly having read his mind. Thane wondered whether it was one of her abilities, like Zann-Xia-Czul could do to anyone. "Our goal today isn't to recruit him. Today, we'll need only to open his eyes to the greater war happening around him."

Shadows of his thoughts played across his face. Despite the uncertainty eating at him, he held his barrage of questions back as she led him to the shop's entrance. As she opened the door, sunlight flooded the room, enveloping them in a sudden warmth. Light enveloped them, but it also gave Thane apprehension. By now, everyone in the Darian Kingdom would have heard how he'd murdered Princess Lydia. So many people had seen him at the wedding and would know his face, and chances were that anyone could recognize him.

"Do you have a cloak or something I might wear while we go?" he asked. "I need to be careful not to be seen by others, as my new armor is eye-catching." The suit's white surface was nondescript, but the emerald lines accenting its edges pulsed with a bright, green light.

"You're in a tailor's shop, Thane Asche," Somnius said, "and you don't need my permission to take anything you want. It's unlikely that I'll come back to this place.

He returned to the rearmost area of the shop, the spot where Bios Auras had teleported him earlier. By avoiding a duel with Somnius, everything now felt simpler. He rummaged through the racks, his hands brushing against velvets and silks before settling on a coarse, brown cloak. The dark green hood seemed to promise anonymity, and as he draped it over his shoulders, he felt a comforting weight envelop him. The woven material was thick enough to block the shining green light that could probably illuminate an entire room. With the hood over his head, and satisfied nobody would easily recognize him from a distance, he approached the door again.

"Thank you, Somnius, truly, for everything."

"No, Thane. It is you who deserves my thanks… and my apologies."

"For what could you possibly be indebted to me?"

The goddess paused for a moment as if she had reached the end of her line of thought. "I've… previously misjudged you. If I'd left my shortsighted understandings unchallenged, I wouldn't have ever reached the truth. You and Lydia would have both been victims of your wedding."

He searched her thoughtful gaze. Her apology seemed genuine, yet the weight of unspoken words hung between them. Thane sighed, the complexity of their alliance clear from the releasing tension in his shoulders.

She was apologizing for something she hadn't done. Maybe at one point or another, she had considered slaying him. That would have been the most reasonable action to take after everything that his family and the Throatian people had done. She must have understood that Thane was not like his parents, and the sequence of unfortunate events had affected his choices and actions. Chances were that she would always know more about everything than what she would tell him. He would have to accept that she had his best interests in mind whenever she revealed something or otherwise withheld it.

To trust her so blindly was a dangerous path, and it seemed just as risky as growing up in a world that worshipped Zann-Xia-Czul. Still, something about her seemed more real, true, and compelling than the dragon who had posed as their god. She appeared human, though Thane suspected it was only one of her forms. The way she carried herself, the intensity of her gaze, and how her voice wavered between confident and forlorn hinted there was so much more about her. If anyone could defeat Zann-Xia-Czul and help Thane return home, it would be Somnius.

"We can leave the past behind us," he said, "but as for the future, I'm not sure what I want. I mean, we clearly need to stop Zann-Xia-Czul and Bios Auras, and I want to save Cereene. After that, I'm not sure. I want to return home and liberate my people, but I'm not sure they will rebel against their god. Only a handful of people tried to stop Grimm Kathaar from claiming the crown when I was imprisoned. Do you think they can be turned against everything they've been born to believe? Should I try to reclaim my role as king there?"

Somnius closed the door behind them as they stepped outside into a narrow alley. Birds chirped overhead, and he could hear the bustling of a nearby market, perhaps the same one he passed through the first time he'd arrived in Last Hope. "What you choose to do is your choice in the end. Take faith in your people, Thane. You learned to open your eyes. That is your proof others might as well. Now, please follow me."

The sun beat down on the two of them as they waded into the waves of crowds traversing through the market. A labyrinth of stalls and tents guided the lines of people through the large chaotic maze. Thane couldn't hear himself think amongst the shouting of the merchants who were trying to gather anyone's attention they could. Each one peddled their barbecued meats, new fruits he'd never seen before, and disgusting cheeses smelling as though they'd been rotting in the sun for years. Locals would know the locations of where the best goods were hidden.

Suspicious individuals mingled in the crowd, hidden in cloaks and hoods. Chances were they were pickpockets or looking to purchase unadvertised goods from the market's stalls. White Boar's Landing was devoid of such common criminals. The ever-present mind reading abilities of Zann-Xia-Czul threatened anyone who might resort to thievery. As he watched one particularly thin man stalk someone carrying bundles of ripe tomatoes, Thane realized that he and Somnius probably appeared just as dubious in their cloaks.

"Fear not, Thane. You're not as recognizable in Last Hope as in Serenity Keep." She led the way toward the main castle but turned left, guiding him down a different path.

"Is someone following us?" Thane whispered. "This isn't the way there."

"Writing this letter may take some time," Somnius said. "We'll be safer at the library than we were at my shop."

She led him to the single imposing building that seemed more elegant, fine, and maintained than even Serenity Keep. Ivory stones made up the exterior, shimmering like diamonds in the sunlight. As they approached the entrance, six statues of scholars, whose names Thane didn't recognize, greeted them in a row. Just ahead, a large oak doorway, wide enough for two carts side by side, opened as two guards let another patron out.

As Thane and Somnius approached, his gut

lurched. Why would a library have members of the city guard watching over it? Were they waiting for them?

"Some of the library's texts are controversial," Somnius explained. "The knights at the entrance are searching for weapons and anything else that might harm the collections or patrons within, not for us. Besides, these guards know me as a frequent patron; they won't search us."

They made their way inside without a second glance, and Thane sighed in both relief and awe as the massive door clunked shut behind them. Inside the library, shelves piled high with books reached the ceiling, using every available space yet leaving just enough room for people and ladders to squeeze through. Cereene had mentioned this to him long ago, and her words didn't capture the vastness of knowledge within. The collection of texts was reputed to house the world's most valuable information, spanning both modern and ancient times. He wondered whether any of it contained information about Bios Auras or Zann-Xia-Czul.

"Can you write in Common Tongue?" Somnius asked without stopping her quick, confident stride.

"Not well," Thane said. "I can try to write the letter for you, but I was under the impression you already knew how."

They approached a tall desk with a small shelf on

top, brimming with various note-taking supplies. Somnius promptly helped herself to a paper, envelope, and quill after dropping a coin into a collections bowl. She then sat down at a nearby study desk and Thane looked over her shoulder.

"Would you mind if I wrote a letter using your name, then?" the goddess said.

"Shouldn't you introduce yourself to Kaine?"

"I must remain hidden for now," she said. "King Ether and I have a complicated past. It's best he not notice I'm involved."

"Assuming Kaine and the King see the letter," Thane said, "isn't my relationship with them just as complicated, if not more? Will they believe anything we've said?"

"Kaine needs not to believe. The purpose of this letter is to open his eyes to the possibilities—possibilities he will eventually realize are truths."

"I don't think there is anything we can do that would make the Darians trust me again," Thane lamented. "What could I possibly say?"

"For today, we only need to warn Kaine of Bios Auras and the importance of keeping the God Stones hidden."

"Wouldn't they already know to do that?"

"They do," Somnius whispered, "but not from you. We will open their eyes to the fact that not everything that happened to Lydia was as it seemed.

This is what will prompt Kaine to join us in the future, despite your involvement in recent events."

Thane glanced around the library to ensure no one was eavesdropping. "I trust you. Please, write the letter. I'll keep watch."

"Thank you, Thane."

Somnius scribbled on the paper so rapidly Thane suspected she'd memorized the words beforehand. Before the ink even dried, she stood from her chair and waved for him to take a seat.

"Is this okay to send him this on your behalf?"

Thane took a seat and read:

Kaine Khalia,

It's important for you to know the truth, despite how much it scares me. I don't expect you to understand or believe everything I'm about to tell you, but someone advised me you might be the only person capable of accepting my true intentions.

You and I were being used for a higher purpose—something greater than we were aware of. Keep this in mind, and please don't resent me for what surrounded the wedding.

Much took place in the shadows we couldn't see. I warn you that a knight in crimson armor sits in the center of it all. Remember this, especially as the inevitable conflict between the kingdoms plays out. Besides the one I've known as my god, there's no enemy with stronger magic than him. Beware the knight—he thrives in chaos.

I failed to stop what's coming, but this greater threat infects all else around it. My mission is to help set things right again, so in the meantime, please protect the God Stones. Find a new location to hide them. We cannot risk them falling into the wrong hands, as I almost let them go. Everything depends on it. Whoever wields their magic determines the future. I regret I couldn't do more to prevent what happened, but it's clearer to me now that everything had to serve its purpose.

There's so much I regret, and so much I've lost, but this is only the beginning. Please forgive me for what I have set in motion. It's my fault for failing to stop it, but there's little else I could have done. I had all the wrong facts.

For now, remember me by this letter, and forget what you saw me do before. None of it matters because none of it was as it seemed. There's a considerable lot to achieve in order to defeat the darkness plaguing our world. A friend of mine—a powerful one—believes you will play an integral role in the greater war still to come. Kaine, I'm unable to determine the specifics yet, but I trust my friend is correct. Hold your heart close in the meantime and be ready when the time approaches.

T. A

Somnius's intention was now clear. It was too soon to put the truth about Zann-Xia-Czul out into the open. The upcoming war between the Darians and Throatians would serve as a distraction, while Somnius used the opportunity to hide within the shadows and let her child be born. Meanwhile, she would set Kaine up to turn to her side later, through Thane.

"I am beginning to understand what you intended now," Thane replied. "It's all about planting a seed. There are certain events you don't want to have happen too early, nor too late."

"You are correct. Time is a major factor in the war against Bios Auras."

"I trust the words of this letter will serve your greater purpose," Thane said. "If so, let's send it. It can't possibly harm us, can it?"

"It's unlikely to cause harm, but regardless, I wanted to ensure I had your approval before I signed it with your initials."

Thane smirked at her formality. He would never have expected a goddess to ask his permission in any matter, let alone something as trivial as this.

"You treat me as though we are equals," he said.

"To become one of my knights grants you that respect," she replied with a graceful smile, "not to mention our shared goals."

"In the short hours I've known you, you've

already given me more respect than Zann-Xia-Czul ever did in my entire life. The tea, the armor, and most importantly, the truth. Thank you for everything."

"Your world is a dark and bleak one, Thane," the goddess replied softly, a comforting hand resting briefly on his arm, "and it is my honor to bring it some light."

She sealed the envelope and led him outside, continuing their path toward Serenity Keep. They passed through a series of decorative trees with bark as white as Mount Sephorr and then moved onto one of Last Hope's main streets. Guards occasionally passed by, the sounds of their armor clanging in a pounding rhythm as they marched on their patrols.

It was then Thane realized the cloaks he and Somnius wore were the perfect disguise. There had been so many suspicious characters at the markets donning similar cloaks that the guards had become indifferent to seeing them. Every guard knew those in cloaks were suspicious, but as long as they didn't draw attention to themselves or disturb the peace, the guards would ignore and quickly forget them. When everyone in a cloak was suspicious, none of them were—the guards were desensitized. As they passed several more pairs of guards, Thane's confidence in their anonymity strengthened.

However, despite his newfound comfort, his

heart began to race as they approached the main gate leading into Serenity Keep. If King Ether, Councilman Merdel, or any of the other Darians he'd met saw him, all their efforts would be for naught. Somnius apparently knew this as well, as she asked him to wait in a nearby alley and pretend to fiddle with the buckle of his shoe.

"It wouldn't be too surprising if I'd accidentally left some of my supplies behind, being the tailor for the wedding," Somnius said. "I'll drop the letter underneath Kaine's door and will return to you soon."

Fifteen minutes later, she reappeared as promised and declared they were done with their business in Last Hope.

"Now, we must travel north," she said. "Far, far north. It will take us many days to travel to central Yaenia, where the Black Moon Tribe resides. We have to cross the Shield Haven too, if you're knowledgeable of that location."

He hadn't heard of it, but surmised it was a considerable distance from where they were now. Still, the farther away they went from people who might recognize them, the better.

"Should we stop at a market on the way out?" Thane asked. "We haven't any supplies."

"I have everything we'll need. Do not worry."

Thane nodded, noticing the glimmer of determination in Somnius's eyes. "Did you always know?" he asked as they passed the signpost marking the border of Last Hope. "About all of this? About me, my fate, the God Stones?"

She looked at him, her expression a mixture of fondness and contemplation. "Being a goddess, Thane, I understand things beyond human comprehension. But remember, even gods cannot foresee the future with certainty. I have a sense of the larger design, but the specifics, like every choice you or I will make, are ours alone. It's a war between fate and free will, order and chaos. Even I can only guess at which will be victorious on any day."

Thane pondered on that, finding comfort in her words. "It's just... everything is so overwhelming. The fate of my people, Lydia's death, Bios Auras, Zann-Xia-Czul... I wonder if there's an end to it."

"Endings and beginnings are woven into the tapestry of what it means to exist," Somnius replied. "But remember, even in the darkest times, you have allies. You are not alone in this."

"And what about you? In a way, aren't you alone? With the immense power you hold and your knowledge of things, doesn't it get lonely?"

Somnius paused, looking off into the horizon. "It does," she admitted softly. "But then, I find souls like yours, and it gives me hope. It reminds me of the very purpose of my mission—to guide, protect, and bring balance."

Comforted, Thane smiled. The two continued their journey, knowing that the path ahead was filled with peril, but also holding onto the hope that together they could bring about change. The world was vast, and its intricacies were endless. Yet, as Somnius had said, even in the darkest times, they were not alone.

BOOK 3 CHAPTER PREVIEW

Next is a bonus preview chapter from Symphony of Crowns and Gods Book 3: Prophecy of Tears and Sacrifice. I hope you will enjoy this glimpse of the next part and what's coming later on in the series. To order Prophecy of Tears and Sacrifice, please visit www.theauthorbrian.com or whichever storefront you purchased this book.

Thank you and enjoy!

— Brian A. Mendonça

NOTE ABOUT THE PREVIEW CHAPTER

Please be aware that the following scene preview is from an early or mid part of Prophecy of Tears and Sacrifice and has not undergone professional editing yet. Details presented here may undergo changes in the final version. This preview serves to provide a glimpse into the story's early development and is subject to further refinement. Expect minor changes and more writing enhancements in the subsequent drafts as the narrative unfolds...

PROPHECY OF TEARS AND
SACRIFICE SCENE PREVIEW

Finnegan, the middle-aged chicken farmer whom Xander had mentioned earlier, set them up in a borrowed shack for the night. Their accommodations smelled of mildew and burned grass, but were otherwise better than no shelter at all. Likewise, the sheets on their beds reeked from exposure to the smoky, yet humid, weather, and Kaine wondered how long it would take for the scents to leave his body.

Later that night, long after everyone had fallen asleep, Kira's scream jolted him awake. He fumbled for *White Oath* from between his bed frame and the wall, flinging the sheath across the room as he glided into an offensive stance. With his eyes already adjusted to the darkness, he saw Kira pointing toward the window, her other hand covering her mouth in shock. Merdel had sat up in his bed too, but was in no position to defend her.

"Stand back!" Kaine yelled as he ran toward the window to put himself between it and Kira.

"Look!" Kira yelled, but the tone of her voice seemed more excited than fearful.

Outside the window, small glowing yellow dots filled the village and were floating up toward the sky. They appeared to be fireflies, illuminating from each of the village shacks. Slowly, each glowing dot floated around before drifting into the pitch-black skies above. It was a sight to behold, but not worth making his heart race.

He lowered his blade. "You shouldn't scream like that unless it's an emergency."

"Sorry, Kaine—I just forgot about the tribute."

"What?"

"It's a local tradition," Merdel explained, fully sitting up in his bed. "Rather than sending paper lanterns into the sky like most Asuras, Gale Village's people capture the fireflies and release them halfway to sunrise. It symbolizes the faint line between death and life, and how one should always strive for Asura's light."

"As beautiful as it is, the middle of the night should be for resting," Kaine finally growled. "If not a single person is to be seen outside despite every household taking part, then we should just sleep through it."

He had never heard of their practice; it seemed the people here were following a distinct branch of Asura's religion of their own making. Even in their midnight rituals, the streets were still void of any people. Nobody would miss that they weren't there.

Gale Village's people, or specifically, those who served Elder Orin, somehow appeared only as they were needed, without being summoned. In all other cases, the entire town's small population had stayed inside their homes for the entire day since they'd arrived there. Kaine considered all the possibilities and decided that perhaps the villagers feared catching disease from visitors. Otherwise, his second explanation was that the entire town was a cult and Elder Orin was their leader. Few other options made sense to explain the oddities and reclusiveness of every single person in town. Kaine hadn't ever heard of a religion where its members otherwise seemed to actively avoid each other.

The next morning, Kaine and the others followed Orin for almost an hour as they hiked toward the graveyard as scheduled. When Kaine asked the Elder for any hints about the Gale villagers' identities, Orin gave a rehearsed answer: "the people here have a closely-knit culture that needs to be guarded." The nearer they got to their destination on the other side of the mountains, the more Kaine noticed Orin staring at him. He figured it was because he was the only one who'd never been to their mountains before. To add to the oddities, Orin had left his cane at home and was walking rather energetically—as if to show his strength and impress everyone, even though there wasn't a discernible reason for it. Kaine decided it was best to ignore Orin's awkward glances, and just keep pace with Kira.

He wished he could find a moment to speak with her and ask if she knew why the God Stones had glowed while he'd been wearing them the previous day. Still, even if he found the chance, Kira seemed oblivious to their real purpose in traveling to the distant location. Bringing up the conversation about her father's enchanted stones would mean revealing his own secret to her, and for whatever reason, King Ether had made it clear he didn't want his children involved with the true purpose of their journey.

Earlier in the morning, Merdel had claimed that the God Stones don't glow, and that there was no reason to believe they had. He questioned whether Kaine had consumed enough water during the final stretch of their hike and if he was perhaps becoming delirious from dehydration. The councilman's opinion had merit—when Princess Lydia had been alive, she'd used the Memory Stone several times in plain sight, in front of Kaine and many other people, and the stones had not shined at all. For them to suddenly activate in a way like never before while they'd hung around his neck and for no magic to happen caused Kaine to have doubts about the mysterious flash that only he had noticed.

As he admitted to himself that perhaps the God Stones hadn't truly activated for him, their group reached a small plateau overlooking a valley of orangish-yellow magma. Scattered about the clearing were several graves. Carved with rudimentary techniques and varying skill levels, each tombstone was different in shape from the others. They all seemed to be made of a natural glass rock, leading Kaine to believe that perhaps someone hadn't crafted the tombstones. Instead, each piece might have been found and hauled to the graveyard by the villagers. They had scratched the names of the deceased onto the surfaces of the tombstones, a laborious process without the proper tools. That was why only the names of individuals were inscribed on the stones, with no additional information about their identities.

Orin led them to a semi-oval-shaped grave with a jagged corner and gave it a slight bow. The frail man's legs seemed to grow tired as he stepped back and leaned cautiously against another tombstone several feet away. "We're here," he said. "Xander, Kira... We'll give you some time to say hello."

"He really should've brought his cane, or at least a walking stick," Merdel muttered.

"It's as though he has something to prove to us," Kaine replied. "He's been such an oddity, ever since we've arrived."

They waited as the prince and princess kneeled where their mother was buried and prayed. Kira removed a small paper lantern from her pocket and her pale fingers trembled as she unfolded it. Kaine was too far away to read the details, but he could see her penmanship covering most her craft. Once she stabilized the paper, she bent the small wire base into a rectangular shape and threaded the base through the lantern's edge slit. After she finished standing the lantern up on the ground, she revealed a flint and used it and some of the dry grass to light her flame.

"I'm doing my best for you, mother," Kira whispered as tears streamed down her face. "The world is so dark, but I'm trying to bring it some light."

She lit the lantern's inner chamber and it erupted into a small ball of flame. For a few seconds, she held it in front of her to let the fire warm the air contained inside. Once it was ready, her small hands reluctantly let go, and Kaine sensed her fear that the paper object might crash to the ground. Rather, it quietly floated up past the princess's face and drifted on its own into the skies above.

With a thin smile, a satisfaction in that the lantern would reach its destination far above them, Kira stepped away from her mother's grave. Xander remained there, tilting his head toward the tombstone at his feet, frozen in silent thought or prayer. Instead of bringing out a lantern of his own, he removed a small letter from his pocket. He used Kira's flint and a fistful of grass to set the paper ablaze, silently lowering it to the ground next to his mother's tombstone.

As the parchment disintegrated into ash, he stomped out the flames and resumed staring at his feet. A moment later, he returned to where Kaine, Kira, and Merdel were standing.

"Let's go back," he said.

"Kaine," Merdel said on cue, "perhaps you would like a moment with the queen?"

"Sure. If the rest of you want to start heading down, I can catch up in a few minutes."

"I'm certain Orin appreciates your offer for the early start," Merdel smirked, glancing at the Elder.

The bald man lacking his cane glared back over at them. "I don't see what's the rush, but fine, have it your way, Merdel. Apparently the upper servants in

Last Hope cannot appreciate the natural beauty of our landscapes."

Orin took the lead for Merdel, Xander, and Kira as they trekked back toward Gale Village. Now, that Kaine was alone in the graveyard, he counted to sixty, just in case either of the children decided to return and keep him company, then removed the small coin purse wrapped around his neck. He delicately poured the four God Stones into the palm of his hand, and examined each of them for the last time.

"Green, blue, silver, and black..." Kaine muttered to the deathly air around him. "Now, there is no going back."

He pinched each of the four differently colored stones, checking again whether any of them would activate or reveal signs of magic for him. When not a single one of them glowed, he tried squeezing them inside his fist, adding as much pressure as he could. Still, the stones gave no reaction. It seemed Merdel had been correct after all—Kaine must have been delusional when he'd seen them light up the first time.

Crouching at Lily von Stonewall's grave, he took a flat stray rock and carved a small hole. He had no intention or desire to dig as deep as where the queen's remnants might have been, but he scraped far enough to where the natural elements wouldn't erode away his work and reveal what he was about to bury. When the deepest part of his hole reached twenty inches or so, he buried the God Stones into the ground, one by one.

"This was King Ether's wish," Kaine said to the queen as he replaced the dirt. "And I'm sorry I couldn't save Lydia... But I promise—no, I swear it on your daughter's grave—I won't let anything happen to Xander or Kira."

Perhaps leaving their father's magic with their mother would help him accomplish that. Nothing about the God Stones was clear to him, but leaving the four of them there where nobody would think to look was probably the best action to take. As Ether had warned and Lydia had demonstrated, the power within was far too powerful and dangerous if they were to fall into the wrong hands.

He scattered some of the ashes from Xander's letter over the newly overturned earth, covering over any signs that it had been disturbed. Once he was sure it was undetectable, he jogged down the mountain path to reunite with the rest of the group.

It didn't take long for him to catch up with the others, but as he approached, Merdel faltered off to the side and slammed sideways into the ground.

"OW! MY LEG!" the councilman howled. "IT'S BROKEN!"

"Merdel!" Kaine shouted as realistically as he

could. "Are you okay?" He wasn't sure what would have been his reaction had Merdel's fall not been an ruse, but what mattered was whether Orin believed it to be true.

"Let's take a look," Gale Village's leader said, pacing over to the councilman. "This happened all the time during the war."

He squatted at Merdel's side and pulled up his pant leg. "It's not broken at all," he commented. "Just a sprain, perhaps?"

"It's awfully twisted anyway," the councilman insisted. "I don't know, but I heard a pop and it hurts. Asura's ass!"

Kaine smirked, as Merdel was normally too formal to yell so crudely, but his act was convincing. Kira offered him some water from her canteen while the councilman caressed his ankle.

"We're not too far from the village," Orin said. "You should be able to hobble the rest of the way on one leg. We'll move slower, so it's not going to be impossible."

"Easy for you to say!" Merdel spat. He then looked up to the sun beating over them. "I feel... dizzy. Did I hit my head? Can someone carry me?"

Xander laughed. "How fragile are you?"

"I'm serious," Merdel groaned. "Something's not right with me."

"I'm too small to carry you," Kira said, "but I wish I could."

"And I've only got one good arm," Kaine said, pointing to his sling.

Merdel stared at Orin and smiled. "We can't ask the prince to carry me, can we?"

"Even if you did, I would have to decline," Xander said, turning to Elder Orin.

"I've carried more than my fair share of wounded warriors when I was younger," the Elder said, "and the years have stolen that ability from me as of late."

"So what should we do about me?" Merdel whimpered, perhaps playing his part a little too well.

"I'll head back to the village," Kaine volunteered, as he and Merdel had planned. "I'll find Finnegan or whatever his name was, and maybe he and some of the others can help us. You should rest there for now."

"It's a waste of time, in my opinion," Orin said. "He should be able to make it home on one leg, especially if he just leaned on you. But if he insists on being a child and a nuisance, may he lay on the ground in pointless agony until you return."

"I'll be back soon," Kaine said with a smile. "Don't die on us in the meantime."

* * * *

Half an hour later, he passed through an open wooden gate and entered Gale Village, which was still devoid of people. This time, rather than pondering the possible reasons for the empty streets, Kaine was grateful for it. No people around meant he had the advantage of having no witnesses for what he was about to do.

Orin's shack stood at the other edge of the small town, alone and unguarded. Kaine approached, moving quietly just in case anyone happened to pass by. A small hole in the decayed wood of the front door allowed him to peek inside and verify that nobody was in the Elder's home. He took one more look at the lifeless shacks nearby before turning the doorknob and letting himself inside.

Kaine closed the door behind him as he examined the room. The advantage of Orin's single-roomed shack was that there were few places to hide anything. The only problem was that the letter was thin and easy to conceal between other items. He searched the bed first, raising the mattress up against the wall and checking its underside. Aside from a small hand-ax strapped there, there were no signs of the letter.

He searched the battered armoire next. Inside it were a few more sets of plain, old black robes, a larger battle ax than the one hidden in the bed, Orin's cane that he'd left behind for the day, and a wooden box of garlic, herbs, and some other medicinal root. The Elder was poor or preferred to live with only his most essential possessions. Kaine suspected it was the latter of the two.

Still, the small number of items within the large wooden armoire were likely a decoy, or at least there was still plenty of space within the furniture piece to stash something. Kaine pushed his hands firmly into the bottommost shelf and instantly felt it give some play. A few seconds later, he managed to slip his fingers into a tiny crevice and pulled out the baseboard shelf from the armoire. There was a small bag made of brown leather and beside it was a letter, folded in a packet of the same hue. He'd found it!

Ether had told Merdel that they should bring the letter back to Last Hope unread, however the king's wax seal was entirely missing. This detail tempted Kaine to read through the letter anyway. After all, there was no way for anyone to know whether he had read it. Nevertheless, the last time he'd snuck a peek at a von Stonewall letter, he'd burned it for being such a blight to their family name. Chances were that this letter was only of sentimental value and not an elaborate deceptive lie as Lydia's words had been...

He promised himself that no matter what he read, that he would not destroy the letter this time, and then peeled back the envelope's lip. Letter in hand, his eyes sped through the words:

> *Ether,*
>
> *I'm sorry I cannot say this to you in person; we both know it wouldn't be right for me to appear at Serenity Keep. I miss you, and I regret that I left to train so far away. There wasn't any other way to do what needs to be done, and the woman who you met last time is doing her best to take care of me.*
>
> *There's something important I have to tell you. We were wrong about the Prophecy of Tears and Sacrifice. It turns out that I'm not the savior who will set things right; instead, I am the one who must die. Ether, it pains me to say it, but I'm fading away. You know as well as I that I am not a goddess, but by using these stones, I've been pretending to be one.*
>
> *It all comes with a price that I'm unsure of whether I'm capable of paying. Using multiple stones at a time is tearing my body and soul apart. The damage is irreversible. Unless I discover a way to use the stones to fix this, then I don't have much time left, and*

nothing else we've tried can preserve my life.

Despite my wishes, you have to take care of Lily Ashthorne if you haven't married her already. I know you won't be happy to hear this, but through the use of the Time Stone, I've learned she and I share a similar bloodline. If I should fall, it might be up to her to take the next step toward fulfilling the prophecy. This was a surprise to me too, but true history cannot be disputed. You know what this means, but it is for the greater good of all.

Please, take the five of them pressed in this envelope and test whether she can activate them. If she can, the one who trained me will try and train her. Perhaps I was never meant to use the God Stones. Perhaps our roles have been wrong in this all along...

There's not enough parchment in the world that can contain everything I wish I could say to you. You took me in your arms and showed me how to be strong. I love you for that, and it pains me so deeply that our circumstances didn't allow our dreams to come true.

Zelia

"What did I just read?" Kaine muttered to the empty room. How had Elder Orin even gotten hold of this letter? Who was Zelia, and how were they related to the von Stonewall family? Even more alarming was that the letter mentioned five God Stones, but only four of them had ever seemed to reach King Ether's possession.

Before he could fully comprehend what he had just discovered or have another chance at reading it again, someone knocked on the door.

"Orin?" It was a woman's voice. "I thought you had gone to the graveyard."

There was nowhere in the small shack to hide. The door swung open, and the woman who entered revealed why the people of Gale Village had been hiding in her homes all along. Her posture was bent from the ages, and for each year of her life she'd lived, she had a long wrinkle on her face. But it wasn't her age that caused Kaine to drop the letter from his hand and reflexively draw his sword—it was her grayish purple skin. To have such a skin tone meant only one terrible fact. Queen Blanche had often warned him that if he ever got captured by a group of them that it would be easier if he simply took his own life rather than subjecting himself to their cruel whims.

"They'll cut your chest open for fun, just to see what you ate for breakfast," she had once said as they had drank wine together. "Most of the time, they don't even need a knife—their mind can cut sharper than a blade, and they don't care how loud you're screaming while they do it."

Lucidians were perhaps the most dangerous beings in existence, and now Kaine was alone in a room with one.

PROPHECY OF TEARS AND SACRIFICE

PEACE CANNOT COME WITHOUT SACRIFICE.

BUT WHO WILL PAY THE GREATEST COST OF ALL?

The Wedding of the Torn Rose may be over, but the costly aftermath has only begun. New alliances are forming in Yaenia, and threaten those who are still licking their wounds. A goddess selects her subjects in hopes they will fulfill a prophecy, but a hero in one kingdom is a villain in another. The exiled Prince Thane is on the run and must find the mysterious Whisperers, those who speak like the dragons dead from long ago. Back in the Darian Kingdom,

Kaine Khalia must come to terms with his new condition, all while tasked with concealing the God Stones, a means to immeasurable magic. Most unexpectedly, the magical Lucidians, previously hidden in plain sight, have revealed themselves, and their scars, as a warning of what's yet to come.

Defensive strategies alone cannot win a war, however. Across the country, a trio of Leilan knights search for a shortcut to ending the conflict with the Throatians—knowledge from the Black Moon Tribe, the previous dragon slayers, may hold the key to saving everyone. But defeating Zann-Xia-Czul will not come easy, especially now that he has joined forces with an invincible knight best known for his crimson armor. Everyone has a different goal, but destiny painstakingly draws everyone into the fray— a legend binding all involved.

BOOKS BY BRIAN A. MENDONÇA

Symphony of Crowns and Gods Series

Wedding of the Torn Rose (Book 1)

Gravity of Obedience (Book 2)

Prophecy of Tears and Sacrifice (Book 3)

Available at most major book retailers.

Store links can be found here: theauthorbrian.com

AN IMPORTANT NOTE FROM THE AUTHOR

As the creator of the Symphony of Crowns and Gods series, my primary aim is to transport readers like yourself on an unforgettable journey. I hope that you enjoyed *Gravity of Obedience* and that it added further depth to what happened in *Wedding of the Torn Rose*. There's still many twists to come in *Prophecy of Tears and Sacrifice*.

I would love to hear your thoughts about it! If this book has captured your interest, would you kindly consider sharing your experience on platforms such as Amazon, Goodreads, BookBub, or any other convenient platform? A few words from you can guide fellow readers and significantly enhance the visibility of the series.

But more than that, your insights serve as my compass in this expansive landscape of storytelling. Your feedback and suggestions fuel my inspiration and aid me in weaving tales that deeply touch your heart.

Thank you in advance for your time and input. You are not just a reader; you are a vital part of my creative journey. And please remember, each review illuminates the path for the next grand adventure someone might embark upon in the Symphony of Crowns and Gods series.

Sincerely,
Brian A. Mendonça

To help, please visit:
https://www.theauthorbrian.com/review-request

Or use this QR code:

JOIN BRIAN A. MENDONÇA'S EMAIL NEWSLETTER

WHY SIGN UP?

It's simple: fans on this email list get my official updates before anyone else, including any other blogs and social media websites. Here's the news you can expect:

- Upcoming releases and previews of upcoming books
- An open dialog about my author journey
- Deals and sales
- Opportunities for ARCs (Advance Reader Copies)
- Info about fantasy books from other indie authors

Sign up link:

https://theauthorbrian.com/join-brians-newsletter

Or use this QR code:

Published by BookPop Media LLC.

Symphony of Crowns and Gods Official Website:

https://www.theauthorbrian.com